The Deaduction Agency

Titles

If anyone cares to read all the books by the same author, the suggested sequence is:

Santiago Tales – where the irascible and incorrigible Terry Tumbler, who is based very loosely on the personality of the author, organises a trip for himself and his cronies to travel to the sacred city of Santiago de Compostela, following parts of the St James Camino, in Northern Spain. En route, as well as swapping stories in the same vein as those related in *Canterbury Tales* by Geoffrey Chaucer, they endure an interesting encounter themselves.

Conceptually, this is a semi-fictional book within a travelogue.

Seb Cage Begins His Adventures – where Terry Tumbler's grandsons come to stay with him and his long-suffering wife, who live on the Costa Blanca, for the entire summer vacation. During this period, the elder one, Seb, experiences a number of futuristic adventures when he joins a summer campus run by a mysterious organisation called *The Sombrella Syndicate.*

The Inlooker – where a presumably unique character, Thomas Beckon, realises his paranormal talents and changes the nature of society in Great Britain, and thereafter of the World, to help shape mankind in its future development.

Magic Carpets, Turkish Carpets – this is where Terry Tumbler experiences the marvels of Turkey in two stages; the first occurring as the preliminary changes in society are being brought about by *The Inlooker,* and the second where Terry and his cronies take a special trip to Turkey and experience a number of futuristic adventures themselves. It is during this second visit that Terry is reunited with *The Sombrella Syndicate* and his grandson Seb Cage.

The Deaduction Agency – Witness at first-hand a group of specialist investigators, as they set up and run a new agency, dedicated to the resolution of criminal cases using paranormal assistance.

Finally, for those who may become more than remotely interested in his upbringing, the author Terry Tumbler's childhood behaviour is recounted in a mildly fictionalised autobiographical work called:

The Rough and Tumbles of Early Years – The author himself subsequently regarded this as a potentially valuable compendium of incidents, which could be serialised in the same vein as *Just William*. Originally, it was prepared for the benefit of his family, who would otherwise have known nothing of his outrageous childhood behaviour

The Deaduction Agency

Terry Tumbler

Witness at first-hand a group of specialist investigators, as they set up and run a new agency, dedicated to the resolution of criminal cases using paranormal assistance.

ACKNOWLEDGEMENTS

This book is dedicated to the professionals who assume responsibility for bringing to justice those who feel no remorse in abusing, torturing and ultimately killing innocent people.

It is a miserable way for investigators to go through life, having to deal with the consequences of the actions of the depraved monsters who roam our world.

It is made worse by the empathy they need to establish with the victims themselves and with their nearest and dearest. Relief only comes, if at all, when they help mete out richly deserved punishment.

Praise be to the heroes concerned, for that is what they are.

CONTENTS

FOREWORD

Do you doubt that psychics are for real? Are you swayed by skeptics in their view that no such abilities exist?

I prefer to keep an open mind. The world-wide web is a wonderful tool to research such topics, and I use it to investigate these matters thoroughly before coming to a conclusion on this and other topical matters.

Below, I present you with some real-life cases of psychics at work, so judge them with fresh, untainted eyes. The names are real, the results are as reported; judge for yourselves, on the web, to do your homework. Truthfully, there are plenty more where these came from.

I should know. My pseudonym is Joe Fraser and I work with psychics on an ongoing basis. These uniquely gifted individuals are part of my regular army of law enforcers.

I hope you never need their services like I do, to find out who 'dunnit' or who's about to 'do it'.

To hell with the 'naysayers'.

The first example concerns psychic Patricia Gagliardi who investigated the disappearance of Richard Eastman, a Missing Coastguard Warrant Officer, who disappeared from New London, CT. in April of 1979. She began to have visions of a man in uniform, water, an eagle and a vehicle.

A girlfriend of hers was told about the visions, and began to search through some old newspaper articles, where she found the story of Mr. Eastman's disappearance. Pat spoke with Detective Ed Pickett and was invited to the State's Attorney's Office, where she was given an item belonging to the missing man; once again she had more visions pertaining to his whereabouts.

In these visions she again saw the car, a dock, two heavy equipment cranes, the man in uniform and an eagle. The State's Attorney's Office and the Coast Guard had been searching for him relentlessly for months. When Pat arrived there at the dock, she knew that he and his car had met with an unfortunate accident, and was in an area that divers had already searched.

At her indirect insistence, the divers returned to the scene, found the car containing the man's body and the valuable equipment that coastguards feared had been stolen. How could Pat have possibly known that the car was there, underwater, by the pier?

In the second example:

a body was found in the US by Psychic Annette Martin. Dennis Prado, a retired US paratrooper, had gone missing from his apartment and police had been unable to locate his whereabouts. With no further leads, the chief investigating officer, Fernando Realyvasquez, a sergeant with the Pacifica (California) Police, contacted psychic detective Annette Martin.

Prado had lived near a large forest, some 2000 square miles. When Annette Martin was given a map, she circled a small spot on the map, about the size of two city blocks. She said that Prado had struggled for breath, had died and his body would be there within the indicated area. She described the path he took, and where the body would be found.

Although the area had been searched before and Prado had not been found, a search and rescue officer initiated a new search with the help of a search dog, as Martin suggested "A search dog is going to find him." They found the body covered with dirt at the location, as Martin had indicated. While the body had deteriorated, there was no evidence that he had been attacked and it is thought likely he had died of natural causes, as she also indicated.

A third example:

in 2001, the body of Thomas Braun was located by Perth

based Aboriginal clairvoyant Leanna Adams in Australia. Police had been unable to find the body.

The family of Braun had been told to contact Adams, an Aboriginal psychic who lived in Perth. The Braun family had requested police to do a search based on Adams' directions but they had not assisted.

Adams went to Alice Springs in the Northern Territory and took the family members directly to Braun's remains, a spot high on a ridge west of the town, some 20 kilometers out. The remains were not immediately identifiable. Police later confirmed the remains to be his, using DNA testing.

A fourth example:

in Sydney, Australia in 1996, a Belgian born Sydney psychic, Phillipe Durant was approached by the fiancé of missing Paula Brown to help locate her.

Durante told police the location of the body of Brown. She was found less than two kilometers from the spot he had indicated in Port Botany, New South Wales by a lorry driver who came across the body.

"Even though the body was discovered purely by chance, the speculation by a clairvoyant appears to have been uncannily accurate," a police spokeswoman conceded. Durant had used a plumb bob and a grid map, combined with some hair from the victim.

A fifth example:

Phil Jordan believes his psychic talent is the sole reason for his first success story. On August 4, 1975 a six-year-old boy got lost in the woods of upstate New York, and had been missing for 17 hours when Jordan successfully led a search team to the boy.

Jordan claims to have achieved this by using a map he had foreseen and drawn the previous night.

Thereafter, the Tioga County Sheriff had him sworn-in as a deputy to assist in other cases. Jordan continues to work with the police agencies at all levels across the country, and his résumé contains cases including missing persons, homicide and arson.

A final example:

in 1988, a young woman named Sharon Gregory was brutally murdered in her Greenfield home. Although never proved in a court of law, a classmate of the victim named Mark Branch was widely believed to have killed her.

There is little doubt that he killed this young woman, and a search of his home revealed an obsession with extremely gory horror movies, primarily Friday The 13th and its central character Jason Voorhees.

Within hours of the discovery of Sharon Gregory's body, Branch's blood-stained car was found in a rural road in a neighboring town, sparking a manhunt that paralyzed and terrified this small town.

Three weeks after Mark Branch disappeared in the woods, the police were hopelessly baffled and the case was brought to the attention of John Monti, a broadcasting psychic from Long Island, New York.

The police worked with Monti for a few days. According to then Buckland Police Chief, Jim Basile, Monti was flown to western Massachusetts and his expenses were paid by members of the local police force, largely from their own pockets.

He insisted beforehand on not being briefed on the case, and only being given a photo of the dead girl to study. He repeatedly stated that the name 'Jason' was coming into his mind.

He was sent packing after fruitless attempts to find the suspect in surrounding, extensive woods. Before that occurred, he did lead detectives to a previously unknown deserted abattoir, where sinister events had occurred; he did state repeatedly that the suspect was hanging from a tree deep in the woods; he also asserted that he was picking up a connection with someone called Kevin who had an Alsatian dog.

As testified afterwards by detectives, they finally gave up searching for the presumed killer's body, when the weather turned nasty and it was getting dark.

When it was found over a month later, it was by a hunter named Kevin who lived deep in the woods and had an Alsatian dog with him at the time. The suicide – or was it an act of vengeance by vigilantes? – was exactly as described, in detail.

The body was actually hanging from a tree 200 meters further ahead on the route that Monti had originally been leading the detectives.

The detectives publicly confirmed that they were subsequently impressed with what the psychic had conveyed to them.

In conclusion, retired attorney Victor J Zammit states with absolute certainty that "the most powerful evidence *amounting to proof* for the validity of forensic psychics is when tough, skeptical police officers and detectives – after working with them – tell millions of viewers around the world that those they recruited are highly gifted."

Don't get me wrong, there's plenty of charlatans out there. It's a case of sorting the wheat from the chaff.

Note

Names of actual individuals have been changed or suppressed in the cases that follow.

The Agency's MISSION Statement

Those who are not familiar with the world of enterprise may wonder: what on earth is a *Mission Statement*?

I am about to tell you.

At its simplest, it defines the reason for the existence of an organization. A didactic soul might be more expansive and state that it should guide the actions of the organization, spell out its overall goal, provide a path, and guide decision-making.

In the case of the 'Deaduction' Agency, the clue for its existence lies in its name. To state the matter simply, the controlling partners within it *deduce*. But what do they deduce?

Well, clients who seek their help are normally in a state of emotional distress. To begin with, the partners use routine, formal principles of detection to root out the apparent, maybe true, causes of their mental agitation.

Now for the interesting, second stage of the assistance that is provided. As I suggested earlier: the clue is in the spelling of the name. You see, the agency partners perform their tasks with *paranormal* assistance; hence, they enlist an unworldly, additional resource for *The Deaduction Agency*!

In effect, they communicate with those who have 'passed on' and now inhabit the spirit plane.

Still confused? I suggest that you continue to read. Sooner or later you'll get the picture.

The First Case is Landed

'Twas Christmas Eve in the Workplace,
Feet were tapping the ground.
The cause of the partners' discomfort?
No clients were to be found!'

"Where *is* everyone?" Honey asked irritably. "We've got the food, we've got the booze. Why has no one turned up?"

She was referring to their new business venture, The Deaduction Agency, which had been set-up on the edge of the busy town center. It occupied the first floor of a refurbished office block, and even had a private elevator for any disabled or aged clients that might care to enter its portal.

Inside, it was tastefully furnished in a modern style, with hard-wearing beige diamond-patterned carpets throughout the five available consulting rooms-cum-offices. In each of these confidential, soundproofed 'work spaces' was a round, glass-topped table surrounded by five exactly-spaced sturdy, beechwood-framed chairs with padded seats and back-rests.

Each workspace was fronted by a metre-wide triple-glazed window facing the outside, secondary road. The exterior wall containing these five windows was uniformly covered on the inside with a cladding of mock dull red-bricks, mediaeval in size and appearance.

This theme was continued on the extreme sidewalls of the two outermost rooms. Per work space, to the left of its allocated window when facing it, was a narrow, beechwood bookcase with matching sideboard underneath.

Partially in front of it and the window, at an angle and facing inwards, was a dual-pedestal green-baize topped desk similarly made from solid beechwood.

This allowed any individual sitting at a desk to gaze outwards to their left and contemplate the external view, if they felt the desire and time permitted.

The four centrally shared sidewalls were constructed from floor to ceiling of reinforced glass panels. These glass walls were in reality folding 'curtains' with almost invisible seams between the narrow panels; when fully parted, this unique feature allowed all five rooms (or fewer) to become one larger area, where the partners could assemble for group meetings and presentations, to cater for visitors.

The innermost walls bordering the public areas were made entirely of fixed glass panels, as were the inward-opening hinged access doors to the workspaces. Hung on the inside of the fixed glass walls were vertical sliding linen strip blinds that could be manually closed to provide privacy. At the moment, they were all uniformly turned half-open.

To discourage any hanky-panky, there were no blinds inside the doors.

Conventional toilets were provided alongside the internal reception area, to the left of the hinged glass access door that faced the shielded receptionist's desk, and there was a separate, small kitchen at the far end of the office, opposite a windowless storage room.

Currently, only four out of the five workspaces had regular occupants, of whom two were present in the building.

Richard, the most senior partner in the agency, was busying himself constantly re-arranging brochures on a side table in the waiting area in reception. It was a quirky habit of his that Honey found most annoying. It also reflected his fussy preoccupation with orderliness and exact measurements.

Naturally, he was the architect of the office layout, which Honey was often tempted to rearrange, solely to unsettle him.

To both their surprise, the high-heeled tapping of footsteps could be heard, ascending the steps leading up to their office suite.

The inner door of the agency had no external handle, and the unannounced visitor paused before pressing the intercom and asking for permission to enter.

It was a woman's voice, slightly high-pitched but without trace of an identifiable accent. The young, female receptionist looked at Richard for approval before pressing a button to unlock the door.

It was a tall, slender woman who entered, pale of face and wearing a dark grey trouser suit under a black overcoat. She had pulled off her tight-fitting black leather gloves before pushing open the door while a warning-buzzer sounded, and advanced forward with her right hand extended to greet the two partners.

The promptness of her advance took Richard by surprise, as did the pleasant smile with which she greeted them.

"*She's pretty!*" was his prompt assessment of her. "*Maybe she's at her peak, in her early forties now, and still fanciable!*" He noted that her skin was porcelain smooth, with the hint of wrinkles at the corner of her shrewd, brown eyes when she smiled.

"Can I help you take off your overcoat?" he enquired, as she began struggling to do so herself.

"Thank you," she said, with a smile, as he hung it up on a wall peg. Immediately, she removed her bobble hat and shook her long, straight black hair to hang over her shoulders. He looked at her slender figure approvingly, which was that of a much younger girl.

Leading the way to Richard's conference room, Honey said, "Come through to the consulting area. There's a spread of food and drinks laid out, so please help yourself."

As the visitor entered, her eyes widened and she exclaimed in mock surprise, "I can't possibly manage all of that, and I'd better stick to soft drinks as I'm driving! If I could have a cup of coffee, white with one sugar, that would be ideal."

Richard laughed, feeling instantly at ease in her company, and invited her to sit down with the two of them, after she'd finished piling her paper plate with cocktail snacks and petite sandwiches. Meanwhile, he asked the receptionist to deliver the requested coffee.

Between serially chewing cocktail sausages, Richard asked her, "You're Nicky Lestrange, aren't you? We spoke on the phone a few days ago, and you had an open invitation to call on us?"

"Yes that's right!" she replied brightly.

Wiping her fingers with a paper napkin, she said, "Give me a few seconds," and rummaged through the black leather satchel she was carrying.

Richard took the file she handed to him, as Nicky explained to them both, "These are the relevant case notes; they contain my profile, my ex-husband's profile, copies of my divorce papers, mediation interviews, and the outcome of the settlement we reached. Also enclosed are the emails we've exchanged and correspondence I've had with solicitors."

Richard gazed through the documents, passing them to Honey for her to look at as well.

Nicky had picked up one of the brochures as she passed through reception and began reading it herself, while she nibbled at a smoked salmon sandwich.

That's nice," she commented, as she detected its seasoning of pepper and lemon juice.

Richard casually asked, as he perused the file contents, "Why'd you choose us?"

Nicky replied, "You've built up quite a reputation, so I'd say it was by 'Word of Mouth' that I came here. In the past, on your own, you've each achieved good results using unorthodox methods of investigation. Together, you should surpass yourselves, once you've got your new venture up and running!"

She said this with her eyes sparkling in anticipation.

Richard decided to test her apparent 'spirit of bonhomie'. Nicky had to be suffering some mental torment, even though it was well hidden.

He placed a laptop PC on the table, so she could see it, and then showed her the client profile he had started building. It stated:

Client status:	Pending
Name:	Nicola Lestrange
Nickname:	Nicky
Status:	Divorced
Date of Birth:	13 01 1973
Hair:	Dark Brown, tinged with streaks of grey

Photo: A passport sized photo was displayed on the screen.

Fingerprints: These were also displayed in a panel, together with a small empty box requiring an 'x' to be inserted, to confirm that they had been verified, and that there was no criminal record for this 'pending' client.

Children: Two boys, born 2001 and 2003; Steven and Robert; known as Steve and Bob; both are Mensa material; no recorded juvenile misdemeanors.

Nicky looked at him indignantly and asked, "Where'd you get that?"

Richard replied with a frown, "What, in particular?"

She answered with a hiss, "That bit about my hair being brown and tinged with grey?"

He said, "Special forensic camera, no flash, as you entered and when you looked towards the laptop. Good isn't it!"

To a giggle from Honey, he added in a tone of reproach, "Bit vain, aren't you, being preoccupied with your looks in preference to matters of substance!" He was feeling disgruntled that she'd apparently not admired his detection skills.

Warily, Nicky asked, "Alright then, where'd you get my fingerprints from?"

He replied, "When you pushed the entrance door open."

With an air of triumph, she challenged him: "What if I'd kept my gloves on?"

He replied nonchalantly, "We'd have turned the heating up. Anyway, there were several times when we could have taken your 'dabs'. That reminds me; we want your DNA as well . . . "

He used a tissue to pick up the china cup she had been using seconds before; cupping it by the base, he gingerly took it out of the room.

"Would you like another drink?" he asked, with a deadpan expression, when he returned.

"No thank you," she said frostily. She put her emptied plate on the table and added, "I'd prefer to continue."

Richard decided, "*Good, she's beginning to lose her Ice Maiden façade!*"

He pointed at her photo, as displayed on the PC, and asked, "Is that you?"

Nicky said, sarcastically, "Once upon a time I'd have said 'yes', but according to you the hair color is rather flattering. I mean, it's totally black, rather than brown with grey streaks."

Richard smiled as the empty box on the screen was automatically updated with an 'x', to confirm that she had used the key word yes. This was sufficient for the PC to confirm that the photo was an accurate depiction of her face, and that the other details were also correct.

She glared at the screen, then at him, and burst out laughing at the impudence of the assumption. He, too started laughing, as did Honey, and they all began to relax in each other's company.

She eventually sighed, saying, "Let's get this over with." As a rider, she asked, "I presume that my health is not in question?"

Richard looked at her wistfully and mulled over what to say. "In the longer term, there are some issues you may have to square up to. For instance, when you smile – as you frequently do – there is a slight blue tinge to your teeth."

"So why are your teeth blue? The simple answer is that the walls of your teeth are so thin after whitening that the black metal-amalgam filling is showing through the translucent enamel. Also, you run the hereditary risk of osteoporosis in old-age, cataracts forming in both eyes and as for your knees or hips . . . "

While Honey guffawed in the background, Nicky rose from her chair in a bit of a temper, and advanced on him with her eyes blazing.

He backed away, alarmed by the transformation in her mood, as she snarled in a menacing tone, "Alright, I get the point. Your deductive powers are very, very impressive, but you don't have to tell me what I'm likely to die from. I've suffered enough from the cruel behavior of a mentally deranged husband; you don't have to add to my woes, do you?"

He could see her rapidly cooling down as she regained her self-composure, and took advantage of the situation to embrace her before she thought of kneeing him in the nuts. She put her head against his shoulder as tears welled up in her eyes, while Honey glared at him and mouthed, "*You swine!*"

Silently, he rushed off to fetch a beaker of water, and then helped his prospective client to sink into a chair. They both consoled her as she sat there, dabbing her eyes, while she recovered her composure.

After a while she felt sufficiently well enough for the initial interview to continue.

Richard tried to mollify her by apologizing, "I'm sorry for the pain you've been put through. Nevertheless, I would say, that I for one want you as a client. Give us the chance to read through your case notes and we'll get back to you with a resolution of the way forward that we think you need to take."

Nicky frostily asked, "What are your costs?" She qualified this by adding, "If I decide to go ahead and hire you!"

Richard stated, "A Grand up-front, to include psychological profiling of you, the potential plaintiff, and your ex-husband, the defendant. That part is always value for money, given the fact that they will be written by experienced and qualified profilers. The remainder will be calculated in advance, payable in stages on results."

As an afterthought, he concluded, "Some of what we find out may not be revealed to you, if there is any risk of it proving hurtful and spiteful. Believe it or not, we are not deliberately cruel, except where we need to prise out your real personality."

They smiled at each other and gave another embrace, more formal this time, before bidding farewell. Honey escorted her off the premises, giving Nicky the chance to broach any other matters, in confidence, such as Richard's intrusive comments.

When they reached the pavement, Nicky asked, "Is he always that personal, when asking questions?"

"Don't worry dear," Honey breezily reassured her. "He does it deliberately. It's often essential, to really get to know who he's taking on! We don't want any fruitcakes on our list of clients, do we?"

As they stood there alone, a group of three men came around the nearby corner, from the direction of the town. They were all over 6ft tall, slim and wearing similar black, casual clothes with leather bomber jackets; two of them had goatee beards and the third wore a Walrus moustache. They were all in their thirties or, thereabouts.

Recognition between them and Honey was instantaneous, as they grinned and she moaned, "Oh hell, not you again!"

"So this is where you've relocated!" said the older one of the three, with goatee; he was a prematurely grey-headed man with a friendly countenance. He asked, "Is it convenient for us to speak to you, now?"

Honey put on a brave smile and agreed, "Okay, sure, you'd better come up."

The moustached man looked sadly at Nicky and asked, "Were you on the point of leaving?"

Nicky replied, "Yes, I took advantage of the agency's hospitality to attend their open evening as a would-be client." She was fascinated by his walrus moustache.

With a gentle, mournful smile, he replied, "My name's Walter. If you've got the time, why don't you come back in with us? You may be interested in hearing what we've got to discuss with the agency."

Clearly, Honey was not happy with the proposal.

Nicky looked at her watch and decided to accept. She reasoned, "*What've I got to lose?*"

Nodding her approval, she said to the others, "Give me a minute to tell the kids that I'll be late and I'll join you in a few minutes." She brought out her mobile and waved to the others to go ahead while she made her call.

She was looking for the chance to get to know the agency better, after her first, bruising encounter. She also wanted to get her revenge on Richard, if the opportunity presented itself. Taking advantage of her isolation, she scrutinized the agency's brochure and her face broadened into a grin.

A Business Proposal is Made

Richard had retreated to the far side of his desk. It was facing the round table laden with a spread of hardly touched party foods. Not that it was much of a party occasion, with no one there apart from himself and the female receptionist.

He was perusing the case notes supplied by his potential client, Nicky Lestrange. As a result of his lack of civility and display of deductive buffoonery, her departure was probably permanent

He thought gloomily about his earlier behavior and concluded, "*What a balls-up!*"

As he read on, his attention pricked-up. "*I see that he and she met as students in a red-brick university, lived together for several years to 'test the water' before getting hitched. He took a degree in Electronic Music, while she took one in Applied Sociology. Both got good results.*"

His interest increased when he read that, as part of her course, she did a stint with the national police doing criminal profiling. He thought, "*That's relevant! It would have given her insight into her husband's future misdemeanors!*"

Skipping the early-years synopsis, where husband Jack's behavior was relatively normal but verging on self-centered obsessiveness, he decided to focus on their relationship in subsequent years.

The tipping-point had started when Jack began to feel thwarted in his lack of professional development. After leaving university, he had worked almost constantly for a very small company. This was run by an allegedly foul-mouthed, bad tempered supplier of electronic sound-system backup equipment and services to the music industry.

Over the years, he gained technical competence in this limited, specialist area servicing sound equipment at gigs for touring live bands. His expertise quickly rivalled that of the boss, who consequently stepped back from day-to-day involvement in the company and deputized Jack. The payroll grew to five regular staff, but these came and went on a frequent basis after an inevitable tongue-lashing from the top man.

Nicky had heeded Jack's constant moaning about his lack of recognition, and decided that his CV needed 'pepping-up'. It was indeed no reflection on his presumed abilities; he had stayed too long in one place instead of spreading his wings to gain more recognizable, broader accomplishments.

He therefore began to focus on possible opportunities in other countries, and chose Canada as their preferred destination. There was no obvious reason to select Canada, other than it being an emotional decision based on hope and desire, and within easy reach of his relatives.

He noted the use of the expression *their* in Nicky's précis, it being Jack's clear intention that they should all go together, at the same time. At this stage of their married lives, the family included two boys, who were in primary school.

He was so desperate that he was prepared to risk all. If the move failed, they would potentially lose the gains they had effortlessly accumulated as property values increased around Oxford, where they lived during the boom-years.

By mutual agreement, Nicky had given up her financial support role in management consultancy, and was providing a secondary income by formal child minding on behalf of professional, dual-working parents. Jack openly resented this, insisting that he should be the sole breadwinner in the family.

Her father advised against the move, worried by the risk, and counselled them to send Jack on his own until success was assured.

Jack would have none of it, and persevered in his application to the Canadian consulate until approval was granted for the whole family to emigrate.

A final visit to the country ensued, primarily to search for job opportunities, but this turned out to be pointless. It was hardly surprising, given the fact that the boys were in tow to see the country first-hand, and the family had travelled at a time when house prices in Canada were rising, whilst those at home were crashing.

There were absolutely no job opportunities in the offing.

By good fortune, a leading equipment supplier in the music industry back home had been expressing a long-term interest in employing Jack over this period, but had been dissuaded by his CV and stated career intentions elsewhere.

When a cautious offer was eventually made, Jack needed a lot of persuasion to accept it. His heart still hankered after the prospect of working in Canada, while Nicky used logic to get him to accept the wonderful, timely opportunity placed in front of him.

"*Silly sod!*" Richard concluded, shaking his head in disbelief. "*The choice was clear-cut!*"

He decided to skip temporarily the intervening paragraphs describing the build-up to divorce and find out what Nicky wanted from the agency, but was startled when a voice at the door said, "Knock knock!"

Honey had poked her head around the frame and was grimacing at him.

"We've got visitors," she announced, "and you may not like them!" As she was speaking, two tall men dressed in black could be seen striding towards his office, and he groaned as he recognized them.

At the same time, he could hear the unaccustomed sound of an electric motor: it belonged to the elevator, which someone was using, for real. That was a first!

Honey stood to one side as the two goatee-bearded men entered the room wearing big grins, and extended their hands to shake Richard's, as he stood up to greet them.

"Jake, Matt, what a surprise!" he exclaimed, with a sick smile as they stood facing each other. "What brings you to our neck of the woods?"

Jake, the older of the two replied, "We've got a business proposal for you and your agency. I suggest we wait until the Walrus joins us. He's gone back downstairs to ensure the safe return of the delectable lady who was departing when we were outside the building. We understand she's your first client?"

He was referring in the first instance to the third member of their team, Walter, whose nickname *The Walrus* had been acquired when people saw his droopy moustache and general countenance.

The prospect of having to face Nicky again, in such a short time frame, filled Richard with dread; she'd find out far too much about the agency for his liking. Still, nothing could be done to prevent it, so let the dice roll.

He had no need to invite his uninvited guests to help themselves to food; they'd already started, and were also popping open the Cobra beers as he looked on.

Before long, Walter ascended in the elevator with a smiling Nicky and could be seen heading along the corridor to join them. He ushered her into the room, and hellos were exchanged again as she took off her coat and joined the increasingly merry throng.

Richard decided to open the 'glass curtain' between his room and that of the adjoining one belonging to Honey, to praise from the 'men in black'. Much to his pleasure, they appreciated this flexible approach to office design, and spread out on the visitors' chairs while they made serious inroads into the food placed temptingly in front of them.

Honey whispered to Richard, "I've called Rose and Chuck on their mobiles, and they're on their way now." She was referring to the other partners in the agency, who were wrapping up their previous business commitments.

Within ten minutes, they too had joined the assembled partygoers and sat down with them, waiting to hear what the newcomers wanted to discuss.

Jake stood up somberly in front of the four agency partners and introduced himself properly, for the sake of Nicky.

"Over a period of three years, we accompanied the members of this agency on their paranormal investigations into unresolved murders. My name is Jake, my colleagues are Matt and Walter, and we are all employed as the camera and sound crew by a television studio. Our dual role was minders of the paranormal investigators."

He pointed out his companions, who gave slight bows as they were identified, and said additionally, "At one time or another, we have all operated in war zones, and are ex-military personnel."

"Woo . . . !" went Honey and Rose in mock appreciation, while Chuck grinned. Richard was impatient to hear the proposal, and gestured to them to be more solemn.

Jake continued, "To our regret, the whole thing fizzled out, with no recorded successes. I would say that this was a failure caused by time constraints, a lack of police resources and universal skepticism."

He looked directly at Richard and Honey and emphasized, "In no way was it a fair reflection of your true abilities. You totally convinced us and the studio that you have a genuine talent as psychic researchers or mediums – these descriptions mean the same thing to me!"

"On the other hand, the local police who became involved often had long lists of unsolved cases to look at, and were in no way as able as the national agencies."

Richard asked, "What is it you now want from us?"

Jake replied, "To take a fresh approach to crime investigation. On behalf of some influential individuals, we've been given the authority to offer you a business proposition that will give your agency proper backing, and access to a broad range of official resources.

"To get your agency off to a running start we are empowered to offer you incentives. These include the following: we will not impose unrealistic time limitations on the studies; you will work in parallel with traditional investigators; you will not be given any more hopeless cases to investigate, unless you expressly insist on them; you will be supported with adequate resources; finally, you *will* be treated seriously."

Rose asked quietly, "And how can we believe you, in making all of these promises?"

Walter got up, and said with relish, "We've been approached by a stonking rich benefactor who not only wants to back you, but who also has faith in you! He's done his homework, I can tell you!"

His curiosity aroused, Richard asked, "Who is it?"

Jake replied in a laid-back manner, "A U.S. philanthropic

billionaire who insists on anonymity. He's not dodgy either!"

Matt looked at Richard and interceded, "There's only one stipulation: you must take on one more partner, of his choice, giving him equal billing."

Richard looked doubtful, asking, "In what role? Who do you have in mind?"

Matt replied, "His name is Joe Fraser and he currently heads a special unit for serious crimes. He would act as an impartial, skilled, lead-detective using traditional techniques. He will smooth the way for cooperation with official agencies, both at local and national levels."

"Do you want to meet him?" He fished in the pocket of his leather jacket, retrieved a smart phone and twirled it in the air.

The four agency partners looked at each other and communicated wordlessly. They had no need to talk, being able to operate in perfect, mental accord. On their behalf, Richard said, "Go for it," while the others nodded their agreement.

Nicky cheerfully lightened the process by quipping, "It sounds like Enid Blyton; meet the Famous Five!"

None of the others smiled, while Richard stared stonily at her.

He asked her, "Is this leading up to something you want to ask? Only, if it is, could you make it quick before our future partner gets here!"

Unabashed, she retorted, "I *do* have a relevant question, yes." She opened the brochure and began.

"It concerns the names of the existing partners appearing in this advertising literature. They read: *Richard Pencil, Honey Linger, Rose Bush* and *Chuck Stone.*" She had the trace of a smile quivering around her lips as she asked, "Are they for real?"

Jake and Matt turned and looked at each other, trying not to show their amusement, while Walter's face was expressionless.

Richard took a deep breath and patiently explained, "The names are not made up. We are fully aware of the mocking that goes on at our expense, and choose to ignore it. Anyway, I would add that any light relief from the awful tasks we have to perform is welcome, and I'm damned if I'm going to change my name by deed poll just to satisfy others. It's the fault of our parents, not us, for causing others to make fun of us."

Honey spoke up, in his defense, "To reassure all of you, speaking from personal experience Richard is no 'Pencil Dick' and he's a straight-up sort of guy!" The three studio emissaries burst out laughing, while Richard had the good grace to blush in embarrassment.

She added with a drawl, "It may also interest you to hear that I have a habit of humming when I'm on the case, and am often called 'Hummer Linger', but don't know why people find *that* funny!"

Nicky looked at her to try to see if she was lying, but Honey's face was a picture of innocence.

Honey followed this up by commenting, "And as for 'Rose Bush', I have no clue what color her pussy . . . " before Richard stopped her dead in her tracks by saying, "That's quite enough for now. We don't want our first possible client to be put off us any further, do we?" This was to uncontrolled gales of laughter from the three male visitors.

Nicky felt a sudden urge to leave; standing up, she announced to Richard and Honey, "Perhaps it'd be better if I say my goodbyes now, and leave you to get acquainted with your new partner."

Walter rose and offered his help. "Allow me to get your coat and escort you out of the building. It's been nice meeting you and hopefully it won't be the last time." Richard and the others murmured their agreement, as she was escorted off the premises.

Little did Nicky appreciate the influence that had been exerted on her by Richard. He was intuitively capable of influencing others by devious methods.

He could also read minds as if they were open books. Like many psychics or mediums, it was not a skill that he was fully aware that he possessed; they often mistook it for communicating with dead people. This was a widespread partial misconception; the rest of it did involve direct communication at some level.

Joe Fraser noticed Nicky as she walked out into the cold night. He waited until she had gone in the other direction before getting out of his black saloon and remotely locking it. He was reasonably fit for a man in his mid-fifties, and entered the agency's office block by striding up the stairs two at a time.

He had his own, clear-cut role to perform, after thrashing it out between himself and their new, joint sponsor.

They had mutually agreed that what distinguished The Deaduction Agency partners from bogus mediums was a seemingly unfailing ability to pick up a so-called 'psychic trail'; victims and perpetrators alike purportedly left this, during a crime.

Joe and the sponsor were open-minded that a trail of this nature could exist; they realized that it might be commonplace, and prove to be a viable investigative option on a par with profiling. It needed formal study and verification, if it were ever to be adopted after any 'buts' had been resolved.

That was to be part of Joe's mission in the agency.

The receptionist could be heard answering the intercom, and Rose rushed out to meet their guest, as requested by Richard.

After exchanging greetings, she said to the receptionist, Alice, "It looks like we're going to be some time here, so put up a closed sign and go home when you have set up the answering machine. We'll lock up when we leave."

Alice nodded and began packing her bag, while Rose ushered Joe down the corridor. She looked back at him with a smile as they walked, noticing that he had a peculiar, floppy gait in his body movements.

"Hi y'all!" he said with a broad smile as they entered the room. "Nice to meet you!"

Brief introductions followed with handshakes all round, as the latest arrival declined the offer of food but opened a beer, and joined them by sitting sociably alongside Rose. This placed him in front of the second desk, in the extended room.

"*At least he's not stand-offish!*" Richard decided, waiting to see how Joe would get down to business. The man was certainly affable, although from the way he looked at people he could be as hard as nails when need dictated.

He didn't have long to wait, as the partnership proposal was broached almost immediately. Joe swigged his beer from the bottle, looked individually at the partners and stated, "From what the support crew have already said, you know what my role will be, else I wouldn't be sitting here now!"

He glanced at them all, with a smile creasing his deeply lined face, before continuing.

"I will act as the traditional lead-detective in the agency, giving you the time you need to complete your investigations, as you see fit. I will 'fight your corner' against officialdom and smooth the way with the various agencies we come into contact with."

Pausing for a few seconds to allow this to sink in, he added, "I also hope to be given the opportunity to advise you, if I think you can do better."

"*Uh oh!*" thought the other partners, which was where Joe offered them a sweetener.

"To get us off to a good start, the sponsor is making the following offer, without pre-conditions: in the first year alone, we will each receive a six figure sum as a retainer. This will be distributed pro rata and upfront, in accordance with a soon-to-be defined new partnership agreement.

"In addition, the entire running costs of the agency will be met without any reciprocal handover of assets.

"The sum will repeat on an annual, rolling basis and be regarded as the basis for renegotiation from the time that you sign the contract; this will be downloaded onto your central computer, for your scrutiny. Renewal will be an annual commitment, by mutual consent. Respond as soon as possible.

"I wish to emphasize that this is *not* going to be a 'scroungers' charter'. The powers-that-be expect a fair day's work for a fair day's pay. It is appreciated that people with your unique skills work better without artificial pressures being exerted on them. We won't abuse you, and we would like the same respect in return.

"How fair does that sound to you all?"

Joe looked around, and was pleased to see that they were all sitting there looking astounded.

The three crew members were equally pleased, having agreed similar, albeit less lucrative, contracts beforehand, subject to the agency partners' formal acceptance.

Richard was trying his best not to jump up and shout, "*Yippee!*"

With a glance at the other partners followed by a slight nod to Joe, he replied, "You'll have our answer tomorrow. It looks favorable to me, perhaps generous beyond my personal expectations. Naturally, we'll pass it to the legal experts for scrutiny and respond soonest."

They were all in a celebratory mood after witnessing the boost received to the launch of the new agency, and chatted away for a couple of hours afterwards. Joe called a halt when he got up and stated, "All good things have to come to an end. I'll await your decision, perhaps tomorrow afternoon?"

He handed out his business card to the partners, and picked up some of the empty plates, asking, "Where's the kitchen?"

Richard replied, "Don't worry about that; we'll clear up later. Let me guide you out."

As they reached the door, which Honey opened remotely, Richard accompanied Joe and the crew downstairs, to wish them a safe journey and hand out his own business cards.

The other partners speedily cleared away the used plates and glasses, carrying them to the kitchen to dump in a sink full of hot water, ready for washing and drying the following morning.

Leftover food was stored in the kitchen, and the entertainment area tidied up, before Rose and Chuck departed, to drive home to their apartments.

Returning to his empty office with Honey behind, Richard turned to face her without warning. She was caught off-guard as he seized her by the waist and kissed her passionately on the lips, growling, "I've been waiting to do that all evening! Damn, you turn me on!"

She dug her nails into his shoulders and gasped in excitement as he started stripping her, before she responded naturally herself.

Suddenly tearing himself away, he said "Wait a second!" and tip-toed out of the room in his underpants and luminescent socks. He could be heard rummaging in the storeroom and pulling something frantically out of a plastic bag, before returning with a brown covered futon, which he unrolled on the floor before his desk.

In next to no time, they were writhing on the floor, locked

together, as they peaked repeatedly in sexual ecstasy. What he found irresistible was her perfect, faintly muscular, totally feminine, rounded body and eagerness to match his demands. She only had to go near him and he was aroused, and when she touched him in any way it was like dynamite exploding in his loins.

By the same token, she couldn't look at him without feeling tingles, especially when he paraded his six-pack around in the nude with his flag at half-mast. He did have some funny habits though, which she regarded as cute when he wasn't obsessing about tidiness.

It had to be said, some would regard one of these habits as a 'turn-off': when he was trying to make contact with the spirits, his eyes would roll upwards until only the whites were showing, before he closed them. For Honey, when they had sex, it signaled that he was about to climax, giving her the chance to anticipate and share in the ecstasy herself.

Afterwards, when his energy began to wane, Richard wasted what little of it he had left by rolling up the futon and hiding it in the storeroom. This was before they put their clothes back on, switched off the air conditioning and left the building, to sleep together in her apartment.

That would give Honey the opportunity to cook Richard's breakfast the following morning. Routinely, he kept most of his stuff there for occasions like this.

Let Battle Commence

In spite of their gymnastics the night before, Richard and Honey were almost the first to arrive at the office. The cleaners were there before them and could be heard clinking the plates and glasses as they washed, dried and put them away. Strictly speaking, it wasn't part of their duties, but they were trying to impress their new employers.

Richard turned on his computer, downloaded the draft contract attached to Joe's email and printed off two copies: one for himself and the other for Honey.

He forwarded the originally emailed contract to their lawyer, with a request to read it and reply urgently.

Placing the contract copy on Honey's desk, he asked her to scan through it and chase the lawyer for a reply to his email mid-morning. He wanted matters resolved later that day.

At 8:55am, Alice, Rose and Chuck came in, looking cheerful and ready for whatever was going to be thrown at them. Richard consulted Honey and they both agreed to pass their contract copies to their partners, unannotated.

Chuck commented, "It promises to be a blank canvas for us, until we get some business coming in."

Rose speculated, "I guess we could start work with that Nicky Lestrange, but it looks like a routine infidelity case to me. I'd prefer something meaty, involving the paranormal, to get us going."

Richard suggested, "Let's select some of our previous, unresolved cases to look at again. I'd bet the studio's got a bucketful of stuff ready to give us, when contracts are signed. Either way, with a bit of luck, we'll be swamped with work before long."

It wasn't until early afternoon that their lawyer consulted the agency's partners; it was good news: they could go ahead and sign the contract. This they duly did, scanning the most important page and promptly emailing it across to Joe Fraser.

Within minutes, Joe was at the front door, keeping his thumb pressed on the button of the entrance intercom.

Alice warned the surprised Richard, who in turn notified the other partners and reckoned, "He must have been waiting downstairs, in his car!"

Richard barely had time to intercept Joe, who had taken aback Chuck by asking, "Which is my office?"

He was being trailed by a grinning uniformed police officer, carrying a stack of files on an upright trolley.

Richard commented to Joe, "You don't hang around, do you?" He pointed at the room nearest the front and said, "This one's yours."

He trailed after the pair of them through the open door. The young officer unloaded the files by the desk, nodded at Richard and left him alone with Joe after saying brief goodbyes. He pushed his empty trolley in front, winking at Alice as he headed towards the exit.

She gave him a conspiratorial wink back, which Richard noticed. He thought, "*That's what I like in a young woman – A touch of sassiness!*" That was one of the qualities that had attracted him to Honey; it still did, along with the rest of her.

Joe sat down behind his desk, broodily tracing the pattern embedded in its baize top, and said laconically, "One door closes, sort of," and adding, "another one opens! Thirty years I devoted to homicide, hunting the wicked, now I do the same in pastures new."

He looked at Richard with a shrug, his eyelids half-closed. For the first time, Richard noticed how pale his blue eyes were. His expression was a reflection of his words: they were those of a man world weary from events that were repeating yet again.

However, there was something in his posture indicating he was not tired of the process. He looked nonchalant, acting like a big cat patiently waiting to pounce on his victim.

Rising from his seat, he picked up the piles of folders from the floor and thumped them on his desk, in three piles.

Sitting back down, he fiddled with the phone system and asked

Richard, "How do I use the intercom on this thing?"

Richard showed him, and he summoned the other partners by barking into it, "Could you come into my office please?"

The others filed in and sat around the conference table, where Joe and Richard joined them. He began the meeting by stating, "Welcome to our first 'Case Allocation' meeting. On my desk are bundles of files containing the initial cases to be distributed between us.

"Others may be added at any time from now on, and be given greater priority as other agencies notify us of their needs. I will act as coordinator in distributing the workload, in consultation with our senior partner, Richard.

"Where Richard is out on a case personally, I will assume responsibility for this task and for liaising with external authorities and the press."

He looked at the others and asked, "You have a new client?" It was a fair guess, having seen a smartly dressed woman hurrying from the building as he got out of his car the evening before.

Richard confirmed, "Yes, a Nicky Lestrange, who has problems with her ex-husband, though I don't think it's anything out of the ordinary." He was implying that there was no *paranormal* element to it.

Joe studied him with eyes widening and said, "She *knew* before she entered our offices what our main focus is; that suggests to me that her husband is not acting normally, in her opinion. No doubt the friends who advised her to come here feel the same, or planted the idea in her mind."

He leaned forward and spoke to Richard directly, "I'd like you and Honey to investigate and clear this matter up. If it's straightforward, then we can move onto another case in a day or two." Richard wondered idly if Joe realized that he and Honey were an item.

Leaning back and pulling the five topmost files off the nearest bundle of folders, Joe glanced at the label on the top one before handing it to Rose, saying, "This unsolved case is a few years old. There's not much forensic evidence in the police files to help resolve it, so your psychic powers are mainly what you'll have to go on. Can you and Chuck establish a trail? Then you can do the same with the other files."

Joe had deliberately placed theses files nearest to himself, for ease of retrieval. Richard noticed this, and thought, "*Everything he does is premeditated!*"

Rose flicked through the contents of the top file, before passing them all to Chuck for scrutiny. She commented to Joe, "We've handled this first one before. It didn't seem to us that the police followed-up what we said originally. Hell, we practically gave them a description of the assailant and his location!"

Joe sighed and said, "I suppose they already had plenty of work on their hands and didn't take you seriously. Prove them wrong! Take two of the crew with you for protection." He inclined his head, to indicate that they should start directly.

Rose and Chuck got up and returned to Rose's office, to contact the crew, discuss their strategy and start making travel arrangements.

Feeling invigorated, Chuck commented, "Good times are a' returning!"

Meanwhile, Honey headed with Richard to his office, to begin their investigation, leaving Joe sitting alone, feeling optimistic. After a while, he began storing the unsolved case files upright in his side unit, from left to right in ascending priority, according to the likelihood of success.

Then he walked across to join Richard and Honey, to see how things were going.

CASE 1.
THE DERANGED HUSBAND

§ 1: A Fresh Approach

Joe eased his way into the room occupied by Richard and Honey, who were sitting at the round conference table. He sat opposite them and asked tactfully, "I don't want to tread on anyone's toes, but I'm wondering how you intend handling the case?"

Defensively, Richard replied, "Well we've got to make travel arrangements first, and read the case notes thoroughly, so there's not much to see at present. Why'd you ask?"

Joe suggested, "I thought it might be opportune for you to take a different approach and see how things shape up. Why don't you start by establishing a 'psychic trail' from the outset? I couldn't help but see the boys' pictures in the client's case file, plus you've got a photo of her on the PC, and her life's history. Won't those do, for starters?"

Honey searched the file and pulled out two small portraits of the boys in school uniform, commenting, "These are of her boys, taken last year I should think. Cute little fellas, so they seem."

Joe's face brightened as he remarked, "I *thought* she might have put them there deliberately. It backs up my view that she chose our agency because of its paranormal associations. Is there a photo of herself included?"

Honey shook the file hurriedly, and looked surprised as two more photos fell onto the floor. She picked them up and confirmed their contents, saying, "Yes, we've got one of herself and another of . . . " She looked on the back and exclaimed, "her ex-husband Jack Lestrange as well!"

Richard looked at Joe respectfully, and agreed with him. "Point taken! We *have* got enough to start with." He pondered some more and suggested, "Let's call this *The Case of the Deranged Husband*."

Honey placed the photos of the two boys, Steve and Bob, face upwards on the table top. Running her fingers lightly over them, she concentrated deeply as she traced their silhouettes.

Richard displayed Nicky's details on his PC and filled the screen with her photo, which Honey also studied briefly, before beginning to focus primarily on the cardboard-framed portraits of the parents. It was when she came to Jack that she gave an involuntary shudder, and felt emotions welling-up inside her.

She said, "I'm beginning to get a rush of remote viewings that make me feel queasy. I'm seeing a snapshot of them with their father, and all three are having some sort of adrenalin rush. I see the numbers '120' in front of them, but it's all fading now; they've survived the momentary danger!"

She paused to reflect on the significance of the sighting and then spoke again, almost as if unaware of those around her.

"Now I'm seeing a holiday with Nicky and the boys in Spain, presumably staying with her parents. Feelings are raw, as their father no longer wants to be with them. It's hot and sunny, and the boys are quarrelling with their mother most of the time.

"They're on their mobile phones every day, for much of the time, whispering and glaring at their mother and grandparents. When they sign off they get really rude, and shout and cry. They're saying things like 'I hate being here' and 'I want to go home and stay with daddy'.

"They must be giving regular reports to their father, who is influencing their behavior.

"The poor grandparents have spent a lot of money on staying at a top hotel on this holiday, to help Nicky and the boys have a deserved break from the shock of the divorce. Not a single day has passed without the boys acting up."

Richard spoke up, "This coincides with Nicky's notes. Her complaint is that in the period leading up to the divorce, her ex-husband was hell-bent on turning the boys against her. It was natural to assume that the boys would stay with their mother, so he bought them each a mobile phone and commanded them to keep in touch with him, using secret passwords.

"If their mother showed any interest, they were instructed to delete all texts and records of calls made; these had to be kept private. In addition, they were not allowed to mention her when visiting him."

Honey continued, in a voice tinged with shock, "I've picked up on him as well, directly. He hates her with a vengeance, and wishes she was dead! He's shacked up with a girl barely out of her teens, and wants to create a replacement family *without* his original partner.

"My God, he acts as if Nicky never existed, and I can hear him shouting as he forbids the boys to mention their mother in his presence. Though he's not living with them anymore, he takes every opportunity to interfere in their tranquility. This is one sick mind I'm reading!"

Richard had continued studying the case notes and said, "From what I've read, his behavior has worsened since the divorce. He won't go near the house he lived in when married, and parks a few hundred yards up the road to collect the boys when it's his turn to have them.

"Nicky's concern is that he's brainwashing the boys into moving in with him and his girlfriend.

"He refuses to communicate with his ex-wife direct, insisting that the boys are old enough to make up their own minds when he talks to them. The disruption he's causing is immense; whenever the boys are with their mother, he provokes arguments between them. He does this by poisoning their minds against her when they are with him.

"The younger boy remains implacable: he is determined to go and live with his father. The older boy's bad language has to be heard to be believed and he is now attending counselling sessions. The schools have been notified of the situation and are involved sympathetically."

Joe pitched in and commented, "It seems to me that he wants the boys to go and live with him full-time. That way he'll be able to eliminate any payments agreed under a court order and get her out of the house.

"He's probably acting as a guarantor on the mortgage she's paying off. He wants to get rid of this huge commitment, so he can obtain a mortgage of his and won't have to pay rent forever. Am I right?"

Richard finished reading, raised his eyebrows and said, "Yes, you are. How'd you guess that?"

Joe replied sardonically, "It's more common that you might think. Modern fathers who prowl for sex outside an existing relationship are often selfish, lack remorse, blame their wives or partners for causing them to stray, and feel no sense of obligation.

"Kids are used as weapons, with mobile phones instead of guns in their hands. In short, the fathers behave like a bunch of shits.

"What worries me more about this case is the residual hatred he feels towards Nicky. I'll bet her lawyers have picked up on it too!"

As Joe got up to leave the room, he asked, "He's in the music industry isn't he? Check if he takes drugs; cocaine is the main contender, when he's away on one of his business 'trips'. That could explain his behavior. The guy's paranoid."

Honey said chirpily, "Will do! By the way, when do you think we should pay Nicky a visit?"

Joe looked at them with a shy grin. "Any time from now."

Feeling cheeky, Honey asked, "And what about the money she owes us if we start investigating seriously?"

Joe answered, "My guess is that she'll want to find out how much this is going to cost her, if we continue uninvited. If she does, tell her we'll let her know *in advance*, when it looks like we're getting somewhere worthwhile. She's a single mother so don't frighten her off."

Before heading back to his office, he gave them a special warning, "You may not realize that the ex-husband's behavior could be categorized as criminal. Where cruelty is regarded as grounds for divorce, this can include mental as well as physical abuse.

"Prison can be the sentence for this type of sustained behavior. Let her know that the police may get involved, officially; that should buck her up!"

After Joe had left them alone, Richard asked Honey, "Can you check if Nicky is home tomorrow, and if so what time's convenient?"

She held her photo up, concentrated hard, and stated in a matter-of-fact way, "It's a school day, she doesn't go to work until 10:00am, so about 9:00am will be fine."

Richard looked at her with surprise and asked, "Are you kidding? You can retrieve all that information without making a phone call?"

Honey nodded with a smirk, whispering huskily, "You'd be amazed what I can do!"

Richard wished he'd had the foresight to put blinds on the doors, and locks on the inside.

§ 2: The Crime Scene is Assessed

Their car drew up outside Nicky's modest semi-detached house on the dot, at 9:00am, and the two walked single-file up the short footpath leading to the white plastic front door. There was no bell-push nor knocker, so Richard rapped one of the frosted glass panels in the top half of the door.

He was studying two large spiders guarding the top of the frame when Nicky came to the door. Following his gaze, she looked up at them briefly, before saying, "Yes, we think the spiders are venomous but we don't believe in killing them. Come on through to the lounge and shut the door after you."

Clearly, their arrival had not flummoxed her, and she briskly led the way into a small, low ceilinged room containing two sofas, one large and the other a two-seater, with a flat-screen TV in one corner by the wide, front window.

There were wood ashes in an open fireplace set in the long-wall opposite the door, and the floor was strewn with debris left by the two, untidy boys.

"Excuse the mess," she said, starting to push the accumulating books, PCs, cables, pencil sets and school notes into meaningful heaps. "You can sit on the smaller sofa, where my sons normally plonk themselves."

Richard noticed a blob of congealed food on one of the sofa arms, and promptly sat the other side, after checking that the seat looked clean. In spite of the disorder, Richard sensed that it was a happy, family home.

Honey sat down unsettlingly close to Richard, trying to keep away from the blob of food, and commented, "You seem to be settled here, and the atmosphere is calm. Are you okay?" Nicky was dressed in a smart, dark-grey trouser suit ready to go to work and sat alone on the larger sofa, looking composed.

It was a pointed question, and Nicky responded by answering it with a smile, "Yes, it's fine at the moment. My other half had the boys last weekend, and for once they came home in a happy mood. Would you like some tea or coffee?"

They both declined, as Richard checked his wristwatch, before stating, "The reason for our visit is get some information that'll help us in our enquiries. It won't take long."

Nicky stiffened and asked, "How much is this going to cost me?"

Richard replied, "Nothing at all. We'll let you know in advance if you're going to be billed, so don't worry. This is only a preliminary fact-gathering interview. I can tell you that the police may get involved anyway, if your ex is harassing you and the boys. Cost may not be a factor."

Nicky hardly seemed to register this information, and Honey interrupted by asking, "One time when the boys were with their father, something happened that really got their adrenalin rushing. It was associated with the numbers '120'. What do those numbers mean?"

Without hesitation Nicky replied, "They told me that he took them out in his Mini Cooper sports car and did 120mph on a stretch of road. He was lucky he didn't get a ticket." Wistfully, she concluded, "Never mind, it's done and nothing will undo it."

It had become embedded in her memory.

Richard softened his tone and asked quietly, "Don't you think that's dangerous?"

She snapped back, "Of course, but what can I say if he does stupid things? Anyway, how'd you find that out? I didn't mention it in my case notes, did I?"

Honey explained, "I picked up on it, out of the ether, so to speak.

Nicky looked at them approvingly. "So it's true then, people like you *do* have visions!"

Richard nodded in agreement and asked, "We understand that you're in receipt of a number of emails from your ex?"

"Yes," she replied, "Plus I've got transcripts of the text messages he hurls at me. I can't get at the texts he sends to the boys, who've told me they are under orders to delete their stuff regularly. Give me a moment, and I'll get what I've copied and hand it over to you."

She left the room for a few minutes, returning with a bundle of documents which she handed over for them to take away.

"When are the boys with him next?" Richard asked.

"The day after tomorrow. He waits for them to meet him, in his car, near the end of the road, at 6pm sharp." She pointed out of the front window, to the left, where there were hardly any parking spaces available at the curbside.

Richard told her, "Keep it to yourself, but here's something you should be aware of: deleted messages can be retrieved. We've got some serious software that's capable of doing it."

That's good!" she said, looking pleased. "If needs be, I can lend you Bob's mobile when he's at school. The young one spies on me all the time."

They said their goodbyes and sidled out of the front door, keeping a watchful eye on the dangling brightly colored spiders. Nicky waved them goodbye with an amused expression, shortly before emerging herself soon afterwards to drive to work.

Honey said, "She's a trainee accountant, gaining professional qualifications and working part-time in a small accountancy practice. Her money should double in the near future. Good on her!"

As she drove away, the others trailed at a discreet distance, to make sure she was being truthful.

Richard commented, "No harm in checking!"

As had been surmised, Nicky passed their impromptu test with flying colors.

When they got back to the office, they sat down at Richard's conference table and began sorting in date order the texts and emails Nicky had provided. Then they scrutinized the contents.

As they ploughed through the small pile, they noticed the curt, dismissive orders being relayed from Jack and the restrained, moderate tone of Nicky's replies. At regular intervals, he would insist that she looked after the boys whenever it was inconvenient for him and would comment rudely if he thought she was neglecting them in some way.

At one stage, the elder son, Steve, had to have an emergency operation, in hospital, for a cut on his back that had turned septic. After reading the flurry of emails about this event, Richard commented, "Would you believe that he didn't even try and visit the boy in hospital?"

Honey speculated absent-mindedly, "I should imagine he didn't want to bump into his ex-wife."

Richard exclaimed, "I didn't think of that! The general tone of his emails is domineering. He doesn't hold back either, in saying what he thinks."

Honey chuckled as she commented, "Nicky sometimes forwards them onto his parents, with a covering note saying 'this is what I have to put up with!' at the front of it."

"What does he do, in retaliation?"

"In the past, he's ordered her never to contact his parents again."

"How does she react?"

"She ignores him, time and again."

"It must be driving him bonkers."

"Hopefully, yes!"

Honey picked up Nicky's portrait, began focusing on it, and then leaned back with her eyes closed.

Suddenly she stated excitedly, "Hey, this is so much easier when I have a living person to deal with! It's especially easy when I know the person concerned; it's like watching a recording of someone. I can skip back and forth at any time!"

She leaned forward, supporting her chin with her hands, elbows on the table, and gave a running commentary that was intended to be fed into the PC.

It was also for Richard's benefit; some of it putting more flesh on Nicky's case notes*.

* real names and locations are rarely reported in the notes, owing to the contentious nature of the truth contained therein.

It was recited as follows.

For nearly two years, Jack had driven two hours each way to his new employer. The prospect of a move to Canada gradually faded, although it was resurrected for a brief period after a couple of months. He was giving a presentation to a New York based agent at his new employer's premises when, out of the blue, the agent impulsively offered him the opportunity to join him on a low six figure salary.

Sympathetically, his boss stepped back, giving Jack the chance to consider what to do next. He knew that Jack was still undecided whether or not to stay, which was why he had not yet made any move to live nearer his place of work.

Emotionally, Jack felt enthusiastic about accepting the opportunity, but was persuaded by Nicky to check out the finances before doing anything concrete.

Fortunately, they had a good friend who was working in New York and were able to consult him. When they told this friend that the agent was based on Long Island, there was a sharp intake of breath; it was an expensive place to live, and the salary on the table would be totally inadequate to support a family.

Reluctantly, Jack broached the matter with the agent, who decided not to improve the offer. As likely as not, he'd got the jitters, regarded Jack as dithering, and left the matter in abeyance.

Jack was not used to being denied his ambitions, no matter how futile they might prove to be, and went into a huge, irreversible sulk. He decided arbitrarily that his marriage was over, and refused to communicate anymore with his wife, to tell her how he felt.

"So much for making a life-long commitment! I wonder if Richard will pop the question, someday." Honey thought, breaking off her recital temporarily.

She resumed:

However, it suited Jack to accept her desire to live nearer his place of work, and committed himself to making the move to live closer. His aim was to get revenge for her perceived betrayal, so he began playing with her emotions. At night, he would turn his back on her and she would cry herself to sleep, bewildered by his cold behavior.

Some months elapsed, during which period the house was

sold and another chosen to rent for six months, some 15 minutes from where Jack worked. Upon leaving their original house, they said goodbye to all the friends that Nicky and the boys had made, packed their belongings and journeyed to their new, temporary home nearer Jack's employer.

It was noticeable that Jack had not acquired any male companions whatsoever in his social life. He was a true loner.

Meanwhile, whilst renting, Nicky found the perfect place to live permanently. It was within the catchment area for a really good school, and not much further than the rented house for Jack and his daily working commutes.

The only observable difference in Jack was his behavior when he returned home at the end of each shorter day. He would come in sullenly, briefly acknowledge his wife and two boys, and immediately slouch in his chair, with one leg hanging over the armrest, and begin texting while glaring around him.

At the time, no one thought to ask: "Who are you texting?"

They trusted him implicitly.

"It sounds like you're having fun." Joe was barely audible, as he announced his presence while leaning on the doorjamb.

The sound of his voice made Honey jump, and she barked an instruction at the PC to stop recording.

Joe apologized, "Sorry about the interruption; I didn't realize what you were doing."

"That's okay, there wasn't much done. I'll tidy it up in a few seconds."

She stared at the screen and made a few adjustments to the automatically produced text.

Sitting upright and sweeping her hair back with one hand, she agreed with Joe's original comment. "Yes, it is fun. Communicating with the living is far easier."

Richard yawned, stretched his arms and rose, ready to depart. "Let's call it a day and resume tomorrow, first thing."

"Okay," she agreed, tidying up the paperwork.

"When are you going to visit the client's home?" Joe asked them. Richard replied, "The day after tomorrow, when her ex picks up the boys for a sleepover. We'll be waiting for him at 6:00pm sharp."

"Good," Joe confirmed. "Either of you fancy a drink this evening, before you go home?"

They could hardly refuse this early opportunity to socialize with their new, senior partner, and nodded in acceptance.

Honey spoke up, "There's a bar a few doors away, as you may have noticed. Give me a few minutes to powder my nose."

Richard asked, "Is that what you call it, what you're going to do?"

"Ha, ha," Honey said over her shoulder as she swayed seductively while heading to the Ladies restroom.

Joe watched her with an understanding smile; this banter had helped confirm his suspicion of the deep relationship between the two of them.

The three of them stood at the long, highly polished counter, holding chilled beers in tall, slender glasses. Joe's contained zero-alcohol, and Honey asked him,

"Don't you drink normal stuff that has a bit of a kick to it?"

"Yeah, I do when I get home. I prefer a couple of glasses of red Californian wine with my family meal." He made a face when sipping his beer and explained, "I used to be much heavier that I am now, and decided to cut back before I got any obesity-related health problems.

"To change the subject; what've you found out about your client's situation?"

She gave him an outline of what she'd established so far, with Richard chiming in when judged appropriate.

Joe rubbed his chin with a gnarled hand and reflected.

"I wouldn't like to see him get nasty, physically as well as mentally. If you could assess her current vulnerability and see how alone she is at present, that would be beneficial."

Then he made an offer of help. "Do you remember that nice young policeman who helped me by carrying my files earlier? I'd like him to accompany you when you intercept Nicky's ex-spouse, and put a gentle frightener on him. He'll be in plain clothes but carrying a badge. Would that be okay with you?"

Richard and Honey exchanged a brief glance, before Honey answered, "That'll be fine."

Richard queried, "I thought you'd left the force, when you joined us?"

"Hell no!" Joe exclaimed. "My empire's been expanded. The Deaduction Agency has the official backing of the government, at arm's length. Effectively, you're a semi-autonomous, outsourced facility. That's great for all of us, since it gets around many legislative hurdles."

They looked cautiously pleased, wondering what the benefits would be; only time would tell.

As the evening progressed, they chatted about other aspects of their lives, and parted feeling contented. They had gleaned a lot of information about each other at a personal level, and were beginning to feel more comfortable together.

Joe also let slip his desire for each of the four of the psychics to work singly. This would double the output of Richard and Honey, who had grown used to working as a team when being filmed. He had watched their shows on TV and witnessed the fact that their 'visions', and interpretations of them, had been identical in almost all instances. His advice came as no surprise to either Richard or Honey, whose years of working together had confirmed that as a fact.

In fact, Honey relished the chance to show her mettle, while Richard vaguely feared the prospect that she might outshine him.

Joe thought it odd that orthodox officers worked in teams and pooled their efforts, whereas mediums nearly always worked independently of one another. "Horses for courses!" he reasoned.

§ 3: Distance Learning Continues

Prior to the second planned visit to Nicky's home patch, Honey retrieved the typed version of the telepathic reading that she had recited yesterday and double-checked it for accuracy. The spellcheck and punctuation software on the PC was near perfect in operation, and a real timesaver.

"Good work," she grunted as she made a few minor grammatical changes.

The two psychics picked up the photos they had used previously as psychometric tools, and began to re-establish the memory trails being left by Nicky and her ex-louse. Honey then continued with her recital.

The notes are reproduced below.

From Nicky's perspective, her awareness of her husband's infidelity was sudden and shocking.

All was revealed when her older sister was warned by their parents that there were problems in the marriage and was relayed examples of his erratic behavior. The instant response was: "He's being unfaithful. That was how my ex-husband started behaving!"

She checked the entries on Jack's Facebook site, and detected a persistent flow of intimate correspondence between him and an unknown female.

The sister asked her own daughter, Nicky's niece, to put her knowledge of social sites to good use and help investigate. Immediately, she in turn uncovered a separate flow of gooey love texts and embarrassing photos being exchanged on the associated Instagram service.

The niece also let it be known for the first time that her uncle

Jack had flirted with her on more than one occasion, which she'd found to be distasteful. She only told her mother after finding this supporting evidence of his bad behavior.

"*He's a closet pedophile!*" Richard prematurely decided, staying quiet not to interrupt. Honey continued reciting:

No one else was aware that this might have been happening, although the niece had a mature outlook and would not be inclined to fabricate occurrences of this nature. To her, the style of writing of the other female was juvenile, putting her roughly in the same age bracket as herself.

Nicky was gently advised of her husband's aberrations by her mother, (excluding the hurtful bit about him flirting with his niece) and the relevant proof was handed over. She was tearful and distressed, but hid her feelings from the boys while deciding how best to deal with the situation.

Nicky didn't want the marriage to end and would forgive him if he showed remorse. She realized at last the reason for his emotional coldness, but hoped that things could be mended.

In that frame of mind, she waited for the opportunity to share her knowledge with him and see how he reacted.

One evening, long after the boys had gone to bed, she summoned up the courage to challenge him, sitting with the evidence of his misbehavior on her lap and told him that she knew what he was doing. His reaction was disappointing and extreme.

His voice had always been loud but this time he started shouting. He vehemently denied any wrongdoing and got very angry, until the proof was set in front of him. Tearfully, she rushed out of the room and found the elder son listening outside.

"Go to bed at once!" she told him, while the boy looked horrified at what he had heard, and rushed back to his bedroom. For the distressed youngster, it was unwelcome validation of a call made by his father to another woman, when his mother was out one evening with her friends. His father was flirting loudly and saying things like, "I love you too!"

Nicky went back into the lounge and said to Jack, "You really must keep your voice down, or you're going to make it worse for the boys. Steve was listening at the door." There was no response, nor trace of guilt in his face.

She asked him, "How old is she, this other woman? She's a lot younger that you isn't she?"

Jack replied defiantly, "I checked, and she's above the age of consent. I've done nothing wrong!"

Nicky looked at him in disbelief. "What you're admitting is that she's young enough to be your daughter! Where is your common sense?"

Tears welled up in his eyes as she pleaded, "For the sake of the boys, get out of the house and sleep somewhere else until this is resolved. I've done nothing to deserve the treatment you're dishing out."

Unbelievably, he continued to deny any wrongdoing as he packed and stormed out.

The trauma that she and the boys went through was sickening to the rest of her family, who were instructed by Nicky to leave *his* parents out of it. This baffled her father, who thought they should be made aware of their son's infidelity and should help to influence him to 'return to the fold'.

Over the months that followed, Nicky swallowed her pride and attempted to seek reconciliation with him. It was futile, as he resolutely insisted that he had done nothing wrong.

He stated that he was staying with a work colleague, a possibility that Nicky could accept, until she started to gather his plentiful, scattered belongings for him to take to his temporary abode. Then she found one incriminating record after another.

First she found a sketch book that contained outlines of a heart with his initials entwined with those of his lover, and instructions underneath for a tattooist. Then she discovered a diary with dates and records in it that coincided with his returns from regular business trips abroad.

Armed with this knowledge, she agreed to meet him on neutral territory. This was a local bar, where they sat alone in one corner. Nicky demanded that he bared an upper arm that she knew he'd paid to have tattooed a short time ago; the receipt was in his records.

He refused at first, but realizing that sooner or later he would have to show his tattoos, he rolled his sleeve up and revealed what was an indelible record of his love for another woman.

Finally, she showed him the proof that he had been wining and dining this other, much younger woman on his return from each and every trip he made.

"No wonder you always refused to give me exact flight details; you were staying with her for days at a time, weren't you?" It was more of an assertion than a question, as she shot down his defenses one after the other.

She concluded by looking at him in the eyes, as instructed by the lawyer that her parents had insisted she consult, and saying "I don't love you anymore and I want a divorce from you."

For the first time, the tears flowed down his podgy face at the realization that he now had to take another path in life. It was a fair assumption that he wanted his dual-life to continue so that he could enjoy the best of both worlds.

One evening shortly afterwards, when the boys were at a sleep-over with friends, he came to the house to collect the remainder of his belongings and they had an almighty row. This culminated in him pinning her by the wrists against a wall in the hallway and threatening to head-butt her. She retaliated by kicking him once in the shin.

He instantly released her, bellowing, "You kicked me, I'm going to call the police and have you arrested for assault!"

"Good, go call them now!" she yelled back.

He fled into the downstairs toilet, locked the door and sat there, sobbing noisily. He eventually left, closing the front door quietly so as not to disturb her, long after she'd retreated to her bedroom.

Richard could hardly believe what he was hearing. "Bloody hell!" he said.

Honey angrily interjected, "Hush, you're screwing up the text the PC is producing ... and my concentration!"

She rectified the recorded text and re-established her connection with Nicky, continuing to read her mind and recite the details.

Once Jack realized the full extent of what his wife knew, he began damage limitation. He blocked all access to her and her family from his Facebook account, then he started deleting the text messages that publicly professed his love for another woman.

The formal divorce took a protracted 18 months to complete, until the decree-absolute was achieved. This was far longer than anticipated, and was due entirely to his recurring temper tantrums when confronted with the financial aspects of settlement.

It was gradually dawning on him what his commitments would be, well into the foreseeable future.

In one mediation session, Jack confessed that he had stripped the family bank account of six grand, leaving them short of money. The purpose was to buy a souped-up mini sports car and impress his girlfriend. This was before Nicky knew about her existence.

It was the one he'd used to take the boys with him for a spin at 120mph. Luckily, Nicky had saved a small pot of money from her child-minding days for a rainy day, and dipped into it to make up the shortfall.

His behavior during mediation was emotionally charged, as the mediator frequently took issue with him when he lost his cool and began shouting his way through each session. He also failed to see any valid legal reasons why he should comply with the expectations of others. Neither did he wish to pay a lawyer, and undertook his own defense.

The suspicion was aroused that he was taking advice from colleagues at work. The place seemed to be full of divorced men with legal awareness, and no doubt they were consulted to help him try and wriggle out of every negotiated obligation, no matter how reasonable.

From the outset of his change in employment, it had been observed by Nicky that the atmosphere where Jack works is dominated by what are called 'alpha males'. There were no gatherings or social events that involved women and children, and certainly none were taken on business trips.

If anyone had any hopes that annual Xmas meals would be paid for by the company, they would be dashed; these were a definite no-no. As the song goes, when staff cross the threshold of their building, 'It's a Man's World!'

The post-divorce period was relatively tranquil, although Jack couldn't resist giving the boys' birthday and Xmas gifts that were intended to get under the skin of his ex-wife. Like a TV set for Steve to watch alone in his bedroom.

Nicky reckoned that bedrooms are for sleeping in, and the boys already had an abundance of devices to communicate with others, and to play electronic games. He must have been picturing with glee the quarrels that would ensue as they rebelled from doing their homework when they wanted to do more pleasurable things.

Eventually, Nicky confiscated their mobile phones in the evenings, and made them do their homework in the kitchen, where she could supervise them more easily. Jack played hell, claiming that she was a barrier to him speaking to his sons whenever he wanted.

He had already interrupted board games that the boys were playing at school with their classmates, and Nicky was determined not to let it happen again. Steve was in danger of becoming a social outcast, whereas Bob was obsessed with football and too young to be aware of the implications of divorce.

Their visits to their father in his rented apartment were substantially more attractive. There, they could sit down in front of an Xbox and play competitive electronic games against each other and him to their hearts' content.

His girlfriend had similar tastes to those of the boys, being scarcely ten years older than Steve. Under his guidance she would join in the fun as well, and began helping them with their homework.

Mind you, she was not well educated and had left school without taking higher education, so her efforts were a struggle. It was amusing to see the results, judging from what Nicky read.

The boys thought their visits to their father were great, and were taken on outings to theme parks, which was something that Jack had refused to do before. They began returning home with duffle bags chocker-full of sweets and chocolates, since the girlfriend loved them, particularly M&Ms.

Even so, the boys were aghast at the frequency with which they went out for meals, and Jack spent money like water.

In contrast, their mother was reduced to buying food labelled as 'Basic' by supermarkets, because Jack would frequently refuse to pay for them to go on school trips, and played hell about the cost of school uniforms. This meant she had to divert money from the essentials or see them get distressed. Her parents ended up paying for these things, rather than seeing their daughter struggling to make ends meet.

On the other hand, many a laugh was had by Nicky as she witnessed her husband's girth ballooning, and saw for the first time the plump girl he was lavishing attention on. His attempts to behave as a young man were regarded as pathetic, and videos were obtained showing him gyrating at a party like Mr. Blobby, and attending company events looking awkward as a stuttering, contributory speaker.

What wasn't as funny was when the girlfriend began signing school homework, instead of Nicky performing this duty, as was her right, or Jack's alone. Then Nicky discovered that the boys were being instructed to report back to their father on the minimal times they were left alone, so he could use this information to report her for willful neglect.

This was only essential for short periods, when she was returning home from work, and the older boy was unsupervised in the house with his 11 year old brother.

If they were living with their father, it would have been for absences far longer in duration. Jack was often away on business and the girlfriend was working full-time at his office as a receptionist, so Nicky was dismissive about being monitored.

That was, until the day that the boys came home from one of their regular visits to see Jack, gushing with enthusiasm. He had offered them the chance to go and live with him forever. They would attend one of the best schools in the country, so they were told, and the younger one, Bob, would be able to attend a local football academy.

Nicky felt shattered; the boys were eager to get to the 'Fun Palace' and be done with the discipline she was imposing on them. Bob especially was determined to leave, and she felt inclined to release him, the ungrateful little piglet. The older one, Steve, was in two minds and didn't want to offend either of his parents.

Jack must have guessed that Steve was wavering, since he casually let slip one day that, 'I am the one with the money'. The implied threat was that he could cut-off Nicky's finances at any time he chose.

Both boys had seen enough of their father to judge him impartially, but it seemed that their hearts were ruling their heads. Good lord, they'd already told Nicky, without prompting, that his girlfriend often walked out on Jack, who got drunk on vodka when the boys went to bed, and could be heard crying and wailing at his plight, whatever that was.

Presumably, it was his increasing desire to see the boys all the time, and he was cold-heartedly working on the girlfriend to enlist her support. That was what Nicky thought he was up to.

"What's the definition of a psychopath?" Richard debated.

Nicky was forced to take legal action, to help counteract what her parents regarded as brainwashing by her monster of a manipulative ex-husband.

Her father commented, "The next thing he'll be doing is cutting your benefits, and forcing you to sell the house you live in, and for which you've been paying the mortgage single-handedly. He wants to get his hands on his share of the profit on the house sale, to settle his growing debts and get a mortgage of his own. You'll end up in Queer Street, and you'll never see the boys again!"

The lawyers were consulted immediately, realized the gravity of the situation and dashed off a letter warning him to desist or face the consequences.

This was the stage that Nicky was now at, this time involving more mediation, including the boys. No doubt, if either of the boys recanted on their desire to swap homes, he would make her life hell and continue to work on them.

Honey barked an instruction at the PC to stop recording, and leaned back in contemplation.

"It's a convenient time to stop," she said, glugging at a bottle of mineral water.

Richard said, "Yes. I don't want to hear any more for the moment. Let's get this lot revised and printed, for Joe to share."

Honey added, "You can take a shot at it tomorrow morning, and we'll have a round-up in the early afternoon before we scoot off to intercept the ex-husband and take things to the next level."

Richard began preparing a list of things to do remotely, including:

- Find out more about his family, mainly the parents, to see what they did to help;

- Check his frame of mind;

- Check what the boys think;

- Check the wife's current status and social behavior.

They both left for the rest of the day, ready to resume their remote viewing the following morning.

Early the next day, Honey picked up case notes they'd left on the table, and selected the school photo of Bob.

She began tracing his silhouette while frowning in concentration. After a few minutes her face brightened and she exclaimed, "I've picked up the youngest son's thoughts! He's in school at the moment, doing English. His attention is wandering; let's see what I can glean."

Honey decided to slip into his sub-conscious. She needed to allow Bob to participate in current activities without disturbing his main concentration. Her focus had to be on the background activities of his brain.

As she had explained to Joe, her logic was this: "we are all capable of thinking at multiple levels. The foremost level is akin to sitting in a public place and studying an item of major interest; the secondary level is being aware of what is going around us. It can be surprising what we pick-up indirectly, with our ears and eyes.

"In a correctly functioning brain, we also possess accumulating memories that we can hopefully retrieve at will. I intend accessing Bob's mental library by planting questions to trigger replies."

In this instance, she had probed by enquiring: "Where do you first remember that there was a problem between your mummy and daddy?"

She switched on the PC, rested in a comfortable position in front of it, accessed the speech-recording software and began reciting into the built-in speaker.

The headings in bold print were inserted afterwards, by Honey. The style of presentation mirrored Bob's recollections as recited in the third person by Honey. This reflects the fact that the boy was accustomed to reading books like 'Mr Stink' as written by David Walliams.

It is an accurate portrayal of the dream-world thought processes of that youngster at the age of 10. It also features a 12 year old central character, and can be considered appropriate for both Bob at the age of 9 and Steve, his older brother.

Get Out of My Sight!

Bob was feeling really grumpy. He hadn't woken up that way. The evening before he had felt excited at the prospect of going to stay with his grandparents in Spain, Bamps and Mam, for less than two weeks in a recent summer.

This was a shorter holiday than he and his older brother Steve would have liked, but their daddy repeatedly said that he couldn't bear to be apart from them for any longer than that.

It was the year before their daddy walked out on them.

To help keep them under control, they were always accompanied by their mummy on their holidays to visit their grandparents in Spain. Maybe she was doing it to keep Bamps in order; Goodness knows he needed to have a watchful eye kept on him. He was childish by any child's standards.

Yes that had to be the reason. Probably, Bob's complaints about being picked on had been noted. That must be it! Mam was enough for one nine year old to cope with, but Bamps as well? That was a step too far!

Anyway, that didn't make him feel less grumpy. He was so grumpy that he had been confined like a wild animal to his grandparents' bedroom as punishment for something he had done wrong.

What was it he had done wrong? He could hardly remember, as he snatched the soft-doll of Smiley the Dwarf from where it had been wedged on his grandfather's side of the wrought-iron headboard. Was it put there to stop the headboard from creaking whenever Bob wriggled?

A poor little raggedy doll was also wedged on his grandmother's side of the bed, and both of them helped stop the headboard from creaking.

There was a television set opposite the bed, placed on a shelf, and it had been turned on by his mother to keep Bob occupied. Unfortunately, before she swept out of the room in a huff, she hadn't bothered to do more than check it was on a cartoon channel. It was showing all its programs in Spanish! That was the cause of him feeling grumpy now!

Placing his hands around Smiley's neck, he tried hard to throttle him, which was not a nice thing to do. He stopped suddenly with alarm, as he saw the dwarf's mouth turn down at the corners and its eyebrows rise. Hearing a sob from the other side of the bed, he looked up and saw that raggedy doll had also put on an unhappy face.

He dropped Smiley onto the bed and closed his eyes tight. "How did that happen?" he asked himself. Opening his eyes, he saw with relief that the dolls' faces had returned to normal. He thought, "Whew, that's a relief!" and turned off the television with the hand control, not understanding a word of what was being said.

As a result of turning off the television, he could hear a noise coming from downstairs. It sounded like it was coming from Bamps. Bob crept out of the bedroom, and peered over the banisters, until he could see his grandfather holding his head with his hands and being comforted by the two women, mummy and Mam. He was groaning as he rocked to and fro, to and fro, all the time.

Ah yes, he could remember now why he was grumpy in the first place! Bamps had ordered him, in all that heat outside, to give the car a clean. Being a good little boy, he had tackled the task in true cub-pack fashion.

He started by trying to wipe the dust-covered metallic black surface of the car with a dry cloth; this had been stored in the main shed next to the house. He had heard it making a scraping sound as he rubbed the car hard with it, leaving marks on the surface without really removing the dirt. The next thing he heard was a howl from Bamps who had come out of the house to see how Bob was doing.

"Stop it at once!" he demanded. He shouted, "You're scratching my car!" looking at the cloth that Bob had selected from the shed. He should have checked it first, because there were pieces of dried paint on it. That explained the reasons for the scratches being caused.

"How was I to know that you'd used that rag to clean paint brushes?" Bob asked him, his eyebrows raised, hands held out and voice pleading.

"Oh blast!" Bamps said and shrugged his shoulders, feeling sorry for himself. "It's too late now! Find something else to do!" and he walked back into the house looking miserable.

The little warrior, not to be discouraged, got a plastic bucket, sponge and chamois cloth from the shed. He filled the bucket with really soapy water, and washed the car with extra hard effort, using the dripping wet sponge to clean the surface in circular motions. Even if he only said it to himself, it was getting to look good, as it steamed dry in the blazing sunlight.

Even Bamps was impressed, as he emerged from the house and looked at the newly washed car drying unevenly.

"Wait a minute, wait a minute"" he exclaimed, taking several steps towards his cherished car and examining it close-up. "What soap did you use?" he asked the now wary Bob.

"This one," replied Bob, holding up a large, yellow plastic container. Bamps looked at it and his eyes widened. "It says Lejia. Do you know what Lejia is?" he growled, advancing on Bob, who retreated at the same rate.

"No! Tell me!" replied Bob, getting defiant.

"It means 'bleach' in Spanish, you numbskull! You've damaged my paintwork forever!" shouted Bamps back at him, as Mam and Mummy rushed out of the house, getting alarmed at the commotion. "What's a numbskull?" Bob asked him, getting ready to run.

"Keep your hands off him!" shouted Mam, stepping between them. From the look in his eyes, Bamps intended throttling Bob like Bob had tried throttling Smiley upstairs. "What's done is done!"

From that point on, Bamps had groaned non-stop, as far as Bob could tell. He was dragged upstairs to his grandparents' bedroom to reflect on his sins.

He yelled to his mummy, "You're gonna tear my ear off if you keep pulling it!"

Bob whined, "It's not my fault!" as the door was closed on him. He rubbed his aching ear for a long time.

Stop Playing with the Headphone!

Every day, their daddy phoned them or got them to phone him at least two or three times. "You don't love me anymore!" daddy would say to mummy in a deep and loud voice that echoed around the large living room. "I'm lonely!"

Hiding from daddy and the boys, Bamps would pretend to stick his finger down his throat and be sick.

Once, when mummy had plonked Bob on her lap so that daddy could see and talk with him, Bob didn't know what to say. He started playing with the headphone cables as daddy was speaking and the connection was broken.

There was panic as Bamps was ordered by Mam to find another headphone in the cupboard upstairs. When he found one, he plugged it into the computer downstairs, and the phone was connected once more with daddy.

When his face reappeared on the computer screen, he was looking very angry and upset.

"You did that on purpose!" he bellowed at mummy.

"Calm down!" mummy told him. She looked calm as always. "Bob was playing with the cable. That was all it was!" she replied.

By this time, Bob had run off, up the stairs and into his bedroom. He was afraid of daddy while he was in a bad temper, which was often when he came home from work, or back from a business trip.

Bamps was getting really fed up with their daddy's comments and grumbles because it was upsetting everyone. He had a nasty habit of phoning them at meal times, which caused ructions at the table when the boys started reacting to what he had said.

Mam, Bamps and mummy would have been even more upset if they had known that daddy had found a girlfriend at that time, a year earlier, and was lying about being lonely.

That was not a nice thing for their daddy to do, when they were supposed to be a happy family. Sometimes that is what happens when a man is left alone, but not with all men. Only some men go looking for other women.

That's what mummy said, anyway.

Honey checked the text and found only minor errors to correct. Then she printed the document, for Richard and Joe to consider before switching-off the PC.

After Honey took a copy to Joe, the two mediums sat down and read through the latest report. They were unanimous in their opinion about one of the corner-stone legal aspects of sharing access to the offspring of divorced couples. This states that the wishes of the children has to be paramount in choosing how access should be shared, with a 50-50 split being preferred.

Honey pondered the ruling and stated cautiously, "It's only valid when both adults act reasonably, in the best interests of the children. When mediation treats the children's wishes as paramount, the law becomes an ass. As can be seen from Bob's thought processes, he is too young to understand all the ramifications of the choice he is making."

Richard said, "I agree. He would never understand the financial implications, even if they were explained in full. The fact is: his father has flourished the prospect of Bob going to a football academy, which is near to the school he would attend, as an overwhelming inducement.

"It looks like this will sway the youngster, who does not appreciate the devastating effect this move will have on his mother, who has gone to great lengths to provide facilities like this, within walking distance of where he already lives. She has slaved her guts out, bringing them up alone, and having to deal with the impact of constant sniping from their father."

Joe came in and overheard the last comment; he was holding the report in his hand, and agreed, "Yup, she's had a raw deal. Some kids can be so immature! I'll have a word with the mediation service and see if independent arbitration can be used, to supervise the process in such circumstances. It'll be too late to take the heat off Nicky though. Her ex-spouse is a really nasty piece of work."

"See what you can do to ease the situation, later today."

§ 4: Nipped in the Bud

Late afternoon, as arranged by Joe, the fresh-faced young policeman returned to their office, ready to accompany Richard and Honey to Nicky's address to stakeout her home. He was in plain-clothes and wearing a smart dark-grey suit, white shirt with quick-release tie and shiny black shoes.

Leaning on the reception counter, he began chatting animatedly with Alice when the two mediums breezed past him on their way out.

"You coming?" Honey asked him, without pausing to wait, as he bade Alice goodbye and rushed to catch up. "We don't want to get there late."

"Sorry, I didn't realize there was a rush," he said breathlessly. "My name's Hugh, by the way."

"Hi Hugh," they both chorused, emphasizing the letter 'H' in each word.

As they went to sit in Richard's car, Honey handed him a file and requested, "If you could sit in the back and get up to date with these case notes."

Hugh apologized, "I'd rather sit in the passenger seat next to the driver, if you don't mind. I get car sickness if I try and read in the back, and I don't want to risk vomiting over the upholstery!"

Honey glared at him and exchanged places.

The journey was undertaken at a law-abiding pace, to avoid Hugh reporting them for speeding, and they parked at the curbside on the long road facing Nicky's home.

All the other spaces were taken, which meant that the ex-spouse would have to reverse into one of the access lanes between each pair of semi-detached properties on the right of them. It was a narrow road, and parking was not allowed on the opposite side.

It was nearly 6pm when an ageing black Audi A6 swished past them, stopped and reversed into one of the access lanes. It was getting dark, but Hugh remarked, "I can see that the driver's on his mobile as he's driving; that's illegal for starters!"

He got out, rushed over to rap the driver's window, and ordered him to open it.

"What'd you want?" the man boomed in a very loud voice.

"Sir, put that phone down now so I can take down your details!" Hugh demanded. "You were observed committing an offence by driving and using a phone at the same time."

"I've got to let my sons know that I'm here, to pick them up," he replied, persisting in trying to get a connection. That was not a wise reaction, as Richard and Honey looked on in amusement and wondered what Hugh would do in retaliation.

The driver's expression changed to one of anger as Hugh opened his jacket and showed him his badge.

Hugh warned him, "For the last time, I'm ordering you to stop using that phone. Now I'm telling you to step out of the car!"

The man ignored him and stubbornly carried on fiddling with the touchpad. It was noticeable that his hands had started shaking, either in temper or in frustration.

In response, Hugh yanked open the door, grabbed the portly man by the scruff of his collar and pulled him out headfirst. He stumbled, nearly fell, and then swung a pile driver of a punch that Hugh nimbly avoided before grabbing the outstretched arm and doubling it behind his back.

The man bellowed in pain and outrage, as he was pinioned face-first against his Audi, while Hugh read him his rights as he formally made the arrest. His free arm was pressed against the car roof, trying to cushion himself from the pressure being exerted on him.

Richard and Honey sauntered across to the struggling pair, and Hugh instructed him, "Remove the handcuff-cord from my waist, and put it on the accused, one wrist only. I want his hands behind his back."

Richard paused to study the new style 'handcuff' with interest; it was of a type that he'd never seen before.

"Is this what you mean?" he asked, holding up a single length of thick cord, which he had pulled off the belt. He noticed that it was highly flexible, and woven with glittering, gold-colored metallic strands.

"Yes," Hugh confirmed, glancing over his shoulder. "That's my 'cuff-cord'. Drape it over the wrist I'm holding, then I'll place his other one next to it."

He looked at Richard, who was studying this new-style restraining-device with fascination, and snapped, "Take your time, why don't you!"

The man was making a ruckus like a hippo bellowing, and the front doors of the surrounding houses began to stream light as the occupants craned their necks to see what was happening.

Richard jerked out of his reverie, and complied as demanded. It was a wonder to behold, as the golden cord slithered like a snake around the wrist that Hugh was holding and then wrapped itself around the other that Hugh pulled roughly back, to join them in a single loop.

The two flat-ends seemed to fuse together invisibly as they met, to the fascination of Richard and Honey.

When Richard positioned the 'cuff-cord', he made contact with Jack's bared wrist and involuntarily shivered. He had read his mind, and experienced the insensitive, mental brutality that oozed from him.

"What's your name?" Hugh asked, allowing the man to straighten.

"Jack, Jack Lestrange," he spluttered loudly.

Honey muttered, "Surprise, surprise!"

Honey could see that someone had opened the door of Nicky's home, and that she and a much taller man were standing outside with the boys, staring in their general direction. She marched over to intercept them, before the boys got upset. Nicky recognized her straight away and gave her a smile.

Honey apologized for the commotion, saying, "The police have arrested a man for a minor offence and will be taking him away." She asked Nicky, "Were you expecting someone?" When the boys looked at their mother, she gave her a wink.

Nicky realized instantly what the likely cause of the melee was, and suggested to the boys, "Let's go indoors and wait until your father arrives."

She asked Honey, "Would you like to join us?"

Honey dismissed the proposal by replying, "Naw, no thanks. I've got to head off. No doubt you'll get a call soon, from him."

Fortunately, they had been shepherded inside before Jack resumed his bellowing.

Picking up Jack's mobile when she returned to Richard's car, she speed-dialed Nicky's number and got through. One of the sons could have answered, but Nicky took the call, as Honey wanted to happen.

The situation was explained, and Honey advised her to give an excuse for Jack's non-appearance, until he was freed and could speak for himself.

One of the householders, who shared the access lane that Jack occupied, rushed over to them.

"Excuse me, are you the police?" she asked, looking at Hugh.

"Yes marm," he confirmed deferentially.

The woman complained, "Well, that man is making a nuisance of himself. He keeps parking in our drive, to fetch his sons. Why can't he drive up to his own house direct? We thought he was a stalker when he first started doing it! And he makes his wheels spin when he leaves! And he shouts all the time. We're all getting fed up with racket he makes!"

Jack glared at her, without showing any remorse, which made her furious. She shook her fist at him and shouted, "Why don't you sod-off and leave us all alone?"

Another voice joined in, from a male adult standing in the shadows, and shouted, "You're bloody evil, you are! Fancy bullying a woman as nice as your wife, and trying to split the family! Come round here again and you're going to get flattened, you fat turd!" There was a rumble of approval from the increasingly madding crowd.

Silently, he hunched his shoulders and allowed his head to be pressed down, as he stooped to be put in the rear seat of his Audi. Rather than wait for an official police car to arrive, Jack agreed that

Hugh could drive him in his Audi to the police station where he was stationed.

It was either that or get his prestige car be towed away and pay for it to be retrieved from the official pound. There was also a risk that persons unknown might vandalize it in the meantime.

He detested his wife, for getting others to think he was the guilty party in all of this. He saw himself as a high-achiever, far more talented than those who lived in this neighborhood, and a good father to his devoted sons.

Richard and Honey were the last to leave, and drove off at a sedate speed, as if Hugh was still with them. Keeping his eyes on the dark road ahead, Richard asked her, "How the devil did we fail to pick-up on her boyfriend? I didn't even know he was on the scene!"

That question was answered when they returned to the bureau, met up with Hugh, and were all debriefed by Joe.

When asked, he said, "The reason is simple. Nicky is a person whose thinking is highly 'compartmentalized'. When she prepared those case notes for you, her attention was devoted to the fall-out from the divorce, and the boyfriend was irrelevant to the situation. Your line of questioning guided her to go along your route. Do you see that?"

Honey nodded, so Joe continued. "When conventional detectives pursue a case, they look at what happened from a wider angle. For instance, the search begins at the crime scene, if I may make that analogy. In this instance, there is no actual crime scene, since we are trying to prevent the crime from being committed.

"Divorce is not a crime, but Jack's strange behavior before and after the divorce has the hallmarks of a crime in the making. His intentions could have devastating consequences on the members of his previous family, if he carries them out. It was good that you visited Nicky's home and found out more of relevance to the divorce.

"Now I'd like you to broaden your enquiries to get the full picture. Find out what Nicky's social life is like, how the boys are doing at school and what psychological scars they have, if any. Hell, let's be positive; there have to be some upsides to their lives to compensate for the downsides they've had, or they'd be driven nuts.

"Also, do the same to the husband, Jack. He's the key to all of this, and is likely to inflict pain on everyone else, or be made to suffer the most."

Joe got up to leave, saying, "Come on, let's go and see how the ex-spouse - or should I say 'louse' - is settling down. We'll take my car."

Richard gave a whistle of admiration when he saw Joe's 'chariot'; it was a sleek, futuristic 5-seater saloon. Looking inside, he could see that the normal, manual controls were still visible, but were flush with the dashboard and floor area. They were there for emergencies only, as a form of reassurance.

Joe sat in the front, where the erstwhile driver would normally be stationed, and the others got in the back, to sit on the long bench seat. Joe gave the vehicle their destination, and magnetic restraints switched-on to give them forcefield protection.

As the vehicle silently gained speed, Joe swiveled his bucket seat around to face them, and asked, "Got any more up-to-date info to pass to me? Since we're about to question the divorcee, it would be handy to know more about his latest antics."

Honey took her photo of Nicky, plus that of Steve the older boy, and another of Jack, from the case file she was carrying, and began her remote-access to their thoughts, before reciting them aloud. The narrative follows.

On the last pre-arranged visit to their father, Jack spent his time endlessly extolling the superiority of the school they would be enrolling at, as if it was a 'done-deal'. When he noticed Steve wavering, he insisted that the school required immediate notification of his enrolment, otherwise entry to the next academic year would be problematic: there were anticipated to be more candidates than places available.

Jack was on edge, hence his persistence. The more he talked, the more his sons felt uneasy; they had already stated their desire for their mother to participate jointly in their future custody, but the father seemed over-keen to get the lion's share of their time.

Moving to Nicky's photo, Honey sensed other influential presences warning her of Jack's intentions. It was the parents, hers to be more precise, pointing out what they foresaw Jack trying to achieve.

This was based on Jack's behavior at the most recent mediation session, where he had frequently lost his temper, talked about her as if she did not exist, and stormed out when told (by the mediator no less), to give his ex-wife the chance to speak. He was undermining his own case, and had left his wife fearing for her safety; she was being intimidated by her ex, and began genuinely quivering with fear.

Nicky now realized, with her parents' help, that she would end up seeing very little of her sons, once their father got them to stay with him and attend a school that was of his choice. It was a direct challenge to her authority as the boys' guardian; they were already attending a good school, and had moved to the area to be close to it.

Recently, Jack had moved from the two-bedroom flat he had been renting, into a rented four-bedroom detached house in an upmarket district near the school he intended his sons to attend. He was intent on them changing house and school, and unwittingly disrupting the routines his ex-wife had established.

Doubtless, his original neighbors were glad to see the back of him, and would have been 'hanging out the bunting' at the prospect of enjoying some peace and quiet. His thoughts indicated that his original rental period had not been extended. The property owner wanted Jack and his baggage out.

He had been a bullying, swearing and demanding father once, who shouted and occasionally hit them. Like a leopard, he showed no signs of having changed his spots. She was determined to stand up to him, but felt the need for physical protection.

At the last mediation session, he also challenged her right to have a boyfriend. This must have been a sore point for him, dating back to the original divorce conditions. He had tried to insert a clause insisting that she could not have one for two years, but the judge dismissed the condition with contempt.

Now he was challenging her to prove that the man she was

dating was not co-habiting with her on a regular basis, as if it was any of his business!

The next thing he took exception to was the purchase of a Labrador puppy, which the boys soon grew to adore. He stated, "Doesn't *she* know how difficult it is to rent a flat with a pet?"

What was irking him was the possibility that she was using this as a way to garner affection from the boys. What this also revealed was his presumption that she would soon be forced to rent and live somewhere else, when he had his way.

Anyway, he was allergic to cats and dogs, and this was the true reason why he couldn't consider having pets in his household. A goldfish might have been acceptable, since he would have enjoyed watching it swim round and round in a confined space; it was the same way that he regarded the people closest to him, as possessions.

Ultimately, what he was after was a reduction in his maintenance payments, to keep her on the breadline. Her parents had urged her to go the police. In practice, this was what she ended up doing.

Joe announced, "We're nearly there. Let's wrap this up for now."
Honey said, "Blast! I should have recorded this."

Joe reassured her, "There's no need; the car has a built-in recording system. I activated it when you started reciting. I'll send it as a voice mail to your mobile."

Honey looked at him with a mixture of admiration and respect, making barely detectable body contact with Richard, who stiffened; he was aware he'd missed a trick.

The car drew up outside the flat-roofed police station, and they all got out at the main entrance. Introductions were exchanged at the front desk with a cheerful sergeant, whom Joe asked to get someone and take them through to the inappropriately named, soundproofed 'observation lounge' adjoining Interview Room 1.

A uniformed officer led them there and asked if they wanted coffees while they waited, and with what complements.

As they sat looking through the one-way glass panel, Jack was brought into the interview room, his handcuff cord was unleashed and he was told to sit down and await company. He looked more composed now, but was checking his wristwatch anxiously.

When the officer returned with their mugs of coffee, served as requested, he asked casually, "So you've met Floppy Joe?"

Richard and Honey looked at each other blankly. "Yes, we know Joe quite well. Why's he called *floppy*?"

The officer explained, "It's because of the way he walks. Haven't you noticed?"

They nodded.

"It happened when some thug caught him in the face with a knuckle-duster. Laid him flat out he did. Instead of addling Joe's senses, it affected the way he walks, but left him with enhanced brain activity. It was the best thing that ever happened, for us. His clear-up rate for crime resolution is phenomenal. Are you some of the mediums who have joined the force?"

They nodded mutely.

"We're looking forward to working with you!" he said, grinning as he left the room.

In a short while, a plain-clothes detective came into the room and sat opposite him, the other side of a square table fixed to the bare, tiled floor. He was a thickset man with a gray crewcut, in his forties, who looked as if he would come out as top dog in any bar-room brawl.

His features were not very pre-possessing, and Honey thought unflatteringly that he looked like a pig, but without the snout; his nose was small in comparison and regular in shape. No one had succeeded in flattening it, up until the present day.

At a click of his fingers, another bruiser, this one in uniform, came and stood by the door, with an old-fashioned truncheon swinging from his belt. His gaze was directed at the accused and was intimidating, as if he couldn't wait to be left alone with him. Not once did he stop staring at Jack, who tried to avoid making eye contact.

The detective busied himself laying his notepad and case notes on the table in front of himself, placing a biro on the right of the pad, ready for writing, and setting-up an old-fashioned digital recording machine to his left.

He flicked on the recorder, squinted at the accused man

opposite, cleared his throat a few times, and spoke.

"My name is Detective Sergeant Ted Spiros. Speak into the recorder and confirm your full name, date of birth and occupation."

Jack was fidgeting uncomfortably as he leaned forward to comply. "My name is John Daniel Lestrange; born 13th January 1973; working as Technical Support Associate Director for Digital Acoustics Enterprises."

Detective Sergeant Ted stopped the recorder and played it back, to confirm that the details provided were fully audible.

He too leant forward, startling Jack as he stared at him from close range with his small eyes slit, and grated loudly, "Using a mobile phone in a moving vehicle is a minor but costly infraction. Assaulting an officer of the law is in a different league altogether. You may well go to jail. What have you got to say for yourself?"

He turned off the machine, and hissed, "**Scumbag!**"

Jack look at him fearfully.

Detective Sergeant Ted shouted, "**Explain!**" and turned the recorder back on.

With tears welling up in his eyes, Jack was finding it difficult to speak. He covered his face with his hands and started to sob uncontrollably.

"I'm sorry!" he blubbered.

Detective Sergeant Ted asked, "Sorry for what?"

Jack replied in a hoarse voice, "Sorry for hitting the policeman."

Detective Sergeant Ted asked, "And?"

"And what?" Jack asked with trepidation.

"Why were you there in the first place?"

"To collect my two sons, to come and stay with me. It's my turn to have them!"

"Why don't you go direct to your previous home to collect them? Are you afraid of something?"

"No."

"I see from the case file steadily being accumulated against you that you cannot bear to be anywhere near your ex-wife. Is that true, and if so, why?"

"I'm not going over past history. All that I will say is that I realized some years ago that she doesn't love me and the relationship has turned sour."

"As far as I can see, you are the one that fell out of love with her, not the other way round. Why'd you hit her?"

Jack exploded in false indignation. "What?"

Detective Sergeant Ted repeated, "Why'd you hit her? My understanding is that you went into her house, to collect your belongings. You had a row, pinned her against the wall by her wrists. Then you threatened to head-butt her, moving your forehead back and forth. Is that not what you did?"

Jack retorted, "For a start, it's not her house, it's *our* house. Yes, we had a row, but she kicked me back, so it's also her that assaulted me!"

Raising his voice, Detective Sergeant Ted replied, "To be exact, it *was* your house before you were kicked out. It is hers now and you were there as a guest, to collect your stuff. You assaulted her, and she was entitled to protect herself. Imagine what a court will make of your claim that '*she kicked me back*' when you attacked her so forcibly? For pity's sake, she's only half your size!"

Detective Sergeant Ted turned off the recorder and said to Jack, "Cut the crap!" emphasizing each word as he spoke.

"If you'd tried something like that on someone who's more your size, me for instance, I'd have beaten you to a pulp, or, I'd have shot you and claimed you'd gone for my gun. I say 'good for her!' It was plucky taking on someone like you."

"Yeah, you're a gutless lardy-arse!" sneered the uniformed officer, holding the handle of his truncheon. "Is it any wonder that you're held in such low regard, you lump of horse manure!" Jack reckoned they were trying to provoke him and grew more fearful.

Detective Sergeant Ted turned the recorder back on and said, "So you admit to assaulting your wife and threatening to head-butt her, and you have no rational explanation for deserting her. Now tell us about the harassment you are inflicting on her!"

Jack was fast realizing that Detective Sergeant Ted knew more about him than was comfortable. "What harassment?" he asked, in a hesitant tone.

"Oh, nothing much," was the response, delivered sarcastically. "The endless stream of emails couched in bullying terms, the coded messages you relay to the boys and insist they respond to, and the rows you provoke in the house by subtle interventions, and so on. Plus the attempts to change schools and bullying of the boys to abide by your 'wishes'.

"You do realize we can restore the records you and the boys exchanged and deleted afterwards? We're working on them now; they make for interesting reading. Even your own mother has said, to Nicky, she doesn't like the emails you're sending. They too are highly incriminating, I can tell you.

"One of the emails from you goes as far as threatening her 70 year old father, who you warned was within easy reach. That too is being included in the list of harassment charges. You've overstepped the mark, Sonny Jim."

Jack said, "I want a lawyer."

Detective Sergeant Ted replied, "You're welcome. He can listen while the preliminary charges are read out. These will no doubt include a driving offence, assault on an officer of the law, and multiple charges of harassment. Hopefully, you will be tagged and put on a restraining order until sentencing."

Looking horrified, Jack asked, "What about my job? How am I supposed to earn a living with this lot hanging over me?"

Detective Sergeant Ted replied, "You should have thought about that before you started misbehaving."

He finished by asking, "Oh, by the way, do you own a gun, or have a license for one?"

"No!" was the defiant reply.

"Good!"

Most of the onlookers in the observation lounge were looking with unrestrained glee at the outcome of the interview conducted by Ted. Joe had joined them, and was being congratulated on getting a magnificent result. Hugh was also there and wearing a broad grin on his face.

Richard however, whilst obviously happy, kept glancing with concern at Jack, through the pane of glass. Observing this, Joe asked him, "What's the matter; have we missed something?"

The reply was, "I believe there's more than one spirit occupying and guiding him. I haven't yet decided how best to prove it."

Joe looked across at Jack, and noticed that he seemed to be wavering between fear and hatred, with a wicked gleam appearing in his eyes whenever he looked in their direction.

Joe replied, "I see what you mean. However . . . "

He rubbed his hands in delight and dialed a number on his mobile phone. "Brains, is that you?" he asked loudly, causing the lounge to become suddenly silent as the others strained to listen.

'Brains' was the nickname given at the station to the head of the regional research and development laboratory. "I've been given the opportunity to test that device of yours, the one that is based on the Spectrometer. Can you bring it with you tomorrow, to my police station? You know the address? That's good. See you then, first thing. Adios amigo!"

Honey took Joe to one side, and stressed the need for caution. "I don't think he should be punished too harshly, otherwise the family will suffer from the loss of his income. In two years' time, Nicky's circumstances should improve as she gains her accountancy qualifications.

"Somehow or other, the fear of God has got to be put in him and his stupid behavior curbed."

Joe looked at her sympathetically, patted her hand, and said, "All will be dealt with in due course. Have faith in me. You and Richard can use my car to return to your offices, with an uplifted heart."

Jack's lawyer never arrived, claiming other pressing commitments. The truth was: fundamentally, he didn't like the man and the way he was behaving. He also had the hots for Nicky's lawyer, and had cunningly been recommended by her to help the Neanderthal he was now lumbered with.

Jack declined to accept any lawyer chosen by the police and spent the night in the cells, after phoning his girlfriend and making a lame excuse for his sudden disappearance. To add insult to injured pride; as well as his personal belongings, he was told to hand over his belt, tie and shoelaces to the duty officer.

Meanwhile, Richard and Honey were delighted to be able to bask in the comfort of Joe's swish saloon car, with its myriad gadgets. Naturally, they sat in the back, to enjoy each other's company, as it transported them home of its own accord.

Richard put his arm around her shoulders, gave her a friendly squeeze, and brushed his lips against her cheek. Unobserved, he brought out his Music Box and pointed it at the front panel, where a blue light flashed once, to indicate that it had received a signal.

The tune he had chosen was the Karaoke version of the enchanting melody '*I PUT A SPELL ON* YOU', as sung originally by Screamin' Jay Hawkins. On this occasion however, he intended singing it himself and had memorized the words.

As the tune started playing, Honey felt a tingle as she recognized what it was, fast becoming mesmerized as Richard sang alone flawlessly. His rendition was perfect in all respects, and she would have defied anyone to distinguish his voice from that of the original singer.

In an unexpected frenzy, she began ripping off her clothes, tearing at his, and turned to face him, her bare legs straddling his. He looked distractedly over her shoulder, thanking the gods for his good fortune and forgetting the words he had strived to remember.

To his relief, he noticed that the lyrics were displaying in mid-air, directly in front of him, and continued singing in an increasingly strident voice. As he lost memory of where he was and became total immersed in her, the voice of Screamin' Jay Hawkins took over. Joe had invested in a clever, reactive sound system.

The three of them continued pounding along in unison until the journey ended, and the saloon magically stopped in the deserted street fronting the agency. Its suspension eventually settled of its own volition as the copulating couple ceased releasing their sexual tension. Richard knew that he was a lucky man, to have come across his peach of a Honey.

At that moment, he wanted no one else on earth, and even thought of making an honest woman of her. On second thought, he decided that she was exactly what he wanted, and at her peak. Unrealistically, he wanted her to stay the same for eternity.

*'I PUT A SPELL ON YOU
BECAUSE YOU'RE MINE,
YOU'RE MINE!*

Let tomorrow look after itself.

§ 5: All Good Things Come, For Some

The following morning, Richard and Honey were sitting in front of Joe, who was occupying his other desk; that is to say, the one he uses when fulfilling his duties as Head of Homicide. They were waiting for 'Brains' to arrive and demonstrate his gadget that could somehow be used to detect specers (or 'spectres', as the Brits called them).

While they sat there, feeling relaxed and drinking their coffees, Joe gazed calmly at the two mediums and said, "By the way. How'd you like my driverless saloon?"

"Fine," Richard replied, sensing no danger in the question. "It goes really well. A super ride!" Honey nearly choked on her drink.

"Yes," Joe continued, placing his feet on the desktop, "I had a tracking device fitted, to prevent anyone stealing it."

"Makes sense," Richard replied, sipping his coffee.

"*And* an internal 3D camera to catch anyone who was daft enough to get caught in the act!"

With a shriek, Honey dropped her half-full cup on the desk, clasped her hands to her head and rushed out of the room, leaving Richard to face the consequences on his own.

"Agh!" Richard cried.

"Yes!" Joe said in a hard tone. "*I HAD MY EYE ON YOU!*"

He continued, "When I generously told you to go home with an uplifted heart, I didn't mean *uplifted* in that way! My kids have to sit on that back seat when I take *them* out for a ride. After we've done here, you can damn well go and get it sponge-cleaned, professionally!"

Richard blushed a crimson color, as he apologized profusely to the person who had indisputably identified himself as his boss.

Joe took his feet off his desk, leant forward, and whispered to Richard, "If you're gonna have a wig-wham erection, do it on *your* reservation in future, okay?"

Richard looked down in embarrassment, while Joe daydreamt about the possibility of trying the same stunt with *his* very attractive wife. "*Yes, it could be worth the effort. However, I'm a Sinatra sort of guy, so it'd have to be something on the lines of, I'VE GOT YOU UNDER MY SKIN, and I'd need the original singer all the way through. My vocal chords aren't up to it.*"

Snapping out his fantasy, he suggested to Richard, "Try and get Honey back in the room; I imagine she's using the Ladies' facilities. We need to make progress while we've still got Jack the Lad in custody. If she's looking distressed, tell her to apply makeup; we need to keep your sexual adventures under wraps."

When the pair of them returned and sat down, Joe noticed that Honey had applied blusher; on the plus side, Richard had lost his shade of crimson. He directed his attention at Honey and said, "Forget about what happened, honey, like I have. What's done cannot be undone."

He was using her name as a term of endearment, and lying when he claimed to have already forgotten the incident; it was etched indelibly in his brain.

She jutted her jaw out, and decided: "*Sod it!*"

Joe interrupted her train of thought, saying, "I want you to give me some last-minute dirt on the accused, to build up our case. Do you want a fresh coffee, while you concentrate?"

She shook her head and referred to the case notes. After a brief study of the documents and photos, she began to recite her readings of the situation.

During his final years as a senior pupil, Jack began self-mutilation. There was also a locally publicized problem involving a female lecturer but this was quickly hushed-up, to avoid him getting a criminal record. Nicky only found out about these incidents later in the marriage, since his family earlier suppressed mention of them; they could have had an adverse impact on her choice of partner.

Steve had noticed the scars, and asked his mum what caused them, but she skirted around the issue.

Joe broke in and commented, "If the boys don't yet know by now what their father's like, they're going to have a rude awakening - if they go and live with him!"

Honey continued mind reading.

Nicky faced up the loss of her husband by socializing with the many women she had befriended in the short period she was living in the locality. There was a considerable number of them, and they banded together to socialize in different bars.

After Nicky regaled them endlessly with horror stories of her broken marriage, the numbers began to diminish; some feared that their husbands might be behaving in a similar manner and preferred to stay at home to keep watch on them. Others couldn't bear hearing the endless saga of emotional torture she had to endure; it was too much for them.

One evening she did the unthinkable. She had noticed one particular man eying her up, boldly walked up to him and asked: "Are you married?"

"No!" he replied, "Are you?" He was fancying her as much as she fancied him, and her slightly drunken rant about her love life, or lack of it, was no deterrent when it inevitably arose.

They proved to be a good match, temperamentally as well, and their fondness for each other grew considerably over the months that followed.

His name was Jason, he was blond, 6 feet 2 inches+ tall and wedge shaped, with a slim waist and broad shoulders. He had a fresh-faced handsome cleanliness about him that indicated an outdoor life.

He proudly informed her that he was an instructor for the Special Forces, had served in the marines and was now approaching retirement age. He was five years older than her

She couldn't have chosen a better alter-ego to Jack, whose aggressive personality had destabilized her. This man was calm, didn't swear in her presence, and was well-adjusted.

It was not long before her parents paid a visit and met him too; it was an instant bond, although her father thought he looked slightly too red in the face. He took Nicky aside and asked, "Does he glow in the dark?"

"No!" she replied with a laugh. "What made you ask that question?"

The answer was, "Because I've seen a program that claims there's a special unit that collects debris and bodies from UFO crash sites, and the soldiers doing retrieval get high levels of radiation poisoning. Ask if he goes to Brussels, on NATO business."

She checked and had to admit that Jason fitted the picture painted by her father, but believed her new beau when he dismissed the claims as a pack of nonsense. Besides, his acquired knowledge of things electronic was abysmal. He was 'Action Man' personified in real life.

To continue to support their daughter, the parents' came to visit more regularly than in the preceding years, but the boys' behavior went from bad to worse. They couldn't make up their minds about Jason, although he took them with him when he went flying micro-light aircraft and that silenced them for a while.

Up until that moment, Bob used to sit near him on the sofa, glare up at Jason and try and provoke him by saying things like, "You're gay!" It was a brave act, considering the differences in size, putting Jason in a quandary; he had to retaliate, but how?

The chosen method was to play 'death football', where the boy was ordered to run across an open goalmouth, and Jason would unleash shots at him with a football. That shut him up, although counter accusations of being gay himself, would reduce Bob to fits of howling at the meal table, and the mud slinging petered out. It was a topic of conversation about Bob: 'how young he is, for his age'.

Steve was more subtle in his digs at Jason, and the source was obvious when the words came out of his mouth. Rather than risk confronting someone as comparatively huge as Jason, he would say uncharacteristic things to his mother like, "He's a sponger!" and "He's a leech!"

It was her ex-husband providing the ammunition.

Army work was not well paid and Jason already had a mortgage on a house that he had bought and restored, and infrequently used as a holiday retreat; it was large and secluded, near dramatic coastline.

Nicky fell in love with the place; it was reminiscent of the peninsula further south in the same region, and was where her parents had been brought up. She dreamt of moving there permanently, but had to be reminded of her shorter-term commitment to the highly respected school which Steve was already attending and which Bob was registered to attend.

Coincidentally Jason was at a crossroads in his life, facing three career options: to quit permanently and take a job in civvy street; to continue part-time in the military; or to resume his previous role full-time, with an increase in rank.

The 'ex' wanted to find out if this interloper was contributing or not to the household expenditure, so he could reduce his maintenance payments. It really got his goat when he spied on his wife's house, and saw Jason's large four wheel drive all-terrain vehicle parked almost permanently on the lawn in front.

Jason wanted to 'punch his lights out' but knew that if he did, the police would pounce on him in an instance. Honey detected a lot of thought being devoted to resolve that matter.

In the meantime, Jason took Steve rock-climbing, which alarmed his grandfather in case a version of 'death football' was intended, but Nicky had the utmost confidence in Jason. The boy was getting plump due to his pre-occupation with sedentary electronic games, and needed to be toughened physically and mentally.

Steve loved the challenge and began asking for specialist gear to tackle his new hobby. Nicky also took it up and it became a family thing for the three of them to do together.

There was one activity that united all three males, and that was participating in Nicky's pastime. First thing each day, she would unfurl an exercise mat in the lounge, turn on the TV, and perform yoga for 20 minutes while aping the movements of an instructor demonstrating set positions on a DVD.

She would stretch her limbs, point in various directions and crane her neck to look upwards and sideways. At strategic moments, one or more of the three males would pass by, and with lips puckered, provide a chorus of accompanying farting noises. After initially collapsing in mirth, she learnt to ignore them.

Undoubtedly, this bonding would have enraged Jack, who began to try and lose weight but couldn't hope to compete athletically with his new competitor for the boys' affection.

Plus, there was her personal, longer-term achievable ambition of following a new, accounting profession. She had already been allocated regular clients, and things were going her way.

No, she had to face these positive realities, and contrast them with her unpleasant, personal circumstances. She had demons to overcome, with the support of her immediate family, before dreams could be turned into reality.

The boys were manipulative, although Jack's parents one day knocked at her front door after returning them from a periodic visit, and made clear their disapproval of the worst excesses of their son Jack's behavior.

That admission was heartfelt and gave her comfort; it was a significant departure from their previous insistence that 'Jack is our son'. They wanted to continue seeing her and the boys regularly, and their only daughter, Jack's highly intelligent sister, was also asking about Nicky's wellbeing.

A light tap was heard at the door, in response to which Honey looked up and asked Joe, "Does that help you?"

He nodded, and beckoned the person waiting there to come into the room. A short, thin man peeped around the edge and smiled at them. He was wearing oversized glasses and an unbuttoned white laboratory coat, with casual clothes underneath. He was pulling a metal case on wheels behind him, which he left upright on the floor, as he advanced to shake hands with Joe.

Joe stood up, exchanged greetings and introduced his visitor. "This is Professor Michael Dawnes, modestly known as 'Brains'. These good people are here to witness your latest invention, which is called the . . . ?"

"It's Mike actually, and the machine is called the *SPECTRACTOR*. Where is the research to take place?"

Joe replied, "In Interview Room 1, down the corridor from here. I want you to be accompanied by Richard and Hugh, while the rest of us sit in the observation lounge next to it, watching events unfold. I'll arrange for the 'study-subject' to be led there and for Hugh to join us. It'll only take me a few minutes, so perhaps you can wait here for my signal?"

While they were waiting, Mike took the opportunity to explain how his invention worked.

He unlatched the case and took out a bulky machine that looked like a portable instrument container, coated in white enamel. It had a lid, which he opened, revealing a top half containing a small screen, and a variety of dials, knobs and buttons. A fold-up lens was placed upright and clicked into a fixed position, pointing outwards and away from anyone using the device.

He explained, "This is based on the mass spectrometer. It emits electromagnetic radiation that is visible to the human eye. It also utilizes the ultra-violet and infra-red frequencies which are beyond the human spectra, that is to say the visible colors of the rainbow."

"Huh?" went the others. "Can you repeat that in English?"

Mike took a deep breath, and stated, "It uses beams of light that are beyond the scope of our vision, to detect unnatural halos around a person. That is, it can detect associated spooks, specters or spirits, whatever you care to call them, *in a small room.* The mass of the detected object is light in weight, and we believe we can separate the good from the evil by using positive ions. That is as good as I can manage!"

Joe appeared at the window of the interview room and beckoned Richard and 'Brains' to join him. They carried the machine through and set it up at one end of the fixed table, before the manacled Jack was led in by Hugh and placed at the other end.

Jack glared at the machine, as its lens was focused on him, and asked, "What's that?" They all ignored him, as Brains plugged the cable into a floor socket and turned on the equipment.

Mike rotated a knob to select different frequencies. Jack turned his head and closed his eyes. Some of the colors were dazzling him.

"There you are!" Mike said excitedly, as he pointed at the small screen next to the dials. They all zoned in on the dark-grey halo surrounding Jack's head and upper torso.

"Now I'm hoping to use the oscillator to separate the good from the bad!" He turned another knob, first left and then right, and the halo lost its clarity as it started vibrating at a specific setting. The halo immediately separated into two distinct, static entities.

"Gotcha!" exclaimed Mike triumphantly. He gestured impatiently to Richard, saying "Try and communicate with it."

Richard brought from his pocket an Electronic Voice Detector and switched it on. He always carried with him a digital recorder.

Advancing towards Jack and concentrating on the presence, which was invisible to the naked eye, he challenged it, "Who are you? Why are you here, in this man? Do you know him?" Then he switched off the recorder.

For a short period, as he played back the recording, the onlookers were beginning to think that he had failed. Suddenly, a deep male voice was projected into the room.

"I'm Daniel. He's my grandson, I'm helping him."

Honey got straight on her mobile and tried to make contact with Nicky. Luckily, she got through after a few tones, and asked her, "Do you know anything about Jack's grandfather, who goes by the name of Daniel?"

Nicky replied, "Yes. He's the one who walked out on the maternal grandmother. He left his wife all alone to bring up their children, including Jack's mother. Why'd you ask?"

Honey replied excitedly, "Never mind. I'll tell you later!" Ending the call, she rushed into the interview room to whisper to the others what she'd found out.

Jack was getting increasingly agitated at what was happening without his knowledge. He demanded to be told, "What're you up to?"

Armed with this knowledge of the ancestral family, Richard stated firmly to the spirit, "You must leave Jack alone. You must leave him NOW. You must join the rest of the family who you deserted and make your peace with them. GO NOW!"

Mike concentrated the beam on the separated spirit, and rotated the oscillator, to get the image vibrating. Whether or not it made any sound no one would ever find out, since Richard had stopped using his EVD recorder, and the spirit abruptly vanished from the spectractor screen.

In a droll manner, Joe speculated, "Oh dear, we might have witnessed the first ever murder of a dead person!"

He leant towards the pane of glass, peered at Jack and commented, "It doesn't seem to have changed him for the better, either!"

Mike was also focusing his machine on Jack and had come to the same conclusion. He remarked to Hugh and Richard, "Blast! His halo remains dark-grey. He's still got anger-management issues!"

From the malevolent glare that Jack was throwing at everyone around him, there was not going to be any worthwhile improvement in his behavior.

Joe went to speak to Hugh, and ordered him to arraign Jack with charges of harassment, assault of an officer in the execution of his duties, and use of a mobile phone whilst in control of a vehicle.

He also confirmed that he wanted him released on bail until a date had been set for his appearance in court. In the meantime, he was not to be allowed to make contact with Nicky, except for the purpose of sharing pre-arranged visitation rights with the boys.

It was also on condition that he made no further attempts to try and directly influence his sons in ways that were prejudicial to the tranquility of their family lives when with their mother.

In the meantime, he additionally tasked his officers with visiting Jack's place of employment, to ascertain who had been giving him advice and support in the harassment of his wife and family.

He also wanted confirmation of all the dates on which Jack would be out of the country, and which might need re-arranging when the court dates were set as the top priority to be complied with. Otherwise, Jack would be arrested for being in contempt of court.

"The same criteria to be applied to his girlfriend and her family," Joe snapped, wanting it stressed that there were potential criminal charges that others could be facing for aiding and abetting the accused to perform criminal acts.

When Honey spoke to Nicky, to explain why she had asked about Jack's deceased maternal grandfather, Daniel, she replied, "I'm not surprised that Jack exhibits similar trends in his behavior. He has no faith to guide him, no interest whatsoever in reading anything other than technical manuals, no moral rectitude, and absolutely no conscience."

Out of the blue, something unlikely occurred: Jack disappeared off the map.

§ 6: Always Expect the Unexpected

The first that Joe knew about Jack's disappearance was when he was notified of it by the police, via the station within whose jurisdiction his employer's offices were located.

His boss, the managing director of Digital Acoustics Enterprises, had reported that he hadn't arrived at work one day, and neither had his girlfriend, their receptionist; it seemed that both were missing.

At first, the police assumed that they'd done a runner, but his parents insisted that something more ominous had happened, like a kidnapping. After a few days, the police arranged with the landlord of their detached house to give them access.

A systematic search revealed that both their passports had been left behind, and there was no paper trail indicating a prior intention to go anywhere other than their place of work.

Seaport, airport and road-border toll-point records were checked, and all of them confirmed that they had definitely not left the country by the commercially available main routes. Simultaneously, their photos and descriptions were posted throughout the country and via Interpol, to no avail.

Neither had their credit and debit cards been used anywhere, at any time after they had gone AWOL. Likewise, their bank accounts had been left untouched.

Joe wasn't perturbed, since he regarded the man as a potentially dangerous individual who deserved the treatment he was about to get: jail time. It was logical that he might attempt to avoid having to face the music for his misdemeanors.

However, he eventually conceded that something might have been done to remove Jack from circulation, perhaps by Nicky's boyfriend, Jason. He was the obvious suspect, and Joe asked Honey and Richard to see if they could trace any intention on Jason's part to deprive Jack of his freedom, or his life.

He had to decide if Jason was worth bringing in, for an interview or two.

Richard and Honey were concentrating on picking up the thoughts of Jason and Nicky respectively. Shaking her head, Honey was the first to respond. "No, she's curious about his whereabouts, but not worried. She's glad to have respite from him, and is basking in the unaccustomed relief he is providing. Frankly, she couldn't care a damn about him."

Richard shook his head too. "Not a glimmer of a clue about Jack, in Jason's mind. He's looking forward to a business opportunity that is coming from a contact of a contact, if you follow my line. I would say he's excited about it, since its right up his street. No, I'd say that Jack is the last person on his mind."

Joe suggested. "Okay, let's try another avenue. Selecting the photo of Jack from the case file, he tossed it to Honey and said, "Try and focus on the missing man; see what he's up to."

Honey studied the photo and traced Jack's outline. After a few seconds she got animated, saying, "He's alive! He's in a small, windowless room, with only a bed in it. I see the color black all around him – nothing to do with auras, but a dominant black.

"I see another man with him, who's come to the door and is indicating to him that he wants to show him something. They're both going into a large, deserted building, where Jack's car is parked in the distance. The building looks derelict, with some of the windows smashed, high up on the sides.

"Now I see more! There's a small group of men, dressed in some type of black uniform, who are all in a row, on all fours, searching close-up for something."

Honey said excitedly, "It's a search, like we see on the TV, and I think they are policemen conducting a forensic ground-trawl!"

Joe inclined his head thoughtfully, and pondered the significance of the 'psychic trail'. "Where is it, that's the question?"

Honey shook her head. "I've lost it now, but black is the color to focus on."

"That's no good to me!" Joe sighed. He was getting used to sighing when mediums were around.

The weeks passed, until Joe received a call from Nicky, dismally notifying him that, "Jack's company is running out of patience. They're going to give it another month, and then they will terminate his employment contract. That means my child maintenance and other financial support will cease."

Joe commiserated with her and put the phone down. Notifying Richard, he passed on the message, and commented, "No doubt her parents will step in somehow and fill the breach."

Yet more time elapsed, and everyone was concentrating on other, newly distributed cases, when Joe received a call from one of the leading law enforcement agencies that made him sit up and pay attention. Jack and his girlfriend had been found and they were alive!

He and two others were expected to go to the agency's headquarters, and fly there to witness what was being gleaned. Joe chose the two mediums to go with him.

After a trouble-free flight, they were met by one of the agency operatives, Ivor Caruso, who fast-tracked them through the airport to his official car. In less than three quarters of an hour they were led through the portals of the prestigious building, and took an elevator down to the basement, where questioning was taking place.

As they approached, they could hear a man's voice angrily booming. Joe commented, "I don't need telling who that is!" Ivor opened a door, and invited them into a narrow observation room overlooking the interview room where Jack was being interrogated.

The three of them sat next to a couple of young agents, both females, busy taking and comparing notes, who greeted them cordially.

There were two agents sitting opposite Jack and already giving him a hard time. After politely knocking, Ivor opened the door to the interview room, walked over to them and whispered to the nearest, who immediately ordered Jack, "Once more, start at the beginning will you? And repeat what you've told us."

Jack rolled his eyes in exasperation and boomed in his deep voice, "It was Monday morning, 8:00am, and Angela – my girlfriend – was opening the front passenger door ready to get into our Audi A6 car. I was doing the same the other side, ready to drive us to work. We were parked in the drive outside our house.

"Three men, coat lapels raised and broad-brimmed hats lowered to hide their faces, marched up to us from the road, and showed us the pistols they were carrying, tucked into their trouser belts. Angela was told to get in the back with one man, who got in himself and put his gun on his lap, while the other ordered me to sit in the front passenger seat while he took over the driving.

"We were handed eye masks to put on, and sun glasses to put over them. We couldn't see where we were driven. It must have taken about 20 minutes to arrive on the outskirts of wherever, and the road surface became bumpy for at least another five minutes.

"You got all that?" he asked sarcastically.

"Keep going!" he was told impassively. What did the men look like?"

"They were all about my height, perhaps shorter, and had similar complexions to mine."

Joe looked at him, and saw that Jack was brown-eyed and olive-skinned with open pores; his nose was fleshy and his lips were full but not puffed-out. His hair was black, tinged with grey, and tightly ringed. He could pass for any number of men whose countries bordered the Mediterranean.

"Before you ask again, their eyes were brown, like mine," Jack added. "Everyone else in my family looks Caucasian except for me."

"When we drove off, the third man was presumably tailing us, since when we got out of the car after our journey, I heard another one draw up behind us. I then heard the sound of a large door opening. It was being pulled by hand, I think, and I could hear metal panels banging as it was rolled back to let us into a building."

One of the agents asked, "Did you notice anyone watching what was going on, like a neighbor? Have you any nosy neighbors?"

"Not that I'm aware of," was the reply.

"We'll check. Please continue."

"My car doors were opened to let us all out, and when they were slammed shut the noise echoed off the walls. I reckon it was an abandoned industrial unit, but I didn't hear anything crunching under the wheels after we entered. Outside was even bumpier, when we swung towards the building. I heard the big door being shut after us.

"I heard Angela being taken to a room, when the door to it swung open with a screeching noise, to let her in, and was then slammed shut after her. I heard a bolt being pulled to lock her in. It was at least 30 yards from where we were standing. I was led in the opposite direction, on the same side of the building where she had been locked up, around a corner so I knew we wouldn't be able to see each other."

"That's good and precise. Please continue," requested one of the questioners, in a pleasant manner.

Jack took more deep breaths and carried on talking.

"I had a slop-out bucket in the room, and a plastic toilet, but no chair. There was only the bed to sit on, and nothing to read. Each day, I saw three, sometimes four men assembling in a row ready to pray in the same posture adopted by Muslims. They would chat briefly before laying down prayer mats and crouching on them.

"How often did this happen; what were they wearing?" Ivor asked.

"I'm coming to that! They did this a few times a day, and wore black robes. Behind them was a short row of black flags, placed in white, plastic parasol stands. On the flags was some type of off-white symbol, in Arabic I guess."

Don't you know Arabic when you see it, or recognize the language when you hear it? Don't you watch the news bulletins?" Ivor was getting inquisitive.

"No. I never read anything apart from articles about the music industry, and technical manuals. Why should I?"

Ivor looked flabbergasted, while Jack ignored him with an air of disdain, before continuing.

"Anyway, the men would then begin raising and lowering their bodies, in unison, and chanting."

In the observation room, Joe leant towards Richard and Honey, and whispered to them, "This tallies with your vision of a row of men crouching in a row, wearing black. So much for your theory that they were police officers trawling for forensic clues! Right idea, wrong supposition!" They were looking embarrassed; he leant back, chuckling to himself, and sighing profoundly.

Jack continued. "This went on for days, with me cooped up most of the time. I could hear a generator in the background, feeding us electricity. The only times I was let out was after each round of prayers, to take exercise, have a shower once a day, and go to the bog in the adjacent toilet block. I made a point of crapping there, or the stench in my room would have been unbearable."

"Did you have any contact with Angela?"

"No." It was a blunt, unemotional statement from Jack, who conclude by commenting, "That's it, really. I heard nothing about being released until the day all hell broke loose. I was afraid they were going to kill me, but they left me alone in my room and scarpered, until you lot arrived and released me."

"Why'd you think they did that? Let you live I mean?" asked Ivor as the two other agents again let him have his chance to speak.

"I dunno. Maybe they feared getting caught and charged with murder. Maybe they hoped for a lesser prison sentence. Who can tell?"

Ivor signaled to the observers to wait, whole Jack was led away in shackles.

A member of the catering staff came in, and offered Joe, Honey, Richard and the others coffees and biscuits, which they gratefully accepted and began chatting about what Jack had stated, in his statement, and the ramifications that went with it.

Joe made a few general observations, like, "He's a cold fish. Did you notice how unfeeling he was towards his girlfriend? And how insular he is, when it comes to world matters?"

One of the other agents, whose metal name badge said she was Natalie something or other, gave him her professional opinion of Jack Lestrange. "I'm a psychological profiler, and that man is an intriguing cross between a sociopath and a psychopath."

Richard asked, "How do you distinguish between the two?"

Natalie replied, "Sociopaths tend to be nervous and easily agitated. They are volatile and prone to emotional outbursts, including fits of rage. Normally they are uneducated, but Jack is the opposite of that. Sociopathy is more likely the product of childhood trauma and physical or emotional abuse, or both.

"Conversely, psychopaths are unable to form emotional attachments or feel real empathy with others, although they often have disarming personalities. On the whole, Jack is anything but charming, but he can be. It is believed that psychopathy is the result of genetics.

"Psychopaths are very manipulative and can easily gain people's trust. They learn to mimic emotions, despite their inability to feel them, and will appear normal to unsuspecting people. Jack fits this category by being well-educated and holding a steady job.

"People with this disorder are so good at manipulation and mimicry that they have families and other long-term relationships without those around them ever suspecting their true nature.

"What we have to determine is how bad Jack's disorder truly is. Psychopathy is the most dangerous of all personality disorders, because of the way he may dissociate emotionally from his actions, regardless of how terrible they may be."

Honey commented, "Jack has definitely suffered childhood traumas, both at school and home; therein lie the sociopathic trends. Genetically? I would say yes, he has inherited some disturbing behavioral problems and a residual personality disorder."

As they were sitting there chatting, Angela was escorted sympathetically into the interview room, with a lady agent supporting her gently by the arm.

"This is where it starts to get interesting," Joe murmured.

The three agents opposite visibly relaxed as she sat down to face them, and they extended her their sympathies in compassionate tones.

"Hello Angela, nice to see you again. Are you ready to tell us once more what happened to you? You can skip the bit about the car journey when you were first abducted. We'd like you to recite your experiences after you were separated from Jack. We have some visitors and they'd really like to hear your version of events."

Jack's girlfriend had apparently lost some weight and was more attractive to look at, compared with her photos, although her face looked drawn and tired. She had brown hair and freckles, blue eyes and looked as if she normally smiled a lot, prior to the kidnapping. Under her boiler suit, she looked well-rounded and had big breasts, so the weight loss must have been significant for it to be mentioned by her relatives, when they were reunited.

She began to speak hesitantly in a twangy, high-pitched voice. "My name is Angela Bevan. When we arrived at the deserted industrial unit, I was led to a row of cells and pushed inside one of them, after my blindfold was removed."

"Do you mean blindfold, or was something else used to keep you from seeing?"

"Yes. They made me put on eye pads, like you get on aircraft if you wants to sleep, then dark glasses on top, for some reason."

"That's fine. Please continue."

"Before I went inside my cell, I looked around and that was when I could see where I was, in a big, empty building that looked old-fashioned. It had brick walls with paint peeling off them, big sliding doors at the end where we came through, windows along each side wall, and a high v-shaped corrugated roof."

"Why'd you describe your room as a cell?"

"Because it was in a row of identical cells. I called it a *cell* because that's what they all looked like, prison cells like you see on the TV. I thought they was empty, but they wasn't, 'cos I heard voices coming from them, female voices."

Angela was relaxing, and her true speaking-voice was starting to come through.

"There was no sound coming from them when you first arrived?"

"No, they was all quiet."

Honey whispered to Richard and Joe, "She is little more than a child; she sounds childish and from what I've read she *is* childish. I'll bet she's done some growing up very quickly!"

Ivor asked her, "What were the others saying, the women I

mean?"

Angela continued her discourse. "I dunno. They was whispering all the time; they sounded scared to me. When a guard came near, they'd stop sudden like. I got scared too!"

"What was your room like, inside?"

It had nothing in it. A bed, toilet for peeing in, and nothing much else."

"No bedding?"

"Oh yeah, a blanket. It was still effing cold at night!"

"Did they let you out at all?"

"Yeah, to have a workout, on the spot, jumping up and down an' things! Also you got to go toilet proper, in the toilets nearby."

"How many times did they let you out?"

"A few times, after they'd 'ad their prayers. Unless you wanted to go toilet sudden like, then they'd let you out special!"

"Where was Jack being kept?"

She snorted, "Him? He was with 'em, the bloody rat!"

"How'd you know that?"

"Cos I saw his fat arse stuck in the air, when he was praying with 'em! I also heard him bartering to buy some of the other women, like we was all slaves!"

"How'd you know it was him?"

She snorted again, in derision, "I came out of my cell one morning, and there he was, in a black robe, crouching on his mat, praying!"

"How'd you know it was him, if he was covered from head to foot in a robe?"

She looked heavenward, as if for inspiration. "Because every normal day, it was the same men praying and chanting. Then one day, when I went to the toilet sudden like, there he was too!" She looked at the agents opposite and shouted, "I'd know his fat arse anywhere! Besides, I heard him speak as he got up suddenly, when he saw me! It was him alright."

"How'd you get away? Please be precise."

She explained. "I could see that the mesh covering the opening in my door was loose. When everything went quiet, I gave it a push on one side, where it was loosest. It came away, so I folded it to one side. That left me with the bars. They was wide-spaced and my arms are on the skinny-side – the only part of me that is!

"I managed to squeeze the left arm through and reach down to the bolt that was keeping the door closed. I just about reached it and wriggled it open. I was bare-footed, but ran like hell on tiptoe through the building to reach the big doors, which were part open.

"I squeezed through and ran hard to where I could hear lots of traffic. It was a main road and I took a good look round, to remember where I was. Then I tried flagging down a car, but they all took no notice. When one did stop, he asked how much I wanted.

"Me, a bloody hooker for God's sake, that's what he thought I was! I let him have a piece of my mind I can tell you. Anyway, once I showed him the scratches on my arm, from where I'd hurt myself, he realized what I was telling him may be true and took me to a police station.

"The silly sods there wanted to book him for child prostitution, until I got going with them too! I mean, do I look like a kid, with my knockers?"

Calming down, she concluded by saying; "Anyway, once they'd looked me up on their records, they took me seriously and here I am now!" She looked relieved to have finished telling her story.

"That's all for now. Thank you for helping us," one of the two original agents said, as the others also thanked her in support, and she was led away.

Joe commented, "Well here's a conundrum. He says one thing, she says another. Either he's a jihadist or he isn't." He was swaying as he spoke and moving his hands from one side to the other, to emphasize the points he was making.

He looked at the other two young agents with them in the observation room, and asked, "Is there something you're still not telling us? I don't know which way this cookie is going to crumble!"

The agent accompanying Natalie, whose name badge told the world that she was Isabel Sutton, chimed in, "We've read the case notes you emailed to us. I think Nicky's boyfriend, Jason, is the instigator of this kidnapping."

Joe agreed. "The facts are indisputable. Three masked men

ambushed Jack and Angela outside their rented house. There were only a few who knew their current address as they'd only recently moved there. Someone arranged for the abduction, and the man with the resources and know-how to do it was Jason Henman.

"The finger of blame points at him as the organizer. **But**, and it is a big **but**, how do we prove it conclusively? I'd bet that if he was to take a polygraph test, he'd come out of it smelling of roses, no lies detected. My gut-feel tells me that the deed was done on his behalf, at full arm's length.

"I don't like depending on probable cause, with his defense lawyers arguing that all he was guilty of was suffering 'temptation'. Who could blame him for suffering that human frailty, when his lovely girlfriend, Nicky, was being mentally tortured by her ex-husband?"

Natalie added her opinion, "There's also the claim made by Angela, Jack's girlfriend, that he was party to the kidnapping. She insists that he was participating in the prayers, and the selling of women for the slave trade. But, she never fully saw Jack, and never caught sight of any of the other women she says were held in her cell block."

Joe agreed. "I think that a body-double may have been acting as Jack, and a good sound system was employed to broadcast voices. They could have used their family members to act as the victims.

"As for Jack . . . Well, we all know how he blasts off at everyone and everything. The gang could have provoked him to say whatever they wanted him to, spliced sections together and played them back to convince Angela of his involvement. I reckon it was all smoke and mirrors."

Isabel provided more information. "When we hot-footed it over to the industrial unit pinpointed by Angela and in the locality identified by the driver who'd picked her up on the nearby main road, we found some interesting pieces of evidence.

"These included a cache of pistols, old grenades, four Kalashnikovs and a lot of ammunition that had been dumped in a rubbish container outside the building. We also found a bundle of black robes and flags soaked in petrol in a dustbin, not yet set alight.

"Guess who's partial fingerprints were found on some of the weapons, and whose DNA was on one of the larger-sized black robes?

"Equally as intriguing, we also found a very comfortable, decent-sized room around the corner from where Angela had been incarcerated. There was a duvet on the bed, Egyptian cotton sheets over a deep sprung mattress, a large carpet covering the floor and traces of Jack's DNA everywhere. Real homely it was."

Joe weighed up the pros and cons, summing up the situation in a stupefying way, by saying,

"The residual problem is: what to do about Jack Lestrange? He is, by any standards, a walking time bomb. It has been professionally diagnosed that he has serious psychopathic and sociopathic personality disorders.

"He could have been the victim of a revenge set-up. Equally, he could be complicit in the kidnapping. That would have been done to cover his tracks as a jihadist, in a plot that backfired because his girlfriend is not as stupid as he thought she was.

"Either way, does your agency want to take the risk of him being judged innocent of the charge of being a threat to the homeland? If he really is guilty, he could end up rampaging and murdering innocent people."

The other agents looked most glum, and were unresponsive as the meeting broke up.

As they were leaving for the return flight home, Ivor informed Joe, "We'll arrange to transport those currently in custody back to your locality, pending further action. The girl can be permanently released, but we leave it up to you with respect to Jack."

Joe was not happy with having to make that specific choice.

§ 7: Look on the Brightside

Jack was in a foul temper. When he was released from custody and returned to his local airport, he was expected to make his own way home. However, en route he first had to make a detour to the official impound lot, to which his prized car had been transported by the police; they didn't want it cluttering up their station car park when it was retrieved after his abduction. Apparently, they had taken it apart searching for clues that would lead them to the kidnappers.

It was money being spent all the time, and he hadn't had the chance to check what was left in his bank account. To add insult to injury, the sullen official behind the counter at the impound lot demanded a huge amount from him, to pay for storage and the cost of transport to get it there.

That would be one more civil action he'd be initiating, to claim compensation for his wrongful detention.

When he found his lost property after several searches along a multitude of deserted rows of dusty cars, his attempts to start it were in vain. He had to call for someone to bring him a portable recharger, link it via his flat battery and restart the ignition for him.

If he wasn't so bad mannered, the guy might not have brought out a credit card swiper and charged him as well as his car. While the assistant was walking away, he kicked at the driver's door in fury, and the opposing passenger door fell off, landing on its side in a cloud of dust after smacking into the side of the car next to it.

The assistant stopped, looked back sideways, returned, took out his smart phone, and photographed both vehicles. Not to give further provocation, he sauntered away and only began whistling *The Colonel Bogey March* when he had achieved a safe distance.

The main words that Jack associated with that tune were: *Bollocks, was all the band could play.* He realized that when the other car owner returned, he would be fully informed of the damage that

Jack had inflicted on his property. He opened the boot and dumped the door inside.

He left at high speed, his foot pressed on the accelerator, unaware of the camera taking a photo as he passed it. "Huh!" the sullen attendant exclaimed as he stood in his booth and watched Jack receding into the distance. He turned to his assistant who was about to store his battery charger, and said, "Some people never learn. Do they honestly think we don't get that sort of antisocial behavior on a regular basis?"

The recipient of this piece of news grinned maliciously, and began generating an incident log of the damage inflicted by Jack on another vehicle.

When he got home, he knew his girlfriend wouldn't be there to meet him; it was a workday. What he didn't expect to find was mounting evidence that she's cleared her belongings and sodded off. Wherever he checked there was no remaining trace of her.

"Damn, damn, damn!" he exclaimed out loud. "I've got to go and find another one now! What a bloody nuisance that is! Her timing couldn't have been worse!"

Reflecting on his future plans for the boys. He pondered, "*How am I going to get them to stay with me?*" It never entered his mind to contemplate defeat; this was a temporary setback.

Later on, his boss phoned him. He said, "Jack, glad you're back at last. When are you coming into work. Tomorrow?" Jack confirmed this. The boss continued, "Good, see you then!" and put the phone down.

"*That was short and sweet,*" Jack thought. "*I'll arrange to pick up the boys, to stay with me this evening.*" He texted his ex-wife and requested to collect them at 6pm sharp. Within the hour, she responded positively; 6pm was the accepted time. He got their beds ready and then went out to get the door in the boot re-attached by his local garage, before doing some essential shopping.

What Jack didn't know was the state of mind his boss was in. He was fed up to the eyeballs with his subordinate, who had landed the company in the soup. The police had sent round uniformed police, to delve into the behavior of some of his key staff. It seemed that they had been giving advice to Jack about how to deal with his ex-wife in his ongoing matrimonial disputes.

It emerged that the advice was contentious and inflammatory. The result was that the employees concerned were laying themselves open to criminal charges of aiding and abetting Jack in commissioning acts of harassment and metal cruelty. No doubt if found guilty, civil action would follow to pay compensation to his ex-wife for the suffering and deprivation he and his cohorts had caused her and the boys.

To cap it all, when the police were formally interviewing these staff, they had provided details of their trips abroad, to fix a date for them to attend court on dates yet to be confirmed. When the listed individuals returned from their travels, they were intercepted immediately on exiting their various airports and submitted to roadside tests for Schedule 1 and 2 drugs.

Unfortunately, they were all found guilty of drug-taking, were fined heavily, disqualified from driving and their licenses were taken away. Even more unfortunately, the success of this exercise led the police to take punitive action of the same type against all of the other members of staff who travelled regularly, including the CEO ('Chief Executive Officer') himself. It was a resounding success for the local force.

The consequences were severe, due to one man who they had allowed, if not encouraged to behave immorally. Curiously, the only one whose behavior was impeccable was the sole female director of the company, and she was about to be promoted to the top job, pending its sale to a publicly quoted rival for a knockdown price.

Jack's days at the company were numbered.

Meanwhile, at the wheel of his repaired Audi A6 car, Jack headed toward his despised ex-wife's home and parked as usual in the path between his neighbors' properties. He didn't care a fig what they thought of him, and would call the police if they dared to defy him; his boys came first in his life.

Suddenly, his door was wrenched open and he was yanked out. With a whimper, he held his arms up to protect his head, and left himself vulnerable to the blows to the body that were being leveled at him. Oh how it hurt, and he let out an almighty bellow for help.

The attacker fled the scene, leaving him doubled up breathless and in pain. He could make out that it was a man, who was making off down the alleyway next to his ex-wife's property. When he stared around wildly, there was no one around to stop him, except for another person who was haring off in the opposite direction. From an open bedroom window, he heard someone jeering.

Staggering up onto his feet, he sat down heavily on the driver's seat, only to let out another scream as an excruciating pain stabbed into one of his buttocks.

"What the hell is that?" he moaned, rubbing himself and groaning as it made the pain worse. Leaning on the open door, he saw a very large spider, flattened and splayed out on his seat; it was a bright gold and yellow color, and hairy with it. Its balloon-shaped central body area had burst, and there were little things crawling around in the liquid oozing from it; he could feel this gunge saturating his trousers.

He felt pathetic, standing there badly hurt and on his own; not one person had come to his aid. He picked up his mobile and called the emergency services to come and assist him.

He felt so sorry for himself that he hadn't thought about the boys, nor wondered why they weren't there to meet him when he needed them.

When the ambulance arrived, he looked at the crew pitifully and explained what had happened. One of them rushed off to get a brush and pan, to scoop up the spider, while the other, her companion, stared goggle-eyed at his naked arse and said, "I'm not sucking that! You'll have to wait until we get to A&E."

Strolling into his office at the agency, Joe used the intercom to ask Richard and Honey to join him. As they sat around the conference table together, he commented, "I guess you've seen the latest news? Jack the Lad has been bad again." They nodded, so he continued.

"Yes, he's recovering in hospital from the bite of a 'Golden Orb Weaver', one of the largest spiders in Australia that has found its way here. It has a neurotoxic effect similar to that of the black widow spider; however, its venom is not nearly as powerful.

"Any ideas on where it came from, or who might have dropped it on his car seat, when he was being attacked in public?"

The two mediums glanced at each other, before Honey volunteered to speak.

"I think it came from the front door frame of Nicky's house."

Joe replied, "I *know* it came from the front door frame of Nicky's place of abode, because she told me it did, as soon as she heard the news. I am disappointed that neither of you came to me first, with that information.

"Why didn't you see fit to tell me something that important?"

They looked at each other, before Richard explained.

"Because we cannot see a direct link between the occupants of the house and the theft of the spider."

"Meaning what?"

"Because, when it happened, Nicky wasn't there, the boys weren't there, and Jason was in Africa on mercenary-related work. He is training a government's army regulars and recruits to fight against terrorist insurgents. They all have alibis and can be discounted from the line of enquiry."

"So who is left to investigate? According to the witness descriptions of the attackers, Nicky is the wrong sex and size; the boys are too small, and Jason was elsewhere. Who does that leave who could have thumped Jack, and who else might have dropped the spider into the car?"

Honey suggested, "The neighbors, or possibly Jason's army buddies? If I may be so bold, you need to employ traditional methods to find out who the culprits are, since we cannot detect anything amiss using our psychic abilities."

Joe groaned, "This looks like it's going to be my first ever career failure. Okay, we wait until we get a lead, whenever."

An indirect break came when Jack was released from hospital two days later, with a patch on his backside and strapping around his ribs. He promptly disappeared again.

Joe warily broached the matter with the two psychics directly involved with this tiresome case.

"Okay, where is he'?" Joe asked them.

Honey replied, "He's still alive, that's for sure!"

"Well that's a surprise!" Joe said sarcastically.

Richard enthused, "I see lots of blue in the picture, from above!"

Joe sighed, "Here we go again! I've told you, I need more explicit information than that!"

Honey confirmed the sighting, "Yes, but I also see green as well as blue! Now I know why: he's in a plane and it's coming into land."

Richard said, "Whew, it's hot!"

Joe commented, "I know, he's working in a pizza parlor!" and terminated the meeting by saying, "Get real, both of you! This is bum information you're feeding me!"

As he was leaving the room, he heard Honey saying, "Now it's all turning brown!"

He continued walking, with his back bristling. "Whatever!" he said, in disgust.

Meanwhile, in Africa, there were thousands of new recruits strenuously exercising under the guidance of very strict NCOs. For the first time in their lives, they were being taught to follow orders blindly, without question and only speak when they were spoken to.

They were being taught obedience and techniques that would help them to survive against implacable zealots, and overcome them with superior skills acquired with the best discipline and equipment that money could buy. They were being turned into fighting machines that were merciless, and sharing a justifiable conviction of their personal superiority in battle.

Forming that army was a special breed of trainer, with experience of training the best men that discerning army officers in his country of origin had hand-picked. At their core was Jason, whose hard-acquired talents had at last been recognized.

There was amongst his deputies a very peculiar person that Jason had been forced to use. It was not because of any talent that Jason would have recognized, but because the man in question was a loner with deep-rooted mental problems, and society had no other worthwhile place that could make use of him.

Jason's eyes bulged as he singled the man out for special attention. "ARSEHOLE, come here NOW!" he shouted.

"SARGEANT SIR, YES SIR!" Jack replied, standing rigidly to attention and saluting his superior crisply.

What an example he was proving to be, to the new recruits. Singularly, to add to his mystique, he was kept apart when not being used to inspire them with his prowess. The logic was: if he did it, so could they, whatever they were told to do, without question or thought.

In a sense, he was their Judas goat, with the obedient flock being alternatively trained to inflict slaughter when they followed him.

Joe was pleased when he was confidentially informed of Jack's whereabouts, as arranged by the law enforcement agency with whom he had liaised on this investigation. With a wry smile, he remembered the colors identified by Richard and Honey, and marveled at their useless accuracy. It had taught him a lesson: make sure to ask the right questions, next time.

Nicky was absolutely over the moon when Jack's financial support continued to flow from his bank account, which was replenished regularly by an anonymous benefactor. Jack was living cost-free in his new role, and had no need for money, so Jason managed it fairly on his behalf.

The boys had been on the receiving end of Jack's temper too many times, and were soon trying their best to forget him.

Angela went back home and lived with her parents until she could find someone that was more suitable for her.

Nicky's father met a man and paid him for services rendered, with deep gratitude. He was the missing link, as Honey and Richard would have realized if they'd met or seen him.

That would have been another lesson for Joe to learn: broaden the search, if the need arises.

CASE CLOSED

The time had come for Joe to report on the case, ready for its submission to the agency's backers. This would give a summary of the reasons for taking on the case, to be followed by an outline of the case itself, what the outcome was, how this compared with the original intentions. and a brief conclusion.

Against the trend of modern reporting, Joe insisted that the findings and conclusions went where they belonged: at the end of the report. His reckoning was that if someone was so strapped for time that they couldn't be bothered with a synopsis of the case, then they weren't worth the time he invested in preparing it.

For example, in this instance it started with an apology for taking on a 'live' case that was purely intended to get some momentum going at the agency.

Joe recorded the remainder of the report into his PC in accordance with a written series of bullet points, illustrated as follows:

- The bad behavior of the client's ex-husband was explained simply and effectively by his ex-wife, who requested the help of The Deaduction agency. The agency found that his actions were entering the realms of criminality, which increasingly justified the agency's ongoing involvement.

- The impact the father was having on the boys was described as seriously intrusive and destabilizing.

- His bad approach to parenting had spiraled downwards until he disappeared for a period, during which time he had either been abducted or initiated the process personally, to follow a terrorist agenda.

- The law enforcement agency that supervised and liaised with The Deaduction Agency itself became involved. It neutralized the father, by taking him on the 'rendition path' and spirited him away to another continent.

- The outcome was that the case gave the two mediums involved, Richard and Honey, the chance to demonstrate their mental skills at reading minds. These had been revealed as prodigious.

- What remained to be demonstrated was their skill at communicating with the spirits of the deceased. Fortunately, a welcome glimpse of this ability had been provided when Richard made contact with the main suspect's maternal grandfather, Daniel.

- The provision of an experimental device nicknamed the 'Spectractor' was also praised as a potentially valuable tool for The Deaduction Agency to use in its contact with the spirit world.

Joe applied the maxim, "Always end on an upbeat note!" as he finished off and transmitted his report

CASES 2–6.
A SLEW OF PRIORITIES

Going back in time, and straight after Joe had allocated the first case to Honey and Richard, he thumbed through a slew (or large number) of folders in his sideboard. He selected five from the right-hand side on the top shelf, and took them to their colleagues Chuck and Rose.

These represented the cream of the handpicked unresolved cases, and had been stored upright, within his easy reach. In Joe's estimation, they were at the top of the 'slew' and were a fair test of the mettle of genuine psychics. It was anticipated that they would easily be able to identify the perpetrators of the crimes.

He looked forward to seeing how well cases 2 to 6 would be handled, and in future would be issuing the same challenge to the other partners in the agency.

It should be noted that other cases of less significance were also investigated afterwards, to fill in any spare slots that arose in the workload of each person. No one lacked for something to do, and these were itemized under the heading of 'Miscellaneous'.

CASE 2 – THE DECEASED COURSE-GIRL

It was a self-imposed pre-condition of each case; as little information as possible was to be passed to the medium tasked with detection of the guilty party.

Catching Chuck by surprise, Rose stated determinedly, "I know what I said earlier about this case. However, I'd prefer to handle this one on my own!" Joe studied her with increased interest.

She was a woman in her late forties, about 5ft 8 inches tall, who habitually wore a resolute, self-confident look on her face and had a disproportionate figure. To be blunt about it, her posterior was larger than her bosom, suggesting that she had little inclination to maintain a healthy eating regime.

Her hair, cut above the neck, was a wavy brown color. She was dressed in a matronly manner with flower-patterned blouse, a plain blue cardigan, a plain grey two-thirds length loose-fitting skirt and brown slip-on low-heeled dark red shoes. She wore standard-sized glasses, and her jawline was formidably square. The lipstick she had applied was barely visible, and she apparently wore no other makeup on her face.

Joe felt uncomfortable, knowing that his critical first assessment of her, based on appearance, was irrelevant; after all, the reputation she had acquired for solving criminal cases was formidable. It would be prudent to wait and see how well she did.

She was preoccupied as she walked out of Joe's office, leaving him with Chuck to select the third case; this was subject to separate scrutiny later on in this book: 'The Case of the Two Innocent Flirts'.

When Rose reached her own office and sat down behind her desk, she removed the photo, placed it face down in front of her, and ran her fingers over it with her eyes closed. She had started trying to build a picture of the person shown on the other side, and expressed her pleasure by quietly saying, "Ah!" as she turned it over for confirmation. She noted that the name of the girl was Danah Snowdon.

There in front of her in the photo was a smiling, self-composed young lady, dressed in a powder blue office suit. She was in her early to mid-twenties, with swept-back straight blond-hair and perfectly proportioned God-given features, including beautiful blue eyes and cupid lips. She was to die for, and unfortunately had.

Rose understood without question that the poor lamb had departed this world suddenly, and began the laborious process of detecting how this sad event had come to pass. It did not feel to her that it was a violent end, which piqued her curiosity.

Closing her eyes, she said out loud, "Danah, Danah, if you can hear me, come and talk to me." She concentrated as strong as she could on projecting that spoken message as far as she could around herself, while broadcasting the same mantra mentally.

Her efforts were rewarded, as a young woman's voice replied that only Rose could distinguish. An unmistakable apparition showed briefly in front of her, shimmering in the office light, and soon disappeared, confirming briefly that it was Danah herself communicating.

Rose was delighted and said, "Danah dearest, how are you getting on, in your new world?"

"*Just fine,*" was the reply, "*But I'd like to know how I got here!*"

"You don't know yourself? You didn't meet a violent end to your life?"

"*Nope. Can you help me?*"

"Of course I can! Listen, you're beginning to fade. Where would be best, at the place where your body was found, or at home?"

Rose was fast losing contact with the earth-bound spirit, who could barely be heard as she replied, "*Where I last remember being alive, at the old hotel!*" She had to strain to hear the last words, and wrote them down.

From his office, Joe could see Rose gesticulating as she talked to an invisible spirit, and was fascinated by the scene. Curious to find out what was happening, he got up and walked over to stand by her door to eavesdrop.

He realized at last why he had taken a poor view of her, subjectively: it was because she bore a close resemblance to a stern headmistress who had intimidated him as a youngster. There had been nothing untoward in that other person's manner towards him; it was purely her size, bearing and status that had kept her alive in his memory.

"How's it going?" he intruded, in a kindly way.

Rose replied, "I've made contact; she doesn't seem to have been murdered, but I need to visit the place where death occurred, to make best progress. I could see a hotel in my vision that that dates back centuries."

Joe was impressed, thinking, "*Wow, she nailed that one!*" since *he* knew where the death had occurred.

He restricted himself to replying, "No problema! I'd like you to be accompanied by two of the crew you met originally. I have in mind Matt and Jake. I will make them temporary, official lawmen, to help you gain easier access to the hotel at which the victim stayed and other places you want to visit.

"Don't announce your role in the investigation to anyone other than those two; keep it confidential. Are you okay with that?"

She nodded, saying, "It would help to know why she was there, for how long, and details of anyone she would have met on a regular basis during her visit. Can you get that information?"

"Okay, yes I will. Also, I'll get the crew to pick you up and drive you to the destination town, which is a few hours away on the coast. Be aware that they will probably want to film you in action, and might also recruit some extras to recreate the actual events.

"I'll aim to get this up and running by the day after tomorrow, if you're all available. Is that alright with you, for starters?"

She agreed, while resuming her study of Danah Snowdon's photo. Then she picked up another case file and started work on that. She was enthusiastic in her attitude to help clear the backlog of cases.

Two days later, Rose entered the bureau pulling a small suitcase and was met by a welcoming committee comprising Joe and the two film crew-cum-official bodyguards.

Joe handed her the requested file about the movements of the victim during the crucial timeframe. He wished them a safe journey and good luck, and she was then escorted downstairs by her two companions, with Matt obligingly pulling her suitcase.

They drove at maximum permitted speeds along uncrowded main roads most of the way, with Rose in the back studying her case file. Occasionally, she would doze-off as they passed through vast tracts of green countryside dotted with picturesque farms and outbuildings, while Matt and Jake took it in turns at the wheel.

It had been a restful journey, and they pulled up outside their destination hotel. This had bow windows and an olde-worlde charm about it, in keeping with the general appearance of the old part of the town in which it was sited.

Jake asked to speak to the general manager, who was a portly older man of genteel appearance wearing a grey suit with suede waistcoat, and explained why they were there, on official business. A bellhop then escorted them to their pre-booked rooms on the third floor, one of which had been occupied by Danah Snowdon on that fateful night, years earlier. Rose had asked to sleep there and was accorded her desire.

There was enough daylight left to locate the training centre, which Joe had advised her was central to Danah's reason for visiting the town. She had been attending a five-day course in computer administration, in the nearby smart, modern district, which was awash with office blocks and shopping malls.

The computer company was still in business, and they eagerly strode into its foyer. At reception, the men showed their badges and asked to speak to the course administration manager. A slim, dark-haired man who was in his mid-thirties came across straight away, smiled and got down to business with them.

When he saw Danah's photo, he said, "Yes, of course, I cannot fail to remember her. A sad day for all of us it was. In fact the course was cut short, because no one felt like continuing when her death was reported to us."

Rose asked, "Was there anyone she got close to?"

He replied, "I'll have to check with the course lecturer. Give me a minute and I'll go get him."

Jake said, "That's a stroke of luck. We get to speak to the main man direct!"

A younger man was led towards them, and they went into a conference room next to reception, to talk in private. Most noticeable about him was his eyes; they seemed to bore right through you as he spoke.

When asked the same question, he replied, "No, there was no one she was close to. She had an aloof attitude and kept her distance. Apparently, they all went out as a group for an evening meal at an Italian restaurant, and she apparently relaxed after a few drinks in her. In class however, she was all-business and keen to learn."

Rose changed tack and asked him, "How did they behave the following day, after the evening meal?"

He answered, "Frankly, they all looked the worse for wear, and the smell of garlic was pungent. One guy was flaked out in front of me. Totally asleep he was, with his head on the desk. She laughed fit to bust at his state!"

"What did he look like?"

"Butch! Every day, he wore the same outfit: tight black jeans and a sleeveless string vest, showing his hairy chest and fat arms."

"Sounds like you didn't take to him?"

"Correct! He was macho man and fancied himself enormously. But he was a good tecky and knew his computer stuff, that's for sure!"

"No one else stood out, as worthy of attention?"

"No, not at all! Some of them tried to put in lines of code to test me, via their shared-access screens and keyboards, but they failed." He looked pleased that he had beaten them at their own game.

Matt asked, "Could you provide us with a list of all those on the course, including yourself?"

He agreed, saying. "Give me a few minutes and I'll print it off for you."

Rose asked, "Before you go, I have to ask: you didn't fancy her yourself, did you?"

He replied with a frown, "Yes and no; yes I did fancy her, and no, I didn't try and take her out, I'm a married man and went home to my family every night, punctually, and stayed there."

Rose blushed and apologized. "Sorry, but I had to eliminate you."

He smiled wickedly and went off to provide the proffered list of names. Rose studied his thoughts and realized he had exaggerated his home life; he was married but there were no other family members other than his lovely young wife.

They said their goodbyes and returned to the hotel.

In the privacy of her room, Rose double-checked the additional information provided by Joe, and was disappointed at her findings; the list of course names was incomplete in comparison with that obtained at the computer training center. It also lacked contact details and descriptions, and had been summarized by the original detectives as irrelevant to their investigation.

Later that night, after a solitary evening meal taken in her room, she showered and got ready for bed. She needed to be alone and preoccupy herself on the task she was about to undertake.

Sitting down, she concentrated on Danah and tried to summon her, in the same way as she had before. It was not long before she succeeded, this time, in making a much stronger connection; it was two-way and the mental responses were precise.

"Did you come back to the hotel with anyone?"

"*Yes, I'd fancied this gorgeous creature on the course since I first clapped eyes on him! He was so sexy, and when he let himself relax at the meal table, he was utterly irresistible.*"

"What did he look like?"

"*He had designer stubble on his handsome face, blue eyes, and a powerful body. Built like a bull he was, filling a string vest ready to busting. Lordy, he was the bees knees! As luck would have it, he was also staying at this hotel on this floor! If I could still blush you'd see me doing it now. We had sex most of the night and it was steamy stuff!*"

"Did you take anything other than alcohol?" It was a shrewdly posed question from Rose.

"*Yup, after all, it was only wine we had with the meal. We took some coke after, but not much. I passed out sometime; I don't know when!*"

"One last question: did anyone see you, when you were approaching your room?" Rose was assuming that it was her room they were heading back to.

"*Yes,*" Danah replied brightly, not contradicting her. "*A security man asked us to identify ourselves. We only had to show our room cards and he let us go on our way.*"

Rose said to her smoothly, "I will let your parents know that I've been in contact with you, and that you're okay and happy, but missing them. Will that set your mind at rest, Danah my love?"

Danah replied sadly, "*It will, but I'm so sorry to have departed in the way I did. I still don't know why!*"

Rose reassured her, "I'm sure I do, and the matter will be dealt with in a few days. I can see no reason on earth why you should choose to stay here any longer. Do you see a light in the distance, growing as I speak?" She pointed to the ceiling, to attract Danah's attention to a location beyond the room.

She insisted: "Go towards it *now*, and meet up with all the people waiting to greet you. You will return here later as your spirit begins the next cycle of your progress. Go *now*, before it is too late. Go *now!*"

Silently, she was aware of Danah's spirit flying off and breaking away from her. It was an easy task to complete, and she slept soundly afterwards.

The following morning, she phoned Joe and advised him, "Arrest and question the course attendee whose name was Cristofer Dunschmidt, and bring him in for questioning." She explained the logic behind her request, and impressed him even more with her assessment of the probable cause of Danah's untimely death.

Immediately after, she spoke to Jake and Matt, and recommended they get in touch with the actors' agency they used to recruit extras. Then she suggested how they should slant the story, to demonstrate how Danah had died.

She explained, "I appreciate this has got to be set up, and when the prime suspect has been found and arrested, it will confirm what I've told you. You can be getting on with the filming, and I'll deal with my role in it afterwards, separately.

"In the meantime, can you get me booked on a flight home? My search here is over, and I want to get on with the next case. Time is precious!"

Matt asked her, "What if the ending changes, and he isn't guilty of anything?"

Rose replied, "It won't matter. He is either guilty of second-degree murder or first-degree murder. You can cater for both, to conclude this episode in your series."

Cristofer was duly arrested at his current address, an apartment hundreds of miles from the scene of the crime, in another town and county, and was transported back to the local police station. It was close to the hotel where the death had occurred.

Joe flew there to interview the suspect in person. Cristofer was dressed in casual clothes, not designed to emphasize his heavy physique, but to moderate it in appearance and present himself in a more mature and sober light.

He looked uneasy, sitting opposite Joe who fixed him with one of his deep, penetratingly cold stares. He looked at him as a predator would look at its prey, getting that familiar feeling in his gut. "*My oh my, you do look uncomfortable. We both know that you're as guilty as hell. All that remains is for me to prove it!*"

He was in his element and knew what he would do to get Cristofer to open up.

"Cris, do you really know why you are here, sitting opposite me and charged with murder?"

Cris could hardly look him in the eye, and replied evasively, "No I don't. I've done nothing wrong."

"Haven't you? Haven't you *really*? May I bring your attention to a fact that you may be unaware of? You were seen with the young lady in the hotel corridor outside her room, late the same night as she died."

He leaned forward and said in a confidential tone, "Do you remember *now* explaining to that witness, a dependable security guard on patrol, the reason why you were with her, immediately before her death?"

He was emphasizing the importance of the chance meeting, and deliberately giving Cris some room for maneuver by using the word *death* instead of *murder*.

"No doubt you also read the coroner's report's first conclusion? It stated that Danah's death was 'due to natural causes'. I'll bet you were relieved when that result was published!

"What you wouldn't have been aware of was the fact that we arranged for a *second* 'virtual' autopsy to be conducted, based on the original, typed autopsy analyses.

"This time round, evidence was found, in those notes, of suffocation that had been overlooked by the person doing the original autopsy.

"This time round, the revised conclusion was therefore

reached that death had been due to 'causes unknown'. This gave us justification to re-open the investigation.

"I ask you one more time: what can you tell us about this newly uncovered 'death by suffocation', and what role did you play in it? I am giving you this one chance to come clean, so get it off your chest. How did that poor girl die?

"If you cooperate with us, your voluntary confession will be taken into account when judgement is passed on you. We want to put her parents out of the agony of not knowing what happened, in that night of passion that ended in Danah's death – or was it murder, by you?"

That was the moment when the accused cracked under the emotional pressure. He cried and cried, his shoulders heaving as he broke down and cradled his head with his arms. Joe let him stew in his anguish, and then interrupted the flow as Cris quietened down.

"When you're ready to make your statement, we will start recording the details you give us. Are you ready now?" Joe sounded sympathetic; he didn't feel it.

Cris nodded, wiped his eyes and began talking.

"We went to bed together and she went absolutely mad. It was pure sex, and boy, did we have a good time. I'd never had it so good!. After a while, I felt she'd got the better of me and was worried that I couldn't keep up the pace. I guess she was feeling the same, because we both stopped for a while, and she suggested we take some coke together . . ."

Joe intervened. "Stop right there. Are you trying to put the blame on her? How can you say that she alone provided the powder?"

Cris stated emphatically, "Because she took it out of her bag. I didn't have anything like that on me. I've never had the need and you won't find any record of me getting busted for doing coke."

Joe clammed up for good reason; Cris had no previous for drug abuse, as he had claimed, but Danah did have a few recorded minor run-ins with the police, for attending wild parties as a juvenile.

Besides, Rose had relayed to him the dead Danah's comments about her night of passion with Cris, and these suggested that she already had a healthy sexual appetite before she met him. There was nothing unusual or wrong with that, in this day and age.

Cris continued, "In the end, we both collapsed in a heap, exhausted and slept like logs." He sucked in a deep breath and finally admitted how she died.

He sounded apologetic as he said, "It was an accident. I woke up on top of her, and she wasn't breathing. I jumped out of bed, and gave her breathing aid, but it was too late. She was a goner! I'd smothered her, and I panicked."

"What did you do then?" Joe asked, to prompt him to keep going with his statement.

"I wasn't thinking straight, what with all the booze and drugs we'd had. I ran a hot bath, put her in it to tidy her up, and washed her from head to foot, with shower gel. Then I shampooed her hair and dried her all over. She looked so beautiful it hurt to look at her.

"Then I put her in bed, all peaceful like, then checked the coast was clear and returned to my own room. I was absolutely knackered all day after, for the second time in a row!

Joe got up and said, "Okay, we'll get it recorded and you can sign and check it. Then you'll spend time in jail awaiting your court case and sentencing. I might need to speak to you later."

He left the room and said to the officers with him, "If it was instinctive, that was a bad move by him, destroying the evidence like he did. A charge of involuntary manslaughter might have been appropriate, now it's second degree murder at the least."

In an admiring tone, he added, "That was a good call by Rose. Some of what we do conventionally must have rubbed off on her way of thinking!"

Cristofer was later sentenced to a minimum of 20 years behind bars, with parole possible after 15 years had been served. Fair or not, that was all Joe could muster by way of clemency.

The failure to call the security guard as a witness was never laid at anyone's door, but it rankled with Joe, who was also annoyed at the inability of the investigating officers to identify Cristofer or anyone else on the training course as potential suspects. Subtle interviewing would have got the investigators nearer a resolution of an undetected crime.

Similarly, the autopsy had reached the wrong conclusion, and this had added to the various failures in getting justice for the victim. It was all too sloppy for Floppy Joe's liking, and he wondered how many times the various, local police forces were at fault.

Joe decided to compile statistics on the unresolved cases at local levels. Maybe that was the way for the agency to go, concentrating on the efficacy of the local officers of the law.

On this occasion, the local Chief of Police was summarily dismissed. Secondly, the performance of his officers was reviewed by a specialist, national team of internal investigators.

In due course, some were subject to disciplinary action, including demotion. Finally, the ageing coroner, who was also a qualified medical examiner, was redeployed.

CASE CLOSED

In his report, Joe praised Rose for the initiative she had shown in volunteering to take on the case, and the acceptance of her need to visit the crime scene; this was in order to establish a firm connection with the spirit of the deceased. This had been achieved, and the voice of the girl was now on record.

Joe remarked that this visit [to the crime scene] was a common requirement of mediums, who failed in most cases where they had not requested to do this at the outset, or not been invited by the police to go there. Often, months would elapse before a visit was made and the connection was made.

Sloppy policing in the beginning was identified as the root cause of the lack of closure.

CASE 3 – THE TWO INNOCENT FLIRTS

"This'll test you," Joe challenged Chuck, as he walked into his office and placed his chosen case file on the desk, "it's been outstanding for 10 years!"

"You think so?" Chuck countered, opening the folder, to find inside two photos and a solitary sheet of paper in it.

Joe scrutinized his face, to see if he was showing any signs of disappointment; there weren't any.

Chuck was a single man in his mid to late twenties, with a tangle of blond, spikey hair sticking upwards at different angles. Joe reckoned that he had to apply some type of setting gel in order to keep it in place, and was sorely tempted to run his fingers through it, to see if he was right.

Sensibly, he refrained from doing anything rash, in case the reaction was extreme; some people were sensitive about keeping their personal space untouched. There was another aspect to his personality that made Joe cautious: he and Richard were reputed to be martial arts' experts, and spent time together competing in this aggressive activity.

Perhaps it explained why Rose felt comfortable with Chuck around; he gave her a special type of protection, like she was a mother figure, in a world where violence could occur unexpectedly.

He was a tall and slim young man, handsome, in a round-faced way, with a tenor speaking voice the higher end of the adult male range. His dress sense was idiosyncratic; by that, Joe meant distinctive. Invariably, he chose high quality natural fabrics, and blended contrasting colors together.

One day, he would mix pale green trousers with a salmon colored long-sleeved formal shirt, left open at the collar; he did not like ties of any hue, printed pattern or width. The next day it would be beige linen trousers with a lavender colored, short-sleeved cotton shirt with tails meant to be tucked-in at the waist.

If the weather turned bad, he would don an all weather, plain - not patterned, golfing jacket, guaranteed to keep out the wind and rain. He was not averse either to putting on waterproof over-trousers, to keep himself fully dry.

His shoes tended to be fabricated from brushable suede leather, with soft soles – except when he was on a case. On those occasions, he favored highly polished black or brown brogues with stiff, leather soles and studs nailed into them.

Today was one of those occasions, and Joe decided to ask him why. "Chuck, I like the choice of footwear you've got on today. Who makes your shoes and why do you choose them when on a case? They look good and solid."

While studying the two photos alternately, he replied, "They're Loakes, that's the name of the company that makes them. If anyone wants to try and tango with me, they'll get a good kicking!"

He said this impassively, and Joe decided, "*If I were Rose, I'd feel especially safe with him covering my back!*" He also concluded, "*There's nothing effeminate about this guy; he's a clothes horse yes, but his appearance is no more than skin-deep!*" It was the same conclusion on appearance (only being skin-deep) that Joe had drawn with Rose.

Then Joe remembered the likelihood that all the mediums he worked with were telepaths, and thought it possible that Chuck was mildly warning him to back-off.

As Joe decided that prudence was called for and beat a retreat, Chuck tried to make contact with the two deceased young women in the photos. He had established that they were dead, but was unable to follow their trail, from his present location.

In frustration, he walked to Rose's office next door and asked her for help, but she couldn't make contact either. Both of them walked back towards Joe's end office, nearest the entrance, and Chuck stated to him, "Neither of us can establish a trail. I need to visit the scene to get started." Rose was peering around Chuck's shoulders, and nodding in agreement.

Joe replied, "Okay. Will tomorrow morning, bright and early, be soon enough?

Chuck agreed, "Fine. How far is it?"

"Five hours plus by car. It's inland and reachable in that time at a steady speed. Take Matt and The Walrus with you, so you can spread the workload and they can begin the preliminaries for filming a new episode of the physics' show. Use my car if you want; it'll be a novel experience. Can I borrow yours for the duration?"

Joe fancied driving Chuck's open-top, vintage MG roadster, and trusted that the all-male team wouldn't abuse his slick, driverless saloon by reckless driving.

Chuck agreed instantly and went back to tie up loose ends before packing his gear. He'd heard all about Joe's wagon and was eager to see what it could do, driverless and without distractions. Joe made some phone calls, with the assistance of Alice, to make the necessary arrangements, including booking a hotel near the destination police station.

Later, Honey poked her head around the door and casually asked him, "Joe, how old are your children?"

Without giving his answer much thought, he replied, "They're in their twenties. Why'd you ask?"

With a solemn face, she said, "All that fuss you made, about getting the rear seat sponge-cleaned after we did you-know-what! You made us think they were kids, not grown-ups. Tut, tut!"

"Damn, damn, damn!" he cursed out loud, repeating mentally, "*I must remember they're all telepaths!*"
"*I must remember they're all telepaths!*"
"*I must remember they're all telepaths!*"

Chuck was finding that he preferred to be the one in control of an automobile. Joe's was scaring the pants off him at times; he was half-expecting it not to stop when it had to, and not give sufficient girth to cyclists it was passing, or moving too far out in the road and colliding with oncoming vehicles. It coped admirably with the unexpected, and annoyed him by strictly observing speed restrictions when he urged it to take a chance.

Matt and Walter agreed with him, but liked the soothing effect the saloon was having on them. As Matt said, "It's the way the future industry is heading, so let's get used to it." He looked pointedly at Chuck and said, "We don't want youngsters high on substances racing around recklessly in sports cars, do we?"

Chuck retorted enigmatically, "Nor do we want older guys racing around in them either!" He had seen Joe at the wheel of his cherished MG sports car with its polished wire wheels blurring, and his feet started flexing in his Loakes hard leather shoes.

The scenery they were passing silently through was changing from lush, cultivated greenery, to broader expanses of arid, brown stony desert with fewer dwellings by the roadside. Moreover, it was getting hotter.

Eventually they reached their destination, a town of several thousand inhabitants divided into a grid-pattern of secondary roads built to house communities. Adjoining the main highway breaking the town in two were the usual convenience stores and an air-conditioned shopping mall. Compared with what they had passed through it was an oasis, and they gratefully stopped outside a modern motel.

After they had booked in, driven to their allotted rooms and unloaded their baggage from Joe's voluminous boot, they strolled to the nearby police station. Previously, this would have been called 'the Sheriff's Office', but there was a trend away from this type of democratic establishment.

The law officers who were employed there were still democratically elected, but not always in the townships that they patrolled; the main contenders for the top jobs were often drafted in from elsewhere.

There was a nationwide push in progress towards better, evenly imposed standards, and a higher quality of personnel in policing. This was underway to get rid of the accumulated deadwood, and to eliminate the influence exerted on incumbents by local politicians. As Joe would maybe have put it, "There is too much graft and not enough grit in many sheriffs' offices."

They walked through the sliding doors of the station and introduced themselves to the duty officer. He phoned through to say that the expected trio had arrived, and a senior detective ushered them into his office. He was a heavyset man with a solid physique.

He said, "Hi, I'm Detective Sergeant Eugene Flowers. Please call me Flower; everyone else does. How can I help you?" The humor of his nickname was not lost on the visitors.

Matt and Walter showed him their badges, and introduced Chuck Stone as a specialist profiler, after which Matt got down to business.

"As you have hopefully been briefed beforehand, we are here to investigate a cold case involving the murder of two teenage girls ten years ago. Could we have copies of the crime reports, brought up to date? Afterwards, we'd like to visit the places where they were last seen, and then where the bodies were subsequently found.

"We may also want to see where they lived and interview their families. This depends on what we find in the interim."

Flower narrowed his eyes and said, "That's interesting. You reckon you're gonna solve this case early on don't you?" He looked at Chuck and said, "You're the man who can do it, aren't you? Mind if I tag along, to see you at work?" He was bright enough to have cottoned onto the true nature of Chuck's modus operandi.

Chuck replied with a grin, "I don't mind, so the others won't, I feel sure!" He looked at them and they shrugged; they were indifferent to whatever was arranged.

Flower led them out of the station, suggesting, "Let's do it the other way round and get the longer journey out of the way. That way, we can have a bite to eat at a sensible time, when we return. Is that okay with you?" They all agreed, and he volunteered to drive, saying, "Let's take my car."

He led them out of town on the main highway, for about an hour. Apart from Flower checking in at regular intervals and monitoring the calls being made by the control center, there was little conversation to be made. He was a taciturn man and didn't bother to communicate much.

At an unmarked side road, he turned slowly right onto the unpaved surface, leaving a billowing cloud of dust in their wake. They ascended into foothills along a windy, secluded track, until

Flower stopped the car and grunted, "We're here," before getting out.

He pointed down at a ledge above a ravine, and announced to Chuck who had now joined him, "That's where they were found, by hikers, huddled in a heap. The wild animals and birds had got at them, so they were mainly bones in their clothes. They'd been tossed over the edge from this exact spot. I hope you find the bastard who did it."

He went and stood by Matt and Walter, who had remained by the parked car, and engaged them in conversation.

Glancing across at Chuck, Flower asked, "What's he doing?" The subject in question appeared to be engrossed in conversation with an unknown person, as if he was talking into an invisible hands-free mobile phone speaker.

Walter replied casually, "At a guess, he's trying to make contact with the deceased." Seeing Chuck starting to gesticulate wildly, he added, "He doesn't seem to be having much luck though!"

Chuck spread his hands despairingly and walked towards them, complaining, "I'm not having any real success here; it looks like whoever I'm trying to contact doesn't like this place! Let's head back to civilization."

They could tell from his sour face that Flower was thinking, "*This guy's a phony!*"

An hour later, as they neared the station, Chuck casually asked Flower, "Don't you get fed up driving an official car? I would, always having to be within earshot of the call center!"

Flower agreed, "Yeah, it's a pain. I also have a pick-up that I use, to get some peace from the job; I use it to go fishing and hunting, with my son, whenever I can."

"Here we are now," he continued, driving into the station car park and stopping in his reserved space. "Let's go get a snack. Tell you what, I'll kill two birds with one stone and lead y'all there on foot. It's the same place where the two girls were last seen alive!" The irony implicit in this statement about 'killing two birds' was lost on him.

As they went into the snack bar, Flower pointed to the curb and said, "That's where the girls were sitting, according to a couple of witnesses who saw them there. No one saw them alive again, and no one witnessed who picked them up, if anyone did. It's been one setback after another with this damned case!"

Chuck paused by the door for a while, pondering long and hard, before moving inside and sitting down to eat with the other three.

"See anything?" Flower asked, in between chomping at a fresh-beef filled bagel.

Chuck shook his head sadly, not bothering to reply to the question.

A short while later, he excused himself, saying he had to go for a pee. Standing out of sight of the others, around a corner at the rear of the snack bar, he made a phone call to Joe, told him he had solved the case, and urged him to, "Join us, '¡Cuanto antes!' - As soon as possible!"

The three of them left Flower at the station and returned to the motel, claiming they needed some time to unpack and have a siesta after their journeying about. This gave them time for Joe to drive down, and for Chuck to brief the others.

He said, "Flower is our man! He killed the girls; now Joe has to decide if he's prepared to make an arrest, using the evidence I can provide. I need both of you to back me up when he gets violent. He's tough and will be fast on his feet, so be prepared."

They looked at him with surprise, and Walter commented, "Shit, that was quick!" Matt said nothing, just gaped. Chuck was in charge and they had to back him up. Matt immediately rummaged through his bag and brought out an expandable baton from his travel bag, and Walter went to look for his taser.

Chuck had categorically said that Flower was going to get violent; he was the man with the ability to foresee such an event, and they were therefore obliged to assume it was going to happen.

Joe reached the desert town in record time, at legally permitted speeds. He enjoyed the privilege of rank on those occasions where normal folk would have had to wait at traffic lights; they magically changed to green for him, and he went sailing through with the siren wailing, in his official police car, driven by a uniformed officer.

This level of official priority applied irrespective of the states and counties though which he travelled.

When he arrived, he ordered the others at the motel, "Come on, let's go and serve up some justice!"

Flower walked out of his office with a beaming smile, to greet them. That was until he came to Joe, who fixed him with a cold stare and arrested him on the spot.

With a snarl, he threw a punch at Chuck, who sidestepped it and stuck his fingers hard into Flower's eyes, blinding him. Swiftly, he followed up the blinder by kicking him in the groin with his left foot, encased in its hard, brogue leather shoe.

Simultaneously, Matt walloped him across a shin with his baton, and Walter tasered him between the shoulder blades.

Joe watched the melee with satisfaction, before saying to the awestruck duty officer, "Get him treated in your sickroom. As soon as he's recovered some of his abilities to communicate, give us a call and we'll get down to interviewing him. Keep him cuffed at all times, with no fewer than three officers present at all times. No conferring!"

Joe sat in the interview room chatting with the local police chief whilst waiting for the accused officer, Detective Sergeant Eugene Flowers, to arrive.

They sat motionless as the accused entered, shackled and escorted by two officers. Unceremoniously, they dumped him in a chair the other side of the fixed metal table, and re-shackled him to the floor. He tried to avoid making eye contact with the two senior officers opposite, looking downwards and blinking furiously.

Clearly, he was still suffering from the damage inflicted by Chuck and the other two, and was trying to rub his groin, shin and back against the nearest pieces of furniture, without success.

"I'll sue you for this!" he rasped.

Joe ignored the outburst, and drawled, "Well, well, well! I bet you thought you'd gotten away with it, didn't you?"

He paused to let this statement sink in.

"You, an elected officer of the law, who was supposed to uphold the law, have broken the trust invested in you by the local community by allegedly committing the most heinous of crimes – rape and murder, *twice* over!"

The police chief intervened by asking, "How can the local community ever again trust the police who serve them, if you are found guilty of these grave offences? If anyone were to deserve to die by lethal injection, it would be you!"

Flowers looked back at them defiantly, his eyes moistened and red, stating categorically, "How do you know it was me? I tell you: I had nothing to do with this!"

Joe changed tack, adopting a more compassionate attitude.

"Listen Flowers, when you offered a ride in your pickup to those two highly attractive, lightly clad young women, the trust was mutual. They looked up to you as a father figure, well known in the community and someone to respect.

"It was a chance for them to see a real-life detective off-duty, as a man, and to socialize with him. They relaxed, feeling safe in your presence. Played some music on your radio, the type they liked to play when in their own circle of friends, and impress you by singing along with the lyrics.

"Gyrating as well, flourishing their bare legs and showing off their movements as they sat in your pickup, within easy reach."

Joe leaned forward in a confidential manner.

"Look Eugene, I can understand what you felt. You were convinced that they were offering you sex, on a plate. They were after a good time."

He leant back, still commiserating. "All that happened was you misunderstood the signals they were sending out. When you reached out to them, they reacted badly, told you how disgusting you were, and for good measure, said they were going to tell their parents you were a pervert.

"All they had to do was comply, not tell you to go to hell, and sneer at you. It was stupid of them, to treat you with such disrespect. Had they enjoyed the sex with you, they'd be alive today, wouldn't they?"

Joe and the police chief sat there, waiting for a reaction. Finally, it came.

Detective Sergeant Flowers broke down and admitted between sobs, "I couldn't stop myself. I went mad, insane with frustration and anger. Took one and half-throttled her, then took the other. Both of them, again and again until the mad spell ended."

Joe sighed as he listened, and intervened when Flowers stopped talking.

"Listen Eugene; you will shortly be asked to provide and sign a formal confession. What you didn't know was that one of the girls, Denise, realized she wasn't going to survive the attack and hid a blood-covered hanky up inside the bench seat you were all using. This key piece of evidence will link you conclusively to the crime."

Flowers looked up at him, his attention focused on this news. "I didn't know that," he said, sounding surprised.

Joe continued, unperturbed. "I will suppress all mention of this in your trial, provided you confess to what you did. I will plea bargain that you be given clemency and not have to face the death penalty."

Flowers looked grateful, and nodded his agreement.

Later, the police chief asked Joe to provide the hanky.

"It doesn't exist, I only said it to put him off appealing later," he admitted frankly. "We haven't got any material evidence, and are dependent on the crime report submitted to us by our psychic investigator. I made it up in order to prevent the accused getting off scot-free, if he was to succeed in opposing the verdict."

The chief further asked, "What if ex-detective sergeant Flowers knew there was no such evidence available, in the first place?"

Joe replied, "The pickup was checked beforehand, and it was in a filthy state. If it had been cleaned any time previously, I would not have made the bogus claim, and would have had to rely on Flowers not trying to get out after rescinding his confession."

Joe was always prepared to tell a lie, if it helped make a guilty verdict stick.

CASE CLOSED

Joe was well pleased with Chuck's performance. Like Rose, he had insisted on visiting the scene of the crime and seeing first-hand what had actually happened, albeit belatedly, all those years before. His recognition of the culprit was breathtakingly swift, and devastating for the local police force.

The comparison of the initial rate of progress that Rose and Chuck had exhibited was in stark contrast with his own, which had spanned 20 years, covered 200 murder cases and resulted in a success rate of over 92% convictions. That gave him an average of 10 cases per year. The mediums were getting through each one in a matter of a few days! He knew it was too early to make a meaningful comparison, but hell . . . they were fast!

It was with a mixture of sadness and pride that he 'penned' his latest report and transmitted it to the senior figures at the top.

He concluded, "*That's two out of four cylinders fully functioning!*"

CASE 4 – THE SNATCHED GIRL SCOUT

Joe complemented Chuck on the resolution of his latest case: "Good work, keep up the pace!" and handed to him another file. "This one is probably just as interesting. It's fifteen years old, the crime scene was contaminated and the assailant remains at large."

Chuck looked inside and picked up a color photo of the victim plus a single page of typed notes describing the incident. The photo showed a girl on the verge of her teens, wearing a white blouse with blue stripes on it, and a matching blue baseball cap with the initials 'GS' emblazoned in white, above the long peak.

She was smiling broadly, showing her even teeth, and had brown hair and eyes, a cute little nose and rounded cheeks on a slim face. If she had lived longer, she would surely have turned into a vivacious beauty.

At least, that was the impression that Chuck gained of her potential life. He had already deduced that she had died prematurely, by studying the photo and touching it lightly.

He read that her name was Alison Greensleeve, and she had met her untimely end whilst at summer camp, which was near a broad cove on the coast north of the agency. That was as much as the single page contained by way of information, and he was happy with that brief overview.

Later on, he would be expected to fill in the gaps by demonstrating his powers of spiritual communication.

Joe instructed him, "Let Jake drive. He's agreed to take the wagon provided by the film company and it'll take you about three hours to get there. Would you be ready to leave in an hour or so?" He knew that Chuck kept an overnight bag containing essentials in the agency storeroom.

Chuck agreed and collected his bag, depositing it in his office while he made a personal call and picked up his notepad, pencils, camera and voice recorder.

Joe was unusually happy when Jake arrived, and came out of his office to say goodbye. He quipped to Chuck, "Don't forget: a rolling stone gathers no moss, so get rolling!" He was playing with words, knowing that Chuck's surname was 'Stone'; those within earshot gave a collective groan.

A Global Positioning system (GPS) was fitted to the wagon that Jake was driving; it should be noted that the so-called 'wagon' was a well-equipped and adapted large van with darkened side windows and an abundance of movie-making equipment. The GPS was guiding them to the exact location of the summer camp that Alison had attended, all those years ago.

To reach the site, they drove to the beach near which it was situated, down a windy, two-lane road, and then followed it around the bay. Through high reeds, they occasionally glimpsed the incoming tidal waves crashing on the sand, almost reaching a steep pebbled ridge against which seaweed was being dashed.

"Awesome!" Jake declared, fighting the steering against a strong side wind. At the end of the bay, they passed an abandoned café, on elevated ground protected by the bank of pebbles, and next to it was an unevenly surfaced carpark. In it was a solitary, decrepit small car, presumably parked there for one of the locals to take a stroll, perhaps with his dog.

They looked down across the bay, and Chuck pointed out a lone individual wearing an anorak; he was leaning against the wind as his Alsatian dog splashed through the incoming and receding rippling shore-waves. Presumably, he was the driver of the car next to the café.

At the far side of the bay, they reached a T-junction, where they were instructed to turn right. They ascended a rising single-track lane and parked at their stated destination, which was on the left. It was a bare patch of fairly level ground on the edge of a forest of tall, well-spaced fir trees ascending a steepening hillside. The former camp had long since disappeared, being only a temporary site for canvas tents to be erected.

On the other side of the lane was a steep, craggy slope leading down to the bay. The wind blowing inland almost tasted of salt, and chilled the sun shining down intermittently through white clouds skidding fast across the blue sky. It was much colder again in the shade of the forest, and the air was scented with a pungent, raw aroma of pine emanating from the surrounding trees.

The two men shivered, making Jake mutter, "There's nothing supernatural about this!" as he wrapped his arms around his body to warm himself up.

Chuck walked off to try to find the exact spot where the girl had spent her final night alive. He was holding her photo and asking her to come to him, while he concentrated on making contact with her departed spirit.

It was never the easiest of tasks to undertake, because there were often conflicting voices vying for attention. That was why he found it easier to journey to locations that were familiar to the deceased, or were etched in their memory. It narrowed the scope considerably, and made initial contact more probable.

Chuck's persistent requests were specific and targeted, and a young voice eventually answered.

"*I'm here! It's me, Alison Greensleeve. What do you want?*"

Chuck replied, "I've come to help you move on in the spirit world. I need you to tell me exactly how you died, what happened to cause your death, and who was involved, so we can trace them. I also need to ask if you have any messages to pass on to your loved ones, your nearest and dearest relatives. We've got a lot to cover as quickly as possible, in case our contact gets broken. Please don't delay."

Alison replied in detail, giving a rapid stream of information that Chuck recorded as well as absorbed in his memory. She also left messages for her parents and much younger brother, and assured Chuck that she was living between physical lives with a group of other youngsters who had died prematurely, and was under the devoted care of adults.

Chuck thought, "*That's sad; has she no older relatives to care for her, on the other side?*" He had heard of this type of spirit life, being a type of pleasant, transitory 'limbo' residence for the young departed who had no family members to give them guidance.

After she had drifted away from the impromptu séance, Chuck caught up with Jake and confirmed that he had finished.

"That's it, all done? You've got the answers to all your questions?" He asked Chuck, who nodded seriously.

"You can film the general location of you like, and use it as the backdrop for an episode of the latest TV series. Otherwise, let's have some lunch locally and head back."

After the somber lunch that followed, Chuck gave Joe a call, and gave him a verbal report on his findings. For the first time in his life and to Joe's eternal surprise, Chuck could be heard sobbing hard as he concluded.

"Take your time," Joe consoled him. "I won't, I can't do anything until you submit your report by computer."

Chuck regained his composure and replied, "We'll be on our way in the hour. There is no more to be gained by staying here overnight. I want the damned case taken forward, by you. I want the swine who did this caught and punished."

The following is a summary of the report contents, as narrated by Chuck, recorded on his computer and submitted to Joe for action.

It was the first ever Girl Scout camping trip that Alison had attended. All of them were driven by parents in a convoy of people carriers to the site, accompanied by a lorry that was carrying the tents that the scouts had to assemble on their own.

It was an exciting holiday for those who were going to stay, especially for the newest recruits who had never been on anything like it before. They stood as a group separate from the others, on the fringe of the site, after the parents had waved them all goodbye. Immediately, the leader allocated them their duties.

She emphasized that the new cadettes were there to learn basic outdoor skills, before delegating personal responsibility for them to selected, experienced girl scouts, who were called 'Sixers'.

Feeling excited, they began their first great adventure. Knowledge was passed on by the sixers and their seconds, as the newcomers were deployed to help spread out the first of several bell-tents on its waterproof groundsheet, which would separate them from the bare ground.

They watched while the base of the thick wooden central pole was inserted in the pivoted column of a sturdy, round base, before the top end was positioned in the roof cone of the tent itself. Then the pole was raised vertically, while they held and tensioned the guy ropes that spread the tent out around it.

Then they participated in hammering the pegs into the ground that held and tensioned the guy ropes, to hold the tent rigid. Finally, they completed the assembly of the door frame, like it was a giant Meccano set.

Their next task was for handpicked occupants to enter the tent, unroll their sleeping bags and place their personal haversacks alongside them. The new recruits were then redeployed throughout the campsite, to help generally until all the tents had been erected.

Afterwards, they stood to attention outside their allotted tents, in groups of six, waiting for their efforts to be inspected and commented on. It was rare for anything other than praise to be handed out.

Long before nightfall, the camp was complete, portable showers had been erected, a central fire had been lit and they were helping peel potatoes.

This was one of the essential chores to fill empty stomachs, and the youngest cadettes watched from a distance as the seniors hung canisters over the fire and poured water in them, to heat up.

Immediately after, they dropped potatoes in and brought them to the boil. When they became fully soft, they scooped them from the water for transfer to large aluminum trays. There they mashed them with butter, before adding seasoning and mixing in shredded beef.

The Sixers dished out the food, and the hungry girls added side salads to their plates.

The water itself came from a huge plastic container, which they accessed by taps on one side, using buckets to transfer it to the various parts of the site. This container came at dusk on the first day, delivered by a local company, which also provided the portable latrines. Going to the toilet 'au naturel' was not on their agenda!

In the days that followed, the food varied between varieties of BBQ meats, primarily burgers and sausages, accompanied by cold salads or baked beans, ketchup and other sauces, with fresh bread that bought at a local store.

Frequently, they went on treks along the clifftops to the right of the bay, and could see the debris washed-up from wrecked ships floating in and out along the stony shore at the base of the tall cliffs. Other days, they would follow the trail left by a few scouts, to help develop their scouting abilities.

Alternatively, they would be deployed on obtaining badges in swimming, first aid and other skills, in order to demonstrate a range of special aptitudes they might wish to acquire.

These were the happiest of the memories of Alison Greensleeve, whose vivid recollections of events were recounted to Chuck.

One night, hours after Alison fell asleep in the warmth of her sleeping bag, she was abruptly woken by a cloth being held over her mouth to prevent her from screaming for help. It must have been laced with something that paralyzed her, since she was immediately rendered immobile and speechless.

She understood what was being done to her, and felt jerking pains in her back from the uneven surface she was being dragged over, but was unable to say or do anything to prevent her movement away from the tent.

A hole had been cut in its side, through which she had been pulled and pushed, while a man was seen emerging to run after them. He helped pick her up, making it easier for them to carry her further into the forest.

They took her to a small clearing, which contained many other men and placed her in the center of it, on her fully unzipped sleeping bag. She could see a lot of them now, in focus as the drug wore off, because the whole site was surrounded with strong lights that made it seem like it was daylight.

This was where Chuck despaired, as she described the horrifying acts they committed on her, under the glare of the lights.

After recording her explicit testament of the ongoing attacks, he added a personal statement that he believed the men were participating in a 'snuff movie, and had dismembered Alison after her death.

There was no need for him to declare how important it was to locate the whereabouts of that vile movie, but he did anyway, such was his disgust.

The good news was that she had recognized two of her attackers: one was her paternal uncle and the other was her school janitor. She also knew the area where they had buried her.

After Alison's initial disappearance, a great deal of time and energy was expended on searching for her, but to no avail.

Joe read the report several times before asking Chuck to come to his office. The other three partners in the agency were out of the office that day, so he arranged an urgent conference call to speak to them.

In the meantime, he phoned trusted colleagues in the police and law enforcement agency to warn them that he was embarking on a highly confidential, far-reaching mission and would need their unquestioning support.

Before long, Chuck and his three other partners had assembled ready for the conference to begin, so Joe started the briefing.

"Our source indicates that we are facing our biggest challenge to date. Chuck here conducted the initial investigation, and he will be sending you an encrypted copy of his report into the murder of a young girl.

"In the next few days, I assume that you will all become available to assist with identifying the members of what could be a major pedophile ring?" They each agreed that this was true, so Joe carried on detailing their responsibilities.

"Trust no one, tell no one, of the work you will be undertaking, and I mean no one. This includes the colleagues you will be collaborating with, who may be in the ring for all we know, or in another one, or have relatives or friends who can warn others.

"I will tell you in advance who to deal with, and you must check that you can trust them. Do this by using your unique skills to read their minds. All of you know how to achieve this, by asking subtle mind-questions that reveal their sexual orientation and tendencies.

"I don't care if they have the potential for perverted sex, as long as they are not attempting to perform acts on youngsters. As the saying goes, 'The evil man does what the good man may think'. However, if you detect any such tendencies let me know and we can decide what to do later, but that is a secondary issue. Don't spend time pursuing something that is irrelevant. Keep your focus on what matters.

"I will make one comment to help motivate you: it is **you** alone who can penetrate the evil minds of these people.

"Do what you do best and we will bring them to justice in record time. Let's go do it!"

He bade them all good day, saying, "Let me or Chuck know when you are ready to join us."

After closing the conference call, he turned to Chuck and stated, "We must keep each other informed at all times. I'm going to send detectives to arrest Alison's uncle, who is still living at the same address, and bring him in for questioning."

He handed him copy Identity Cards, saying, "These are the names and ID's of the detectives' who will be supporting us, so check them out by digging in their memory banks, to see if they have deviant tendencies and are aroused by children or teenagers."

He handed him two more document and photos, one for the uncle and one for the janitor, saying, "I've also arranged to bring in the janitor from her old school; he's retired now and living locally to the school. Give top priority to making checks on the detectives I'm sending there."

Chuck looked at the copies of the cards and documents passed to him and studied them.

"Okay," he said, looking up, so Joe continued.

"Neither suspect is going to be told the reason for his arrest, or be informed of his rights. Alternatively, if they prefer, the arresting officers may choose to 'invite' them to help with trumped-up enquiries. In addition, they've been instructed to swoop on both men unobserved, to prevent any else from tipping-off the ring that they may have been rumbled.

"After arrest, the two detainees will be kept incommunicado

in separate 'safe houses' provided by the main official agency. By 'safe' I mean that they will be incarcerated there alone until we have finished with them, without any means of communication with the outside world. The agents are preparing the 'cells' for them as I speak.

"It's all highly irregular I know, but I intend mopping-up the lot of them, no matter how powerful and influential the members of the ring may be. Later on, they'll all be transferred to a converted maximum security mental institution, where they'll stay before and after sentencing. That'll play hell with their sex lives!"

Joe sat down opposite Alison's Uncle Gordon, in the interview room, staring hard and long at him. He savored the man's growing unease, having already kept him waiting unattended for twenty minutes, while he observed him from the observation area the other side of a two-way mirror.

The agency personnel had done a good job of mocking-up the inside of a real police station. They were even wearing police officers' uniforms.

In the next couple of days at most, Richard, Honey and Rose would be joining them. In the meantime, Chuck was showing his mettle by gathering vital information from the unwitting pervert, Uncle Gordon.

He painlessly extracted the names of Gordon's fellow collaborators, in great numbers; the uncle fondly remembered the gatherings they attended, with the purpose of sharing their sexual gratification.

It completely escaped his awareness that these 'recollections of past events' were artificially induced by Chuck, who fed on them avidly. He knew what buttons to press in his target; thereafter it was a busy task, recording the unfolding memories for use against the other members of the illegal ring.

As Rose, and then Richard and Honey concluded their separate cases and returned, their help too was enlisted. They compiled a list of the individuals named by the janitor, cross-matched them to those provided by the uncle, and began to delve into and verify their diverse backgrounds, to substantiate them.

Where considered necessary, they would go back to the two sources and seek greater clarification. To help with this, they employed 'distance hypnosis', ensuring that neither man would remember having been subjected to this intrusive method of interrogation.

As the list of names grew and the information became comprehensive, the investigation moved to the next level. Further clandestine arrests resulted, and more suspects were spirited away in increasing numbers, for similar, painless interrogation.

In a short space of time, officials laid charges that could stick against all those arrested.

The Deaduction Agency was beginning to impress those who had previously doubted its value to modern policing. Its modus operandi was a pleasing contrast to water boarding, which had proven to be comparatively ineffective.

Spin-offs were also being achieved, as other pedophile rings were penetrated and dismantled, and the question increasingly being raised was: what to do with all the prisoners? They had to be kept under lock and key, owing to the gravity of the charges they were facing.

The solution adopted, for their own protection, was – as planned – to house them in a currently available, decommissioned maximum-security mental institution. It would need updating, but the inmates could help with that activity.

The advantage of this arrangement was that the guilty parties would serve their life-sentences in the same institution after sentencing.

As the investigation continued, there were salient aspects to Alison's death and previous home life being uncovered.

In due course, Joe and Chuck went to Alison's family home. Her mother opened the front door and they could hear the sound of children playing inside the detached house. The father heard the visitors introducing themselves, sensed that they were more important than normal and came out to see who they could possibly be.

Joe told them the purpose of their visit, and they were invited into the downstairs study, where Chuck conveyed to them Alison's messages from beyond the grave. They were distressed at first, but became more composed when he told them that her body had been found in an improvised grave that had been dug in the wooded slopes behind the campsite. He didn't disclose that she had been dismembered.

He also advised them that the perpetrators had been apprehended and were now serving life sentences. This disclosure brought them more comfort.

Afterwards, they moved into the large kitchen and sat around a pine table drinking coffee. It was there that Alison's mother revealed that she was their first child and had been adopted. That explained to Chuck why she felt no immediate kinship with the family, and had returned after death to people she knew already, in the spirit world.

The mother also made a proud announcement: she was pregnant again; years after her other, natural children were becoming teenagers.

Chuck hesitated before surprising the parents further. "I think it only fair that I tell you something special. Your next child will be a baby girl. It will be a rare occasion, because it will be Alison's spirit in her. You are specially blessed by this return of someone you loved and cruelly lost."

Joe was almost in tears when he heard this, while the parents could have reacted badly, but were delighted at this news from a gifted stranger. Chuck had realized the risk he was taking, but knew instinctively how they would take it.

As time progressed, there was one overriding question still to be resolved in Joe's mind, and that was, "*Why should society have to pay the costs of housing these monsters endlessly?*" There seemed to be no end to the people they were finding who suffered from this perversion.

Unexpectedly, there sprung into his mind one word that summed up the solution: SPECTRACTION. He was immediately suspicious that the thought didn't originate from him, but none of the mediums he was working with admitted to being the architect.

The more he thought about it, the more he admitted to finding the idea attractive. It was simplicity itself in execution: use a spectractor to identify an evil spirit, separate it by oscillation, and press a button to destroy it permanently!

He began speculating on the theoretical consequences of using this technology.

"*Surely the physical body would become a useless husk?*"

"*Not necessarily. Sufficient elements of a 'good spirit' could be retained to help the physical body function.*"

"*What would we do with the barely functioning physical bodies? They wouldn't need to be kept isolated from the rest of us, in a prison environment, would they?*"

"*They could be used as beasts of the field, and to do any of the tasks that no one else wants to perform.*"

"*It's a bit drastic isn't it? I mean, you'd be killing the part of the human being that transcends physical death. That would be very, very permanent!*"

"*Not necessarily. The spirit may multiply for all we know. Nothing ends up being nothing, it always transmutes into something else.*"

"*Alright then, what if someone were to have sex with a zombie-like human body? Wouldn't that genetically reproduce another twisted pervert?*"

"*We'd sterilize the bodies after spectraction.*"

"*You're making this up as you go along! I don't know which of you is doing this, but I'm sure as hell not speaking to myself!*"

There were the occasional light moments like this that they enjoyed.

CASE CLOSED

This was a watershed moment in Joe's life at The Deaduction Agency. It transcended everything else that they had achieved to date, and confirmed his belief in the capabilities of his partners. As a consequence, the report was gushing in its praise of all four mediums, and in particular of Chuck.

They had disbanded a number of major pedophile rings, and made over a hundred arrests that included some powerful figures in politics, medicine and legal circles, plus snaring accountants and other professionals.

"Unbelievable!" exclaimed the sponsor and Joe's immediate superior in unison, when they read the report. They were cock-a-hoop at the resulting arrests, which were kept out of the press.

CASE 5 – THE NATIVE INDIAN NOMAD

Joe felt that the next case he was dishing out was a bit lame after the previous one, but took a deep breath and began his prepared spiel with forced enthusiasm.

"For many of us in our teens, the short-term prospect of living a wandering existence comes naturally. This transitory desire may be regarded as the last chance to see more of the world first-hand, before starting full-time employment.

"Alternatively, it may be felt necessary as a 'gap-year', taken by a pampered student as an essential antidote to the mental rigors of higher education; this can occur either before, during or after the allotted period of study.

"In the second instance, the parents of the privileged students may wish their offspring a safe journey, warn them of the dangers they face, and say their fond farewells. It is rare for any harm to come to their loved ones.

"It is even more rare for the parents to take advantage of the innocent youngsters by selling their own worldly assets and doing a runner.

"However, it can happen," as he had commented previously to his team of psychics, "when the family bonds of love, generosity and tolerance – or any combination of them – are stretched beyond endurance."

On this occasion, Joe was sitting alone in his room with Rose and handed the file over to her, saying, "This is a tragic case involving a teenager of Native American ancestry. It fits none of the conventional criteria that apply to youngster leaving home, to see the world. This one left school with only a basic education in reading, writing and arithmetic.

"He had the same aspirations as his tribal ancestors, which were those of a true nomad. All he wanted to do was to wander, and see more of the U.S. His desire to do this was unquenchable and his loving parents could not stand in his way.

"They hoped he would eventually return home, after satisfying his need to travel, if he survived. His father fatefully warned him: 'Beware who you travel with and who you associate with. Not everyone will like you, so take great care.' They wished him well and let him go with heavy hearts."

Joe concluded with the sad comment, "He did not survive. They last thing they heard from him was a phone message, asking for the bus fare to be forwarded so he could attend his sister's wedding. He confirmed where he was, at a service center, which was only 90 miles from the reservation and was on his way back.

"For two years after his disappearance a search was conducted by the local sheriff's office at the scene and beyond, without success. It was discontinued when trekkers, in a remote area a few miles from where he had phoned home, found his remains, scattered by wild animals.

"He was identified from the documents contained in his haversack, which had not been scavenged to any serious extent by wild animals or birds of prey. An autopsy was performed, and the body was forensically analyzed. Death was concluded to have been caused by murder; his ribs had been broken inwards by repeated, deliberate blows, presumably caused by a blunt instrument. There was a single indentation to the skull.

"That was 8 years ago, from the time that the body was found, and there has been no progress whatsoever in resolving the case. To help you more than I normally would, I am providing the following." He handed over a big, badly faded backpack.

"This contains all the items of clothing the search team could find, at the scene where his body was found. His name was 'Kajika', which means 'Walk without sound'. The best of luck in your endeavors!"

As soon as Rose reached her own office, she began selecting items one by one from the backpack, and placed them in sequence of recovery on her conference table.

It was not long before her attention was drawn to a battered and corroded wristwatch, which she transferred to her desk and place alongside the tattered identity card. She focused on these two items, while stroking them lightly to try and establish a psychic trail that would be meaningful to the investigation.

At times, she reached over to touch the backpack, and this also helped her to form a mental picture of what Kajika had been doing in the hours leading up to his death.

She was set on recreating the exact circumstances of the murder, not to lead the detectives on wild-goose chases that would make them lose faith in her. What she had clearly seen so far in her remote viewing is documented as follows.

Kajika was a slender, shorter than average young man of pleasant countenance and with a cheerful smile. He was easily identifiable as an American Indian by his dark skin and black hair, but otherwise his features could easily have been mistaken for those of those of a regular featured brown-eyed Latino teenager. He had encouraged his hair to grow shoulder-length, and usually plaited it straight back down to cover the rear of his neck.

The one day he wore his hair loose, having washed it that morning, gave him the appearance of a pretty girl with a high-pitched voice, without facial hair, and that was probably his undoing.

He got to talking in a bar, which was laid out for breakfast, with a couple of men in their forties, who were drawn to him by his appearance. They were odd individuals to begin with, and he should have avoided them, but they bought his breakfast.

One was dressed like a make-believe cowboy, all in lilac colored matching clothes, with a Stetson on his head, and a bolo tie (or 'shoestring necktie') at his collar, held in place with what looked like a solid silver skull clasp. His belt was made of broad, black leather and he wore black cowboy boots, lacquered to give a lilac tint. He was lean in the face and body, had long, swept-back grey hair showing at the edges of his hat, and wore a grudging smile on his lips.

His companion looked like a conventional cowboy, wearing a check shirt, a leather waistcoat, jeans and brown leather boots.

He looked dusty and in need of a good wash. He had no hat on, showing a very short crew cut over his round, unsmiling face. He was more squat than the lilac cowboy and built like a bulldog, down to his bowlegs.

Both were taller than Kajika, and they started talking pleasantly to him. One introduced himself as a ranch owner by the name of Mitch, the other man was his foreman, whose name escaped his attention. Kajika was fascinated by the ends of the ranch owner's bolo tie, which were held down by matching silver end-weights.

This was happening as they drank coffees in the bar at the service area where Kajika had made his call to his parents. In return, he told them that he was trying to get home, which was some distance away. At no stage had his sexuality been identified, and both men assumed, from his name, which ended with the letter 'a', that he was a Latina.

When they offered to drive him some of the way home, in that direction east, he was ecstatic. So were they, for a different reason; they hoped that she (in reality *he*) was on the game. The teenager got in the back, in a talkative mood, while they sat in the front of their big, old style Cadillac, with the boss man at the wheel.

They listened as the voice in the back droned on about everything under the sun, from the moment they left the service bar. It rapidly dawned on them that they had a 'sissy boy' sitting behind them, rather than a tasty young female. That didn't go down well, and their replies got hard and disdainful.

They had driven only a few miles, when the driver swerved last minute to take a detour down an unmade side road, which became a dust track. Before long, the two men got out, and the foreman yanked Kajika out of his side of the car, flinging him to the ground.

Rose could see all of this while it was occurring, and thought, *"Oh you silly, silly young man; you should have got out before now and run like the wind! They'd never have caught you!"* She watched in despair as they took it in turns to kick him hard, as he rolled up, trying to protect his vulnerable, breaking body.

Rose watched in despair as his life force expired, and he lay there with his eyes open but not seeing. She felt his spirit join her, watching the scene of his own death.

She heard his voice, fading as he said, "*Catch them for me. Prevent them from doing this to anyone else!*"

She barely heard the rest of what he was telling her, but it was significant enough for her to record it on her PC, as contact with him was lost for eternity.

Joe read the report on his own PC. His face was grim as he called Rose to come and discuss its contents with him. He said to her, "Rose, I can't thank you enough for getting to this stage. You've shed light on what was a unresolved mystery. I think we should take this to the next stage and start searching for these men. Any thoughts on how to do this?"

She reflected on the matter briefly, before suggesting, "How's about putting a notice in all the local newspapers? It will state that a firm of lawyers is looking for a rancher who dresses in a distinctive style, and is the potential beneficiary of a substantial amount bequeathed by a distant relative. State that specifics will only be revealed when the respondent correctly identifies himself."

Joe replied, "That's a good one! Perhaps we could also broadcast this notice on local radio stations, if we don't get a response from the newspapers."

Rose enthused, "Yes, and put it on the country music stations first! I got the impression the ranch owner is a Johny Cash fan!"

Puzzled, Joe asked, "How did you figure that out?"

She frowned and thought some more, before her face brightened. "Ah, I heard his records playing in the background, when the rancher was driving!"

Then she looked glum, saying, ""I should have put that in my report, shouldn't I?"

Joe nodded. "Yup! Put in as much detail as you can, no matter how trivial. But that's why I'm here, to help you!"

Joe arranged for the notice to be worded and placed, using a dummy firm provided the law enforcement agency with whom they liaised. Now all they had to do was sit back and wait, hoping to catch their prey by duplicitous means.

Joe pounced on the phone when the dummy firm's number lit in red letters and a warning buzzer sounded.

He briefed the receptionist, Alison, to intercept it, using the fictitious company's name and put his own phone down. When the call was put through, he answered it.

"Hello. I'm the senior partner here, Who is this calling?"

A deep male voice the other end replied, "I'm calling after seeing the notice you placed in the local newspaper. I don't think you'll see a style quite like mine, and it's a fair assumption I'm the man you're looking for!"

Joe thought, "*You betcha!*" and said, "Carry on!"

The man said, "I'm referred to as Mitch, and I dress all in Lilac colored cowboy clothes. How's that for distinctive?" he sounded triumphant.

Joe said cheerfully, "You are exactly who we've been looking for! Give me your full address and we'll send our trained legal staff along to fill you in! By the way, when you come here at a later date to sign the paperwork, is they anyone there who can look after things in your absence?"

"Sure, my foreman's around, so he can look after the ranch!"

Joe thought, "*That's two for the slammer!*"

He arranged for a couple of police cars to go and collect them separately, deputies riding as shotguns. A he popped into Rose's office to give her the good news, he rubbed his hands in delight.

When they were brought in, Joe personally interrogated them separately. Neither man would break, and they refused to accept any of the evidence presented to them.

Joe moaned, "The trouble is, they know damned well that no one who saw them is likely to remember anything. It was 10 years ago, and they're insisting that I produce the witnesses I claim we've got. I'm stymied!

"I'll give it one last shot, and if that doesn't work I've got to release them. The testimony of a dead person isn't good enough!"

When he told Rose this bad state of affairs, she didn't bat an eyelid. With a shrug of the shoulders, she said, "Win a few, lose a few! We tried our best and know they did it."

Two blank-faced officers were given the memorable task of driving the released men back to their ranch. They sat in the front of the police car, while the two ex-detainees sat next to each other in the back, where they could be heard sharing jokes and laughing.

It was gut wrenching for the agency partners, having to free suspects that they knew were guilty of murder but couldn't prove it. Joe took it better than most, having been forced before to let people go free on a technicality, or see them receiving a derisory sentence for a despicable crime.

He would give the same, stock answer to those who took it badly, saying, "It's a tough world we live in. Sometimes you've gotta take the rough with the smooth, and remain positive. Always be positive and believe in Karma."

Shortly after reaching the main road, the police driver pulled over to one side. He and his fellow officer were getting fed up with the jolly attitudes and quips of the two ex-detainees. They both got out and opened the rear doors, and leant over to look at the two men, who went silent.

"Give us your mobiles," the driver commanded the nearest one, holding out his hand and placing the other one on the butt of his pistol; his fellow officer did the same, saying, "We don't trust you. You'll get them back the other end, if you behave."

The men clammed up and handed over their phones, after which the officers got back in the front and resumed the journey.

"I don't like the way they're behaving. It's weird," whispered the foreman to his boss.

"Shut up, back there!" the officer in the passenger seat shouted at them, glaring in their direction.

After that, the journey continued in silence and they didn't even stop for a leak or cup of coffee. Eventually, they turned right off the highway onto a dirt track, raising clouds of dust behind them.

The two in the back were relieved to have travelled this far without further incident, knowing that the their destination was less than a couple of miles away. Unexpectedly, the car stopped well short of the ranch, and they were told abruptly to get out.

They were fearing for their lives, but this didn't stop Mitch demanding that the officers give his and the foreman's phones back. They were tossed out of the nearside window and fell into the road as the car did a rapid ninety degree turn and sped off back to the highway, covering them in dust.

The foreman opened his mouth to complain about their treatment, but his phone was dead. He opened the back panel and found that the battery and SIM card were missing. Mitch checked his as well, and found that his were missing too. "Damn!" he shouted, shaking his fist at the police car, which was now almost out of sight.

They started walking, but heard the sound of hooves clip-clopping in the distance, coming from a hillside not far away. They screwed up their eyes to focus on the source, and could see a group of riders picking their way down the slope and heading towards them.

"Hey, they look like red Indians to me!" exclaimed Mitch. "They've got brown tunics on and feathers stuck at angles in their hair!"

"Yes, and they're carrying rifles, and bows and arrows!" the foreman exclaimed, in rising panic. "Let's make a run for it!"

It was not easy, running in high-heeled leather boots only intended for ornamental and riding use; they were soon lassoed as the warriors galloped level to them, and fell to the ground.

An older man, who they presumed was the chief by the row of Eagle feathers stuck in his headband, dismounted athletically and advanced towards them with a large knife in his hand. They inched away as he came up to them, and spoke. "You killed my grandson. Now you will pay!"

While the other well-armed warriors held their bows and arrows at the ready, with their rifles holstered to one side of their horses, the chief sheathed his knife, removed their captives' boots and repositioned the loops of rope around their ankles. He remounted his sturdy warhorse and tied the precious boots to his saddle pommel. They set off at speed, whooping and dragging the two men bare feet-first with the ropes attached to two of their saddles.

By the end of the journey, the two dragged men were more dead than alive, and their backs were bloodied and bruised, with bones broken from being pulled a considerable distance.

Waiting for them was a group of native women, who revived them with water. Any gratitude they may have felt was short-lived, as they were unceremoniously spread-eagled, bound and pegged over two large ants' nests. Soon they started screaming as they were vengefully bitten by the large red insects streaming out of their entry holes, bent on retaliation.

Impassively, four of the 'squaws' gathered around them and used sharp knives to strip slivers of flesh from their victims torsos and upper thighs. Their increasingly loud screams would have been heard for miles, if the women hadn't stuffed soft cloths into their mouths, but the victims bulging eyes and arched bodies spoke volumes for their anguish.

When either man showed signs of fainting off, they would gently revive him with water and a wet cloth to dampen his forehead. Immediately he was conscious, they would show him his flesh being fed to their dogs, and then resume the torture. It went on for hours, before they died in agony, and were flung down a ravine to be left for the wild animals to dissect and consume.

After a few days, the two men were reported as missing, and the officers who had escorted them home were interviewed. They vehemently denied any wrongdoing, insisting they had dropped them outside the ranch; to an extent this was true. Under hypnosis their account of events remained consistent, and they were allowed to return to duty with notes of the occurrence added to their records.

Joe asked his mediums to try and make contact with the missing men, but to no avail. Rose said, "I'm sure they're dead, but I've no idea how or where this happened."

Joe looked at her suspiciously but made no comment. What was the point? He could check if Kajika's tribe had involved itself and committed a crime, but was sure they would be tight-lipped about it as well.

He hoped that his partners had remained aloof from taking vigilante action, but had no way of finding out. Their skills were increasing at a phenomenal rate under his tutelage and he didn't want to disrupt the process.

CASE CLOSED

Joe was pleased to report a successful closure again, but refrained from passing judgement on his psychic partners. He suspected one or more of them was capable of applying the 'justice of Solomon', and didn't want to cloud their prospects by making a possibly wrong assumption.

Privately, he didn't think he could take the law into his own hands, having read about the Brazilian police who themselves acted as hit squads, to eliminate criminals. No, he would stick to the straight and narrow road he had always taken.

"Huh!" Chuck snorted when he read Joe's mind. *"Holier than thou, you are!"*

CASE 6 – SPONTANEOUS ERUPTION

Joe passed the next case to Chuck, his currently favored protégé, saying, "I've given this one a short description, because of the savage nature of the attack. The victim, a 17-year-old teenage girl, was knifed repeatedly in the chest. Whoever did it must have been in an absolute frenzy, and there was blood splashed everywhere.

"The attack happened a few years ago, and DNA evidence was obtained from the scene. A snapped-off kitchen knife blade was found embedded in her chest. It had presumably been taken from a set of knives kept in a wooden block, which was on a table next to where the onslaught occurred; one slot in the block was empty. The handle was not found, and no fingerprints could be traced on what was available of the murder weapon.

"The DNA was not matched on the databases of known criminals, so the investigation has reached a dead-end."

Chuck picked up the case notes and read them without comment, before looking at the photo of the dead girl as he returned to his own room. There was also a small envelope in the file, which contained a red satin pull-string bag, which he opened to inspect the jewelry inside after he had sat at his desk.

He alternated between touching the enclosed necklace and Pandora ring, before closing his eyes and picturing her smiling face in the photo. With a look of surprise, he studied the notes again and then walked back to Joe's office.

Joe looked up to listen, as Chuck poked his head around the open door and knocked politely, to ask, "Sorry to bother you, but have all the neighbors been questioned?"

Joe frowned and then replied, "It's my belief that the enquiries were thorough. Was that not the case?"

Chuck shrugged his shoulders, saying, "I can't say. The notes are incomplete. If you don't mind, I think I'll make a call and ask for the original notes on the investigation?"

Joe agreed. "Be my guest." He was getting a queasy feeling in his stomach that Chuck was onto something that might have repercussions.

Later that same day, a uniformed officer dropped in with the requested official file, passed it to Chuck, and gave a wink to the receptionist Alison on his way out. It was the same Hugh Politino who had accompanied Richard and Honey on their investigation into 'The Case Of The Deranged Husband'; he was dating the lovely girl on a regular basis, and it was obvious that they were enamored with each other.

Joe caught sight of the flirtatious couple and made a vow that he'd never lend *them* his driverless car.

Meanwhile, Chuck studied the original, complete file with increasing attention. Halfway through, he came across an FBI profile of the suspected assailant. It stated some key facts of significance to the original investigators:

- given the repeated stabbing, it was probably sexually motivated;
- it was done spontaneously, given the impromptu nature of the weapon;
- it was conducted by someone she knew, since the attacker was facing her;
- it was probably someone in her age range in school, say grade 11 or 12;
- it was not premeditated.

Carrying on reading, Chuck was building his own profile of the victim, as he recited it into his PC.

The notes are reproduced below.

Olivia Braithwaite, who was 17 years old when she was murdered, was born into a middle class family and had a younger brother and an older sister. Owing to a cyclical trade depression and its adverse impact on their income, the family had moved into a less affluent neighborhood than they would have liked, but could still afford to send the children to good quality local schools.

The change in circumstances was a move from a large detached property with specially commissioned architectural features, a tennis court and a pool, to a row of identical, clapboard covered but still detached houses with no external add-ons possible; the plot sizes did not permit it.

It was a pleasant enough area, with plenty of families sharing similar aspirations, with the kids going to the same schools and sharing the same social facilities.

Olivia had a number of kids of similar ages nearby, but only one living directly next door. He was a 16-year-old boy, who was interviewed by the detectives leading the investigation but had been declared of no relevance to the inquiry; he had moved away since the attack.

This individual was drawn to Chuck's attention by his age and close proximity. Clearly, the detectives had been easily satisfied with his responses to their questions.

Her personality had been established as one of charm and friendliness, with a smile constantly playing on her freckled face. In essence, she was lovely, without being exceedingly pretty. Had she lived, someone would have undoubtedly been drawn to her inherent good qualities and intelligence.

As with all her friends and acquaintances that they had interviewed, there was no one who stood out as having the motivation to hurt such a pleasant girl; she didn't seem to have an enemy in her circle, and it looked like a random killing.

What they did have was the DNA of the killer, from various blood stains and the knife blade itself, but – as Chuck already knew - the person concerned was not on any database of previous offenders.

That also added to his unease, and he felt the need to pursue matters by asking for the police to take further action. He concluded his report by controversially stating, "At the time of her death, she was 17 years old, and the younger boy next door was infatuated with her. I *saw* him attack her. Find him, get his DNA and you will have the killer."

When Joe read the report, which Chuck handed to him along with the bundle of files he had accumulated, he sat up with a jolt. "*That was quick!*" he thought, and immediately made a call to the law enforcement agency.

After a brief search for the boy, with the assistance of his family who were still living next door to where the crime had been committed, he was found in another area over 100 miles away. He was staying with relatives and working as an apprentice mechanic at a garage.

The police arrested him for the alleged murder, insisting that it was early days, but they wanted to question him about the murder of his neighbor's daughter, on the basis of new evidence that had come to light. One of the arresting officers commented how cold he had behaved, as if the death of the girl had no impact on him whatsoever or his alleged involvement in it.

When Joe interviewed him personally, he was struck by the emotionless behavior of the young man, and decided to 'play it cool' as the interviewer, seeing if he could draw a confession out of him.

Information was slow in forthcoming, and as the time rolled by they both felt the need for some refreshments. Joe relaxed and started chatting to the suspect about matters in general, and he began to loosen his tongue a little bit at a time.

There was as yet no sign of a confession ready to be made, and the empty drinks glasses were taken away and exchanged a few times, before a police officer came into the interview room and whispered in Joe's ear.

He brightened up, and looked the suspect in the eyes before saying, "I've just had some good news for me, and bad news for you. Do you want to hear my news first?"

The suspect shifted uncomfortably and shrugged his shoulders indifferently, while Joe stared at him with a hard face and said, "Guess what? Your DNA matches that found at the scene of the murder. You're under arrest for the murder of Olivia, your beautiful young neighbor."

Another police officer entered the room, and Joe ordered him, "Make the formal arrest, officer, then take him back to the cells."

After the charges were read out, Joe watched as the emotionless and silent teenager was led away in handcuffs. He said to Chuck, "I'm glad that one's been taken out of circulation. He's a nasty piece of work if ever I've met one! A true mental case, that's for sure!"

As an afterthought, he asked Chuck, "What was it you actually saw?"

Chuck replied grimly, "Him going into a frenzy. All she did was reject him, but there was a tone of scorn when she did it; it wasn't much, but he was looking for it and it drove him mad. A little touch of sympathy and she would have lived through the danger."

"Yes," Joe agreed, "I think that many lives could have been saved if the victims had handled the situation better. Don't get me wrong, I'm not advocating 'docile submission', but I do wonder if schools could add a course on 'emotional understanding' to the curriculum. Perhaps it would help prevent some of these mass shootings that take place far too often for my liking."

Chuck nodded in sympathy, while Joe decided he had to attend to another matter; he wanted to find out why the original detectives on the case had failed so abysmally to investigate the obvious culprit for the murder.

CASE CLOSED

Joe was well pleased with Chuck's perfoJoe wrote a case report that contained the usual synopsis, and confirmed that Chuck and Rose had met his expectations in exemplary fashion. He also expressed confidence that Richard and Honey were 'snapping at their heels', and would soon shine.

The only note of caution he sounded was his worry that their lives would become drab, if they continued to whittle away endlessly at the large number of cases he had brought with him.

What he was hinting at was the need to take them to a higher level, although he couldn't envisage what that might be. At least, that was before his brain started churning over.

CASE 7 – THE HONEY TRAP

Going back in time, Joe was relieved when he could finally close 'The Case of the Deranged Husband'.

In his estimation, Richard and Honey had taken far too long in its resolution. He was determined that the next cases he allocated to them, for individual pursuance, would be capable of much quicker resolution. He needed them to focus harder on enhancing their psychic skills, under his direction.

To keep things going, at the outset he had simultaneously handed a bundle of cases to Rose and Chuck, labelled between 2 and 6, which they were sweeping through in record time.

Meanwhile, Richard and Honey were now going to be deployed on their share of unresolved cases, allocated with the numbers 7 and 8. However, in some instances, things never quite go to plan; this was one of them.

He called the two of them into his office, and once they'd settled comfortably handed the next case to Richard, stating, "I've given this a provisional title; I'm calling it 'The Case Of The Rampant Serial Killer'. It's supposed to be for you alone, and you can give it a better name later, since I've little doubt we're likely to come across more serial killers as we progress."

Honey's expression was a picture of indifference as he checked her for a reaction. He continued, drawling in typical style, "If you can bring this monster, this prolific killer of young women, to justice, I'll be a happy bunny. If you can do it in days rather than weeks, I'll be a happy Easter bunny!"

It was that time of year, and the weather outside was rather chilly but bright, although the forecast warned that snow was on the way.

Richard looked briefly at the slim folder of case notes, which provided the identities and backgrounds of six women, in their teens and early twenties, who had disappeared under similar circumstances in a major northern city a few hours away.

He thought initially that they were probably prostitutes (or 'prossies' as he liked to call them; he didn't care much for the term 'hookers', since it had connotations of drug abuse about it). He was surprised to find that they were all respectable city workers holding down promising career jobs, and had been snatched off the streets at dusk, when the light was fading.

"Does anyone know what happened to them?" he asked Joe, who had also considerately provided a small box containing their personal effects.

"No, " Joe replied, as Richard took the lid off the box and started examining the labelled items one at a time and comparing them with the photos of the girls. "The police have received no communication whatsoever in any of these instances. They could have upped and left of their own volition, or been kidnapped by people traffickers, or whatever. We are hoping you can shed some light on the matter."

Joe looked at him enquiringly, while Richard passed the items one by one to Honey, for verification.

Richard looked at his sidekick for confirmation before concluding, "Joe, I'm sorry to tell you this: they're all dead. Some sick psycho, who is seeking warped, sexual gratification, has murdered them. Have *any* of the bodies been recovered from the river?"

Joe looked serious as he replied, "Yes, two of them, miles away and badly decomposed. Identification was extremely difficult. I didn't tell you this beforehand because…"

Richard interrupted him, saying, "I know; you wanted to see how well I could do with my 'special' abilities. I understand."

Joe looked relieved, and said, "Okay, let's continue, shall we? Based on your reading of the situation, I'll inform the agency we work with and ask them to warn the girls' nearest relatives to expect the worst. We need to get started on finding the culprit or culprits straight away; the rumor mills are getting to work in the city and the natives are getting restless."

While Richard carried on perusing the various items, Joe gave him a few minutes before saying what was on his mind, "I suggest that you involve the city police and let them guide you around the various places where the girls were last seen. This is no time for academic tests to be placed on you."

"Sure," Richard replied with his eyes closed. "Anything that will help me to understand the situation on the ground is appreciated. The man or men concerned are elusive."

Feeling buoyed, Joe made his key proposal. "The police are keen to use a female as 'bait', to draw out the culprits from hiding. Some of their cadets have volunteered. Would their services suit you?"

Honey piped up, "I could do that!"

His eyes opening, Richard said emphatically, "NO...I will not permit it!"

Why not?" she asked indignantly. "With our rapport, I'm ideally placed to undertake this job. It would be a clincher; we stand a far better chance of luring them into the open, working as a team, than you teaming up with a trainee police woman."

"No, no, no! I will not have you putting your life at risk. That's an end to it. Full stop!"

She pouted. "It's not up to you, it's up to me and that's *my* final word on the matter. I'm going to do it because it's the best solution."

Joe purred, "Now, now children, stop quarreling. We will all ensure that Honey keeps safe. Richard can take special safeguards on your behalf, Honey, won't you Richard?"

"Like what?" she asked.

Richard reassured her, "Leave it up to me; I'll safeguard you as discreetly as you wish. Nothing will be done without your prior permission, I promise you, Honey. It'll all be done 'under the radar'."

Inconsequentially, Joe said, "I propose that from now on, we call this "The Case of the Honey Trap. I know I said that I didn't want you two working together, but this is a really special case and you have my blessing."

They returned to Richard's office, and Joe watched as they both sat next to each other at the conference table. "*At least they aren't quarreling,*" he thought anxiously, as Richard briefed her, while she looked happily at him. "*She seem to be spellbound by him. That's a good sign, I wouldn't want them to get off on the wrong foot; it's too important a mission for bad relations to set in!"*

Later that morning, after Richard spent time on a mysterious shopping expedition, he returned armed with provisions, collected his and her emergency kit bags from the agency's storeroom, and he drove her in his car to the big city further north.

After a few hours of travelling, they parked at the police HQ in the city and made their way to meet with the Detective Inspector O'Malley, who was spearheading the investigation.

After another in-depth review of the case, with other officers attending, O'Malley took the two visitors to the suspected scenes of the abductions. He was curious to see how the two psychics behaved, never having worked with this type of operative before.

They came with impeccable credentials, and he had high hopes of them proving successful, whereas previously he would have scorned their presence as irrelevant to true policing.

He watched as Richard showed the whites of his eyes, feeling sick until he closed them and extended his hands outwards. Blind in physical sight only, he searched the surrounding, high apartment blocks that dominated the various districts they visited, on the broad, tree-lined pavements.

Honey adopted a more conventional approach and restricted herself to staring at the buildings without making any gestures or bizarre facial expressions. O'Malley was staring at her for a more down-to-earth reason. *"What a peach of a honey she is!"* he reckoned.

She looked back at him in a disquieting way and whispered confidentially, "You reckon I'm a peach, do you? Be careful, my companion is a black belt in the martial arts, and he fancies me something rotten! But thanks anyway." She gave him a seductive smile.

"Bloody hell!" he whispered to himself, looking thunderstruck. *"They are good!"*

At each place they stopped, Richard repeated the same conclusion, "There's a number of people around showing an interest in us, but nothing more than ordinary inquisitiveness. Let's try the next one on your itinerary."

With relief to the retinue of officers waiting for a better result, he made a different announcement at the penultimate stop on their tour of the city. He stated, "There's someone nearby who is looking out of his window with bad intentions. He's like a tiger seeking his prey. He's hardly showing us any interest, and he's trying to single-out suitable, youngish women to satisfy his appetite."

O'Malley asked, Where is he?"

Richard replied, "I don't wish to draw his attention to us, but he's high-up in that block on the corner opposite, next to the traffic lights. *Don't* look over there; I'll pinpoint it on the map, when we're out of sight."

As they walked away, Honey gave Richard a nudge and asked quietly, "Was that a dig at me, that quip about *youngish* women?"

He didn't reply, confining himself to pointing out on the street plan, the building where he'd identified the predator.

"What does he look like? Can you identify him?" O'Malley asked, with his big hands held out in a pleading way. Neither medium replied, and Richard closed his eyes to focus on the target.

Honey concentrated hard herself, trying to coax the man to look at himself in a mirror; after a few minutes she looked at the nearest police officer and said excitedly, "Grab a pencil and paper, I've got a description of the one who's been looking out of the window!"

As the officer stood there, waiting for her to provide the mugshot, she described who was possibly one of the serial killers, "He's got greasy black full head of hair, with lots of waves in it, swept back. He's got a low forehead, sideboards, narrow glinting dark-brown eyes and a long, narrow face with a lantern jaw.

"He looks to be in his late thirties or early forties, Mexican, or he comes from another South American country. His upper body looks thin and stringy. I haven't a clue how tall he is, but he's having to lean down to look at himself in the mirror. Ah, wait a minute! He's looking at someone else and speaking Spanish. Now he's walking away! I've lost contact, blast!"

Someone asked her, "What was he wearing?"

"As far as I could see, he had on a dirty white t-shirt with a crisply ironed plain, pale-blue long-sleeved shirt over it."

Someone asked Richard, "Did you see anything?"

"No. I was busy trying to get him aroused, so he'll be wanting to do something tonight." He turned to Honey and held her by the shoulders, and asked her, "Honey, could you take your overcoat off, walk back into view, stand there for a few minutes pretending to be thinking about something, then turn and walk back to us? I'll be tempting him to look out of the window, and will shout to you when I know he's feasted his eyes on you. Will you do that for us?"

She nodded, took off her overcoat, shivered in the cold air and strutted off, sauntering seductively. She stood in the open, in her short mustard colored skirt, slinky yellow sweater with polar collar and long red leather boots, gathering admiring glances, until Richard shouted to her, "It's done, he's hooked! Come back now!"

She came back and stood out of view, while Richard hastily helped her to pull her coat back on. She was shivering after her skimpily clothed exposure to the cold air, and with her teeth chattering, reported, "I broadcast a simple message intended for him; it said that I'd decided to put on my black overcoat, and needed to go back and fetch it! That'll help him pinpoint me later."

"Let's go and prepare. Is there an empty flat in the vicinity, for us to keep watch?"

O'Malley replied, "Bound to be one we can commandeer! Give me a few minutes to set it up." He made a call from a nearby doorway, and came back beaming. "Yes," he said, "It's right behind us. The janitor's going to get us the key; it's a fully furnished condominium on the ground floor. I'll arrange to get your bags brought over to you from the station, after we've got you booked in."

They both ate a brought-in meal, which Richard insisted be served with red wine and bottled gaseous water. Afterwards, they relaxed for half an hour, before showering together in the walk-in unit, luxuriating in the power-jet spraying them hard with very hot water. It was like Honey had the need to purge herself in case the rapist succeeded in overcoming her, while Richard felt an overwhelming desire for role play.

She stepped back for a few minutes to appraise him, and said, "This case is turning you on, isn't it?"

"No, certainly not!" he protested, looking the picture of

innocence.

"Huh!" she exclaimed, nestling up to his naked body. "You're a kinky koo, aren't you? You forget I can read your disgusting mind!"

"You reckon?" he replied, and had sex with her again before continuing to shower away his sinful daydreams.

They were starting to prepare themselves for the fun to begin, when Richard presented her with one of his special purchases.

"What's that?" she asked, holding up a flexible round object, with a Velcro clasp at the back.

"It's a neck protector. You wear it under your polar neck collar. It has the texture of real skin, it's flexible on the outside with a titanium layer inside, so if the guy tries to throttle you he won't succeed. He'll get the impression he's done it, so keep your eyes closed and gasp before fainting off."

She tried it on doubtfully, but said after a few jerks of the neck proclaimed, "Okay, but what if he stabs me instead?"

He brought out a lightweight body protector, and she stared at it frostily. "Forget it, there's no way I'm wearing that thing! It'll show through my sweater and give the game away before it's even started! We need to act genuine in front of this monster! No, I'll feed the desired reaction into his or their brains; we mustn't forget there could be more than one attacker."

"I guess that planting listening devices are a waste of time too, for the same reason?"

"Absolutely! Why should we need them when we can communicate using our brains?"

Richard glared at her and then brought out two more items: a pair of sexy underpants and a pair of thermal long johns, saying, "These are a must, in this weather; they're meant to keep you warm, outdoors."

She looked at them doubtfully, "Hmmm…it'll be unlikely they'll get that far, but anything to keep warmer is appreciated. I've got my creature comforts to think of!" She put them on, bounced up and down on the bed and proclaimed them to be satisfactory, before getting on her feet and donning her bra, a green T-shirt and the yellow sweater.

She put on her makeup, then her boots and overcoat, with a

bobble red and white ski hat pulled over her ears, and announced with a flourish and a pose, "I'm ready!"

"You look gorgeous!" Richard said, and guided her out into the cold dusk air, as she placed the long strap of a red leather satchel bag across a shoulder. "Do you want a peppermint sweet to suck?"

She glared at him. "Are you saying I've got bad breath?"

He tutted and put the small container back in his coat pocket. "Good luck!" he whispered and let her walk around the corner alone, as he stood out of sight, trying to pick up a psychic trail from the apartment block opposite.

The plan was simple in its proposed execution: she would walk two blocks past the apartment block they were staking-out, sit and have a coffee at a pre-designated up-market designer café; she would stay there for half-an-hour and return to her apartment hurriedly, as if she had forgotten something. The she would repeat this once only before packing up the operation if they didn't succeed.

If unsuccessful in luring out the attacker(s), they would narrow-down the search by tackling each apartment in turn, which would surely flush them out, but take longer. It was reckoned to be far more effective to catch them in the act, and give the force a much better chance of nailing them once and for all. Otherwise, they could be apprehended but get off scot-free.

She started her walk, swaying her hips, sure in her confidence that the police were watching her every movement. She had no time to react before someone came up silently behind her, muffled her mouth with a large hand cupping a chloroform-soaked pad that made her feel faint.

She sank to her knees as the pad was removed and she felt herself being lightly strangled by the assailant, using both hands, stinking from the drug. Barely conscious from the ingestion of the primitive anesthetic, she heard a car boot lid being raised, and she was scooped-up like a featherweight and dumped inside with a thump.

"Ouch!" she said, as she landed hard, remembering that the street light she'd passed under had not been lit; it must have been tampered with! Then her mouth was taped. Afterwards, she felt someone grabbing her feet, and using something to fasten them together at the ankles.

They repeated this with the wrists, and she realized that the kidnapper was using a long, self-fastening plastic strap, similar to that sold at garden centers. The pain she suffered brought tears to her eyes, as he fastened them together by pulling the looped strap until it had been tightened to the limit.

For at least twenty minutes, she endured the journey in total darkness, as they rumbled through the streets, stopping and starting at the endless traffic lights. She could hear other vehicles and pedestrians passing but the ducting tape across her mouth stopped her from crying for help.

Finally, after driving off the road and travelling a short distance over bumpy ground, they stopped. The lid was raised, and she was dazzled as her kidnapper shone a torch on her. Before he attempted to lift her, he paused for a moment, presumably to admire his latest trophy.

She gasped as he ran his hands over her, savoring her shapely upper body, before moving down to touch her legs; there he stopped, as he reached an unexpected layer of material, and chuckled when he realized what it was. He tried removing the long johns, but gave up trying, in order to take her out of the boot and lower her to the ground, where he could work unimpeded.

She could make out her surroundings now, and believed that they were in a park; this must have been bordering the broad, deep river which the city bordered, since she could hear the distant sound of passing ships and waves lapping the shore.

She didn't pay much attention for long, as the man was distracting her. He was kneeling to one side of her, and rolling her around as he cut her ankle strap with a knife, and began struggling to remove her long, red boots. She made it more difficult by curling-up her toes, and he gave her a hard clout when he realized what she was up to.

Then he fumbled at the waist of her skirt, while occasionally gripping and stroking her covered legs. This was driving him into a sexual frenzy that made it difficult for him to concentrate on both activities.

She heard him cursing in Spanish, and was comforted by this confirmation of her earlier statement of his probable nationality.

Eventually, he figured out how to use the belt clasp, and tore off the skirt triumphantly, which annoyed her; it was a new garment and he had damaged it. She vowed never to use it again.

Then he started to tackle the long johns, trying first of all to reach inside from her belly and gain access to her inner thighs. It was not easy, since Richard had insisted she tie and knot the extra layer of underwear at the waist, after putting the long johns on, so he tried tearing them off along the seams. The man's rage became fearsome as they refused to part under the strain. Clearly, Richard had the foresight to have chosen a non-rip material.

He finally succeeded, and positioned her on her back as he straddled her. She looked back at him fearfully as he brandished a wicked looking Bowie knife in front of her face. With his free hand, he began undoing his trousers, while she asked herself, "*For pity's sake, where's the team?*"

Then he decided to remove her panties, but again they wouldn't tear. "*Crafty Richard!*" she though, tears welling up in her eyes as she began to regret volunteering for this foolhardy venture.

His language must have been vile, from the look in his face, as she felt the back of his huge blade running across her bare flesh. With another expletive that she understood this time - it was one of joy - he cut off through the extraordinarily strong material and she lay there bare and cold waiting to be violated and disposed of.

Whether or not her body was developing a mind of its own, she couldn't fathom, but her stomach started to contort and growl in a violent manner. Even her attacker stopped and listened as it made a series of pronounced rumbling noises, before the trapped air escaped loudly from her. His body moved away and he started fanning the air in a vain attempt to quell the stench that was emanating from her.

"Madre mia!" he exclaimed, turning his head away as he gulped in fresh air from another angle. It must have been most off-putting for him, but he was determined to finish what he had started and resumed his task urgently.

Suddenly, his body jerked backwards, he dropped the knife, and clutched at his throat. He was gasping for air for only a few minutes, and she could see another man standing behind him, silhouetted against the sky and holding something around his neck.

From his agility, she believed that the newcomer was younger and more powerful than her attacker, and using a garrote to kill him. This last assumption was based on the steady stream of blood falling on her, which indicated that a wire was being used to throttle the man, and she could see the outlines of the two handles he was heaving at.

His head sagged forward onto his chest, his body went limp, and he was lowered to one side of Honey. She knew the man was dead, since she felt his spirit leaving his body, but now she felt even more alarmed at the prospect of rape by one of his accomplices.

However, the man showed no interest in her, and began pulling the deceased away from the scene and towards the river. She heard two splashes, one louder than the other, and she thought that the first was the body being dumped first into the water, and the other was the garrote being thrown in afterwards.

With a sigh of relief and a tremble of her body, she heard the sound of feet running towards her and familiar voices shouting her name. Clearly, the second man was making a break for freedom, and she silently prayed for his soul.

Richard was the first to arrive, and he gently peeled off her gag and covered her with the overcoat left lying on the ground. Holding her tightly, he was clearly overcome with relief and they clung to each other like limpets. O'Malley stood by them patiently waiting for clarification of events, while his officers sealed off the crime scene and searched the rest of the park for clues and witnesses.

Richard told her how much he loved her, and apologized for arriving late, saying, "I put a tracking device in your handbag, and it didn't transmit a signal because of all the metal around you. I should have used a stronger device. I'm really sorry!"

Eventually, she released herself from Richard's embrace and, in a trembling voice, told O'Malley a restricted version of what had taken place. He listened attentively, using a recorder since it was too dark to take notes, and ordered some of his officers to guard the site in rotation until dawn, when a full search could be undertaken. Photos were already being taken, and the associated, artificial flashes were occurring all around them.

An ambulance had been called, and arrived to take Honey to the central hospital, with Richard in attendance. Her ripped undergarments and bloodied clothes were bagged as evidence for forensic analysis later.

Neither medium said anything in the ambulance, as Honey pondered the significance of what had transpired. However, her sudden, fortuitous escape of trapped wind had made her think about several, associated matters that led to one source, and the cause of a lot of her problems became apparent.

She sat bolt upright and uttered one word: "Richard!"

"What's the matter?" he asked, bleakly.

She sank back, without replying.

A couple of days later, she was judged fit enough to return to the station and wrap-up the case. It was a disappointment to the city police that the missing rapist's body had left them with no one to interrogate and no resolution of the previous murders. Or, to put it another way, no 'credible' resolution that could be published.

However, they were confident that the right man had been served his just desserts, and a search of his apartment revealed a family life that, to all outward appearances, was normal and law-abiding.

Honey reassured them that, in spite of their original suspicions, the man who had attacked her was not a member of a larger group of predators. She stressed that whoever had come across them in the park was not a party to any wrongdoing other than subduing her abductor as he sat astride her. No mention was made of the use of a garrote on him, or of the death that resulted.

The newcomer had headed in the same direction as her would-be rapist, to the riverbank, and both of them may have fallen into the river. He was probably an innocent passer-by who had stumbled on them by happenstance.

The river was being dredged, but no bodies had been recovered. Still, it was early days, and they optimistically expected to receive a positive result sooner or later.

She never mentioned the garrote to anyone, and the bloodied clothing was confirmed as matching that of her attacker, after he had cut himself on the huge knife he left at the scene, which also contained his bloodstains.

The first evening after Honey was discharged from hospital, she sat alone with Richard in the rented apartment, eating a romantic meal together. After the meal, she casually asked him, "The evening before I went on duty, what did you put in my food, to give me that discharge of wind?"

He looked at her guiltily, replying, "A laxative."

"Now tell me truthfully: did you use hypnosis on me, to activate the laxative under extreme circumstances?"

"I had to protect you somehow, bearing in mind the potential for you being abused!"

"Can I therefore assume you have used hypnosis before, to get me hyped up for sex? By saying something like *I PUT A SPELL ON YOU!* - is that what you've been doing to me?"

"God no! I'd never do anything like that, to you!"

She got heated as she shouted, "Richard, you're a lying, cheating scumbag!" More calmly, she added, "Move your stuff out of my pad straight after we get back. While we're here, you can sleep in the other bedroom. You will use remedial hypnosis on me to undo your evil act, or I'll muddy your name publicly."

They met Joe in his office after she and Richard had been debriefed by the city police, who expressed themselves satisfied with the results of their investigation. They confirmed that they looked forward to calling on The Deaduction Agency when some future calamity merited their remarkable skillset.

Joe noticed that there had been a cooling of the relationship between the two of them, and reckoned he could deduce one of the reasons for it.

"*What a cheapskate!*" he thought. "*He couldn't bother to buy a decent tracking device and save her skin!*"

CASE CLOSED

MEETING EXPECTATIONS

Joe decided that he would refer in future to the supervising law enforcement agency as 'the Bureau', since that was part of its official title.

The time had come when Joe was due to report in person to those who pulled his strings at The Deaduction Agency. These consisted of the sponsor, and the coordinating director (this was not his official title) of the Bureau. Each of them had one or more designated assistants who could attend as a last resort.

Both top men had decided to attend in person, which Joe preferred. It was supposed to be a progress meeting, but Joe didn't like using that title. It implied that it was an onerous, yawn-inducing task, to be grudgingly fulfilled as a necessary burden.

He aimed to view it in a positive light, as an opportunity for each participant to specify what they wanted from each other, and measure precisely how far they were getting in achieving those clearly defined objectives.

It was Joe's practical application of classic 'Management by Objectives', Peter Drucker style.

As soon after the meeting as he could arrange it, the process of 'meeting expectations' would be reenacted with the staff reporting to him, as the middleman in the reporting chain. This would ensure that none of the links from top to bottom became broken or misinterpreted.

At the top level, the sponsor was providing the funds for The Deaduction Agency to resolve unusually difficult crimes by employing paranormal assistance and extra-ordinary mental skills, like telepathy.

In essence, he was experimenting with novel methods of

crime resolution, in the belief that they would be integrated in mainstream policing techniques. At least, that was in the stated mission statement. Joe suspected he had deeper motives and intended finding out if this was true.

The coordinating director had enlisted Joe's help to translate the mission statement into precise objectives, for measurement against achievements in meetings like this. His role was simple: it was to ensure that the sponsor got 'bang for his bucks'; that is to say 'best value for his investment'.

It was dry stuff, but it kept tempers and nastiness at bay, at least a long as Joe and his new partners performed as measured. Otherwise, he would have to accept that he was not up to the job, and would resign. In that circumstance, the agency would be disbanded.

Patiently, to put matters in their correct context, Joe reiterated facts that they already knew: "I work with four mediums or psychics, call them what you wish. Two of them, Richard and Honey, were previously employed by a film studio, which showed them getting to grips with unresolved murder cases. Before that, they were practising solo and successfully.

"I have reviewed all of those cases shown on TV, none of which reached a satisfactory conclusion, and concluded that the formula was wrong; it did not give them any chance of success.

"Since I came and worked with them, I can confirm that they have demonstrated the skills we expected them to possess. The initial proof is in the typed notes that are in front of you."

"Now for the other two mediums, Rose and Chuck. While Richard and Honey were occupied on the prolonged 'Case of the Deranged Husband', I was liaising with the other two independently, and shared out five other cases, according to the time they needed as individuals. These have been provided previously to keep you up to date, and now lie in front of you for inspection, numbered from cases 2 to 6."

The sponsor thumbed through them and nodded briefly, clearly waiting impatiently for Joe to sum up his findings. The director could contain himself so longer, and with a broad smile asked, "So, you can now confirm that they are *all* the genuine article?"

Joe replied with a grin, "I take it you've both read 'The Case of the Snatched Girl Scout'? That alone has placed us on the map! The number of pedophiles caught as a result of our participation has been phenomenal; the number of men who were in positions of power and have since been dismissed is amazing.

"The results exceeded my wildest expectations, and all four mediums became embroiled in the investigation. I would add that their capabilities are improving in leaps and bounds, largely because of the environment they are now in; I think it is conducive to their best performance. I hope you will see this for yourselves, by the next time we meet."

Joe came to the most crucial point on his list of 'things to do'.

He stated, "At your joint acceptance of my proposal, I will be implementing a further category of crime prevention that will confirm the full extent of their skills, and I will be passing its details to them in the next couple of days. Any questions, before I move on?"

They shook their heads.

Both men made a special point of shaking Joe's hand with vigor as they left, as a sign of their approval of the way things were going. The director took Joe to one side and said quietly, "They are being spoken of in hushed tones, as living legends. Give them all my special congratulations for a job well done!"

What Joe didn't elaborate on was his intention of giving Honey one final case to mature her mental abilities; he felt that he hadn't provided the opportunity for her to excel, when he used her as bait in 'The Case Of The Honey Trap'.

Honey was away completing this additional one-off case as Joe began the next phase of the communication process, by speaking to the other partners in the agency.

He gathered what was left of his flock around him in his office and enthused. He was indisputably on a role, and gushed about their achievements in glowing terms.

"I'm pleased to convey to all of you the congratulations of our sponsor *and* my boss at the bureau. You have covered yourselves in glory – which is better than horse manure!

"The cases you have tackled have yielded The Deaduction Agency unparalleled recognition, for what is a new venture. We have entered the hall of fame, and you are being described as 'living legends'! Who could ask for anything more? I am basking in reflected glory!"

They were all looking perplexed, and Richard leant over to ask Chuck quietly, "What's he on? He's behaving like a medicine man trying to flog us snake oil!"

Chuck whispered back, "I dunno, but I wish he'd give some of it to me!"

Rose muttered, "I've got mixed feelings about this. I can't help feeling that there's something in store for all of us!"

Joe obliviously continued, announcing, "When Honey completes the case I have given her, you will all be going to prison, yes, prison!"

That made them sit up, and start over-speaking each other.

Joe made a hushing sign with his finger pressed against his lips and then pointed at Rose. "You first," he said.

She asked, "What'd you mean?"

"I'm splitting you into pairs, to visit one of the most notorious penitentiaries in our wonderful country. There you will be confronted by inmates queuing up to get your undivided attention. They all claim to be not guilty of the murderous offences they have no recollection of committing.

"One of you will determine if they are guilty or not of the crimes for which they have been incarcerated, and the other will confirm or deny the accuracy of their partner's final judgement.

"It's a dry run in the legal system, as an alternative to costly, full-blown appeals and parole boards. *Plus* you get to find what other crimes they may have committed and not revealed, *and* you get to use the spectractor on a trial basis.

"It is entirely possible you will decide there is no further value in keeping the offenders in prison, after our expert operative, 'Brains' - that is to say the eminent Professor Michael Dawnes - has 'washed' them of their unpardonable sins with his spectractor."

Richard leapt to his feet and protested, "What! You intend giving *us* carte blanche to cleanse their souls of sin and release them into the community?"

Joe replied solemnly, "Yes, on a trial basis. I am reliably informed that some of the Scandinavian countries do this already, not having enough jails to house even the most violent of offenders. At least we have *you* to allow Brains to negate any future anti-social behavior of the released convicts."

He looked at them with a smile and added, "You will be clearing the jails and making enormous inroads into the crippling costs of maintaining an expensive prison system. We will be covered in glory if it goes well!"

Chuck asked, "What will society do with them?"

Joe expanded, "They will partake in every menial task under the sun, such as cotton and grape picking, painting care homes, changing bedpans in hospitals and looking after the aged amongst us! Social departments are preparing lists as I speak, on a trial basis. You've got to admit, this is a far better use of your talents than tackling single cases of murder. "

Rose admitted, "I can see the logic in this, but…"

"No buts!" Joe intercepted. "This is the start of vital roles for all of us. We can extend your responsibilities later to vetting abusive parents, hospitals, doctors' practices, police departments, et cetera. Your lives will be far more interesting, once we've hidden your true identities, I promise you!"

He looked at his watch and, before rushing out of the room, excused himself by saying, "I've got to catch up with Honey and see how she's doing."

The psychics sat there looking stunned and trying to assimilate their future prospects.

CASE 8 – THE PRODIGAL SON

Joe handed the case to Honey, emphasizing the rarity of the crime it centered on. "It's a kidnapping, but not of a girl; it was a healthy teenage boy, on the verge of adulthood who disappeared two years ago.

"He came from a prosperous family that lives in a large house on acres of land. It is surrounded with grazing pastures and paddocks for the horses they love to rear, and riding is their passion and secondary source of income. The father is an advertising director of a prestigious agency and the mother is the boss of this miniature ranch.

"The boy, Oliver, is 17 years old and has an older brother, Nathan, who is 20. There is also a sister, Rebecca, aged 13. They are all protestant Christians, go to church each Sunday, and organize events on behalf of the pastor and his parish council.

"From the photos passed to me, the entire family comprises a handsome bunch of folks, especially the missing youngster. He is blond, tall, and must be a hit with the girls; he reminds me of Elvis, but with different hair coloring; similar features too. I wish I'd been that good looking at his age!"

Honey commented sourly, "Good looks aren't everything in a man, you know!"

Joe replied testily, "You've been blessed with them, so snap out of whatever's troubling you!" He knew that she was having difficulties in her relationship with Richard, and hoped she could leave matters in abeyance for the case she had been given.

He ignored her gloomy face and continued, "One fine Saturday after breakfast, he was walking to the end of the long drive, intending to meet a male friend's family and go out for the day. His mother kept watch fondly until he reached the end of the driveway; when he turned to wave goodbye, she saw with alarm that he was having an altercation with someone, so she raced out to see what was going on.

"She got there, too late to see what had happened, his haversack was laying open on the ground, its belongings scattered as if it had been dropped hastily, and a pool of blood was next to them.

"She kept running around shouting his name, frantically hoping he was still in the vicinity, until the family he was waiting for drove up. They joined in the search, but quickly gave up and took her to the house, to phone the local sheriff.

"A search was instigated for many miles around, by car and on foot with volunteers, but no trace of him was ever found. DNA evidence proved that it was his blood at the scene of the crime. The family has been devastated by his disappearance and are desperate to find out what occurred.

"Over to you, Honey!"

She picked up the folder with its notes, selected the photo of the missing teenager and began concentrating on it. Looking up at Joe, she said, "You do understand that I'll need to go there? It's not easy to make contact with the spirit world from a distance, and even then no one can be sure if the person wanted has died."

That observation filled Joe's heart with hope. He realized that she had met his expectations and was functioning the same as the other three psychics would have done, under the circumstances.

"Okay, I'll get onto it. Would you like a couple of the camera crew to drive you there?"

She said in a low voice, "Yes please," before leaving the room to collect her overnight bag from the storeroom. Joe wondered how she would feel, working without her regular partner for the first time in ages.

He needn't have concerned himself; she was as mad as hell with Richard and the way he thought of her, as a sex toy. She had a good head on her shoulders, and knew how to use it. The film crew intuitively knew she was pre-occupied and left her in peace, to enjoy her own company.

The two men with her shared her high opinion of herself, and Walter commented in a low voice to Matt, who was driving, "It's rare to find someone who's got everything in one bundle: brains and beauty. That Richard is a dope for not making her an honest woman. I don't understand how anyone can be that stupid!"

Honey sat in the back and smiled at the compliment. Her self-esteem had been damaged, but was now restored by that estimation of her. He was completely out of her system from that time onwards.

They reached the general area after a long drive south, and followed the GPS instructions to reach the house. They parked for a while at the end of the isolated drive, where the abduction had taken place. The two men stretched their legs by the side of their gleaming wagon, while Honey surveyed the area in silence, soaking up the atmosphere.

She found that the two of them were a distraction, watching her to see what she would do, and asked them to go for a walk while she performed her magic. When they had left the scene, she brought out the photo and the haversack and focused on making contact with Oliver. It was to no avail, and she then refocused on establishing the psychic trail.

After a few minutes of using her mental faculties to search for him, she exclaimed "Pay dirt!" and shouted to Matt and Walter to come back and fetch her. When they came into view, she abruptly changed her mind about driving to the house, and invited them to join her in walking there, to get some needed exercise.

She was 'smelling the roses', as she set up a smart pace they had difficulty matching, and could detect happier mental pictures as the approached the two storey detached dwelling. It had a nice, homely atmosphere to go with its charming ranch-style appearance, and the door opened as Honey reached for the old-fashioned brass knocker, to rap its matching shiny brass plate for attention.

"Hello, you're from the agency, I trust?" the mother asked. At least, that who Honey assumed her to be.

Honey held her hand out, saying, "And you are the mother, Mary, I presume?"

She reminded Honey of one of Charlie's Angels, Farrah Fawcett-Majors, from the original TV show. Not that it was her, of course, but she was almost her twin.

They exchanged greetings warmly, although the mother was slightly on edge, realizing the purpose of the visit. They went through to the large kitchen and sat around the central, large oak table to drink coffee and chat.

Seeing that Mary was nervous, Honey got down to business immediately. She stated firmly, "Oliver is *not* dead. He's very near here and is unharmed. In fact, he's living the life of Riley, and all we've got to do is find his exact location and reel him in. Have you got a pencil and paper, so I can describe the place where he's staying?"

The men gawped at her, as the mother beamed with pleasure. After hearing her deepest prayers being answered, she got up, her hands trembling, and fetched the requested writing materials from a drawer by the sink.

Ignoring her reaction, Honey busied herself sketching out what she had witnessed in her mind, while Matt and Walter sat opposite, stunned by the revelation and not certain if they could believe what Honey had told their client. What if it wasn't true?

Mary leapt to her feet, her voice shaking as well as her hands, and cried out in surprise, "I know that place! It's the Miller house, in the woods a few miles from here! They only use it some of the year. Her Glam-Rock husband died some time back and his widow still visits when the mood takes her. Loaded she is! Let's get over there!"

Honey calmed her down by putting a hand on hers and saying, "No! *Don't* let's go over there right now. I'll call our agency and they'll set wheels in motion; you have to do nothing for the moment. Let us handle it."

Matt excused himself and rushed outside to contact Joe, and told him about Honey's conclusions on the situation. He qualified these by adding, "My concern is that she may have been premature in saying that Oliver was alive. We don't want a repeat of the bad press the studio suffered when she and Richard were going round the country, failing to resolve any of the cases they investigated."

Joe replied, "I've got every faith in both of them; take it from me, they really are psychics. I will arrange for a couple of my officers to call on the local sheriff, and check out the location where Oliver is believed to be living. We'll review the situation after the place is searched."

Not fully convinced, Matt went back to the kitchen, where Honey was asking, "Is there a B & B to be found near here, where the three of us we can stay for a night or two?"

Mary answered with a smile, "Yes, here! We provide accommodation for people who take a holiday with us, to go horseback riding. It's quiet at the moment, for an obvious reason, so you'll get it for free if Oliver comes back safely!" That comment did nothing to assuage Matt's discomfort.

Later that afternoon, they received a special call out of the blue. Mary picked up the phone, thinking it may be a caring neighbor at the other end of the line. She stiffened when she was told who it was, and cupped the phone to turn and tell Honey, "It's the sheriff!"

She jumped in the air and shouted in excitement, "Yippee!" as she was given good news. "He's been found!"

Rushing over to Honey, she gave her a big hug, and then ran into the hall, to call her children and share her joy with them. "Now you *must* stay here, at least tonight!" she insisted to Honey, Matt and Walter. These two were stunned by the rapid turn of events; Matt sighed with relief and Walter gave a faint smile of support.

Within half an hour, a police car drew up, and Mary was the first to rush outside, followed by Nathan and Rebecca; they could see Oliver sitting in the back, looking ahead without expression.

Nathan commented, loud enough for the others to hear, "You'd think he'd at least *look* glad to see us!"

As the rear car door was opened and Oliver was allowed to get out, his mother embraced him, while he maintained an attitude of complete aloofness. Honey, Matt and Walter had decided to stay in the kitchen, and were watching from the front window.

Matt said, "That's odd!"

Honey commented, "You ain't seen or heard nothing yet! He's an ungrateful, selfish, pampered swine!" Matt wondered why she felt like that, until he realized she allegedly had these mind-reading skills; if it were true, she probably knew him better than anyone else, at that moment.

It was noticeable that he had shot up in height and filled-out, and was now a prime specimen of manhood.

Walter said drily, "He seems to have done well in his two years of captivity. He looks well-nourished to me!"

As Oliver was led into the kitchen by the sheriff, he left him with his mother and siblings and singled out Honey to speak to her confidentially. He said, "He was unwilling to come back here. Treat him with caution. Check if there are any guns here, or in the other buildings; if there are any, make sure they're kept under lock and key."

She asked, "Why? Is he suicidal?"

He replied, "Could be, if he thinks he's going to be forced to stay here. Equally, he could go on the rampage. We had one helluva a struggle to get him to come back. He's one angry young man, unstable too! Also, tell them to put the knives away, out of sight."

As the sheriff left the house and drove off, Matt came up to Honey and said, "Joe sends his regards and congratulations, and tells you that it's okay to spend the night here, to support the family, more if required."

Feeling pleased, she went to confirm the initial bookings with Mary, who got them to fill in the register. As they were being shown to their guest rooms on the first floor, it was noticeable that Oliver was following them at a distance, accompanied by Rebecca; both were deep in argument.

Before Mary left Honey, who began unpacking her travel bag, she informed her in a whisper, "Ollie's asked to go to his room and be left alone for a while. We'll be having dinner at 7:30pm, in the dining room if that's okay?"

Honey wasn't in the habit of staying at private houses offering B & B, let alone dinner, and was pleasantly surprised at the opulence of this one. Her room was large by any standard, and was furnished with 19th century restored furniture and tasteful, patterned soft furnishings; on the walls were oil paintings depicting the regional scenery.

She bounced on the bed, after first removing her shoes, and found it to be supremely comfortable, whilst promising herself a future treat. It was her dream to come back one day and have one of those riding holidays with Mr. Right, whoever that would be. No doubt, it would be far in the future, if ever.

After a shower and change into her one set of evening clothes, she descended the stairs and found the wood-paneled dining room, with its blazing log fire absorbing the evening chill.

As she entered, her two male companions, who had been chatting animatedly to Nathan and Rebecca, greeted her. Matt introduced her to a slim, handsome older man, who put down the soft drink he was holding and gave her a hug, as if he had known her all his life. "Hi, I'm Roland, Mary's husband. Many thanks for all that you've done for us!"

They all made up a circle to join in conversation, while Mary kept toing and froing, making final preparations with staff she had summoned to serve the evening meal. There was no sign of Oliver.

After a brief prayer, they got down to eating one course after another, washed down with wines and water, although Mary and Honey only picked at the wonderful dishes laid out in front of them. They were both on calorie-controlled regimes designed to help them keep their figures, and were teased by the others on their vanity.

"I don't care what you say," Mary responded with a smile. "It makes me feel good, and that's what counts. Watch what you eat and it'll watch over you. What do you think, Honey?"

Honey nodded, commenting, "I'm happy with the way I am, and want to stay that way. I've found it helpful to stay off wholegrains and only eat two meals a day. I'm on 'The In-Sync Diet.'"

Mary looked across at her with increased interest and asked, "What, no breakfast tomorrow? I'll have to pay you stay with us! Tell me more about this diet…" They both chatted together on the subject through the meal, leaving the others to their own topics.

After the meal, when they paused before leaving the table, Nathan caused heads to turn and look at him when he asked his dad, "Why do you accept Oliver back so easily? He's been away two years and told me he wants to return to this woman who he's with. He doesn't even like us anymore!"

Roland replied in a gentle tone, "It's because we love him as much as we love you and Rebecca. It's an unconditional feeling."

Rebecca blurted out, "Which means he's going to share everything with us when you and mom die, even though he pushed off and we didn't! That isn't fair on us, is it?" She looked tearful, as her father got up, went to her and put a consoling hand on his daughter's shoulder.

He explained, "Becky, look what you've had in the meantime. He's lost his education and the opportunities I've given both of you to help me in my business. I haven't told you this yet, but I'm going to be setting up on my own soon. You and Nathan are developing a good understanding of what I do for a living, and what your mother does as well, here at the horse-riding center.

"It is our belief that when we die, both of you will have enough savvy to make your way in the world on your own. What has Oliver got to offer? He will be infinitely worse off, lacking education and will probably screw-up whatever he inherits! That's my take on things as they stand."

Rebecca stood up and hugged her father, and Nathan joined in to do the same. Neither of them may have liked the situation but they now understood it from their parents' viewpoint.

He said to them all, "Shall we go into the lounge and have some coffee?"

Mary replied, "Lead the way Roland, and we'll follow you!"

This was when the two reassured offspring made themselves scarce, leaving the visitors to talk to Roland and Mary in private.

Honey wanted to tell Roland and Mary how their son was taken.

Mary asked her, "Did the sheriff tell you what happened?"

Honey said, "No. I saw it taking place, like it was a dream, as I stood at the entrance to your drive. No doubt, the sheriff will tell you himself, if you ask him. Or you can ask Oliver himself. I know what I saw."

The following details were as recorded by Honey into her PC, after she took up residence in her room. She wisely chose not to relay all the sordid details to the parents, conveying to them only the less juicy parts.

Oliver had only been standing at the entrance of the driveway for a few minutes, when the nymph who had been waiting out of view for him to arrive rolled-up in her open-top 50s classic curbside cruiser. She stopped, gave him an appraising stare up and down, and made it clear she liked what she saw.

"Get in the front!" she demanded; she was used to getting her own way and was anxious to make up for lost time since her husband had died sniffily of an overdose.

For his part, he fancied her too, enormously, and decided to play hard to get. "No!" he answered.

She got out of the car, walked round the other side, and opened the rear passenger door, to invite him to get in. That way, she figured he'd feel safer with a bit of distance between them.

"Will you get in now?" she asked, tapping a foot impatiently.

"No I won't!" he repeated, slouching against the wooden fence surrounding the property. It was the lip turned up in a sneer, at an angle, that did it for her.

Losing her rag, she approached him on the run and caught him off-guard. He staggered after her as she pulled his arm, scattering the contents of his haversack across the driveway surface. It was as she leant over the seat and fell back deliberately, in a twisting motion, that she caught his nose with a whack of the elbow as he landed on top of her.

It wasn't intentional body contact, at least not of the type she hungered for, and resulted in a shriek of, "Don't bleed over my upholstery; hold your nose and bend over the road!" This was as she tried to remove the specks of blood from her tight silk blouse.

They drove away, with him holding his nose and his head back, sitting in the front. After a while, she felt his hand running up and down her bare, nearside leg, and noticed that his interest in her was growing. The car stopped three times on their way back to the Miller's home, with them driving into the woods each time to make best use of the bench seat in the back.

Afterwards, it was sex, sex, sex, roughly, as the song goes,

> *We did it in the bedroom,*
> *We did it in the hall,*

We did it in the bathroom,
Leaning up against the wall.
A-singin' do lolly, lolly Shicky bum, Shicky bum.

Oliver thought he was on route 66 for the rest of his life, and his recapture was a real blow to him. Sod the relatives, with their 'holier than thou' attitudes. He knew what he wanted, and boy was he getting it, with the hottest chick he had ever met. She wasn't much older than him either and was loaded. Whew!

Honey commented in the report that she could see things clearly from his point of view, and thought it best that the couple be left alone, for the lust to run its course.

As the evening wore on and just before they decided to part company, Honey got a glazed look in her eyes and surprised them with another reading.

She had been studying the wide, panoramic photo on the sideboard near her; it contained a faded group shot of a family wedding, and at its center were Roland and Mary, the happy couple, with her in a wedding dress. Now she had made a connection with the spirit world.

She asked the parents, "Do you know someone with the name 'Joshua'?"

Mary answered excitedly, "I had a great grandfather named Joshua. Why?"

"Because he's here with us now, and his wife Rachel is standing next to him. They want to give you some advice about Oliver."

Mary became emotional and pleaded, "Yes please, get them to communicate with us!"

Roland looked skeptical and asked Honey, "Get some more details first, to ensure they *are* her great grandparents."

Helen stared in the air for inspiration, before firing off a volley of questions provided by Roland, and relaying the answers to the couple, for verification. These questions included;

- Dates of birth and death of Joshua and his wife Mabel;

- Where they were born, lived and died;

- Where they first met;
- Schools attended;
- His occupation;
- How many children, of what sexes;
- What caused them to die.

Roland nodded solemnly and thanked her for the information she provided.

"Please continue," he urged her.

Honey relayed the gist of the message she was receiving, saying, "Joshua urges you to let Oliver to go back to his older lover. He needs to get the sex out of his system. He takes after me, so I should know. He could not care less what you think and that is the way he is.

"Keep fond memories of him in your hearts, of his upbringing. He will never play a willing part in your lives until he wants to, and his siblings let him. 'Forgive and forget' is the best motto I can muster. God bless."

Honey said, "They've gone now.

They left the house the following morning, after Matt and Walter had eaten all-American breakfasts that would have given Honey severe indigestion and windy puffs.

On their way back, Walter turned to face her within the confines of his seat belt; she was sitting across from him, behind the driver and reading a book.

He asked her, "Were you making up that story about Joshua and his wife Mabel?"

She retorted, "Would I ever! How did I know those details about them if I'd made it all up?"

Walter said suspiciously, "It would be almost impossible for anyone to check the veracity that far back, especially if they didn't write the details down!"

Honey asked him, "Then how did I know their names? Mary confirmed them, didn't she?"

The journey continued in silence.

Joe read the report in its totality and chuckled at the graphic descriptions it contained. Picking up the phone, he dialed the number of the sheriff who arrested Oliver and his abductor.

Explaining who he was, he requested, "I'd like you to let them go. It's for the best, since Oliver's at a vulnerable age and they think they're in love."

The sheriff replied, "Not a chance! He's a minor and she's a predator. I'm not risking letting her loose."

Joe: "His family are willing, and she's no threat to anyone else. He could be made for life, with her, and she'd make sure he gets a good education."

Sheriff: "I'm still not doing it. For two years she made me look a damned fool and I'm not about to give her a free pass."

Joe; "Is that your last word?"

Sheriff: "You betcha!"

Joe put the phone down and made a call to his director at the Bureau.

Within a few days, the sheriff had been booted out of office for neglect of duty. He had failed to search properly when Oliver first went missing, and left a prominent family in the community unnecessarily distressed for a long period of time.

As Joe said afterwards to Honey, "Hell, they were living next door to each other! He could have sent a car round and probably found the son laying on a lounger, on top of the widow!"

CASE CLOSED

A few months later, there was a twist in the tail. Oliver had learnt to strum the guitar, and had an instant hit with the record he'd released of him singing and gyrating like Elvis. It was a re-arrangement of *The Telephone Man* that Honey heard bawling out in her remote viewing. He was famous, and his parents were so proud of him.

MULTIPLE CASES
CATEGORY 1

CONVICTED KILLERS

When they set off, before waving goodbye to them, Joe was trying to inspire his partners, by giving them a parting line of rhyme:

"Off you go and fight the foe!"

Judging from their reaction, it was a tasteless, demotivating comment. They were about to be driven in the film studio's wagon to their first rendezvous at one of the biggest, toughest penitentiaries in the whole of the Unites States.

Their mission was to interview the most dangerous of inmates: the killers waiting on Death Row, and decide if they were guilty or not of the crimes for which they were locked up. In the former instance, if guilty they would be subjected to a novel form of remediable treatment.

They were to tackle this in pairs, with both psychics in each team using their telepathic powers and ability to communicate with the spirit world to confirm or deny the original sentences passed on the convicts.

If found not guilty, each prisoner would be evaluated to decide how to arrange his reintegration back into society.

If found guilty, Brains would use his 'Spectractor' to find and remove the evil spirit resident in each condemned man, thus rendering him harmless enough to be released back into society. Thereafter he would perform menial tasks on behalf of local communities. Literally, he would be brainless.

Alternatively, unless an objection was lodged, he could be drafted into the military as a 'Universal Soldier' and undertake suicidal combat missions on behalf of his country.

Joe had chosen Rose to partner Richard, and Honey to partner Chuck. They could choose between themselves who did each interview first.

The four couldn't fail to agree with Joe: this was an opportunity not to be missed. It would demonstrate their skills to the full, and give them influence far beyond the current restrictions of any psychic on the planet.

It was global penetration, and they could thank their benefactor, Joe for coming up with this brainwave.

They were sitting on rows of bench seats in the back of the wagon, with the film crew in the front cabin, on their way to jail, as Joe had promised when allocating this type of case.

"I'll thank him one day," Richard vowed to the others, "With a brain-frying burst of energy from the spectractor!"

"That's not the attitude to adopt," Chuck replied sternly. "It *is* the best use of us, as a resource, and the savings to the state will be enormous."

Honey reminded them, "Yeah, then we can move onto a host of other institutions, like care homes, hospitals and social departments, whatever, as Joe told us."

Rose commented, "I'm looking forward to it, whatever you think! It *is* a wonderful opportunity and will give us credibility, if we handle it properly."

Gloom descended on them, as the wagon stopped at the main gate. The rear door was opened from the outside, and a couple of armed guards stared in at them and checked their IDs. In a few minutes, they received permission to proceed to the signposted main wing, where the interviews were to take place.

As they walked through the corridors leading to the specially set-up interview rooms, they could see a queue forming of prisoners waiting to see them, and were given a rousing cheer and handclap, like it was the Oprah Winfrey Show they were on.

Those waiting looked intimidating; some of them were huge,

others looked as mad as hatters, virtually all had tattoos on their arms and some had them covering parts of their faces as well. One stuck his tongue out at Honey and showed her the piercings on his tongue. They clapped louder when the film crew came into sight carrying their equipment.

One old lag shouted, "We're gonna be on the tele!" to a renewed bout of clapping, accompanied by piercing whistling.

Chuck approached one of the guards and asked, "What are they doing here, queueing up like this?"

He smiled frostily and replied, They're waiting for treatment, to be administered by you."

Chuck nearly had a fit. "What! Who told you to do this?"

The guard said, "The Assistant Governor."

Richard, who was listening to the conversation, angrily intervened.

"Take these men back to their cells or we're leaving! Either we go to them, with bars separating us, and select who we're going to see, or you can face the music for doing things this way."

The guard stormed off to contact the man who had given him his instructions, while Richard and Chuck explained the situation to the others and the crew stacked their equipment on the floor. Richard took the opportunity to phone Joe and explain what was happening at the prison.

Within a few minutes the guard returned with a tall, skinny man in a grey suit and wearing round glasses. "What's up?" the newcomer asked.

Richard answered, "I've already told the guard we are not accepting this way of doing things. We do not want a queue forming outside our areas of work, when we are expected to make crucial decisions. They are already making a racket. I am asking you to send them back to their cells, and we will select who we want to see, **or** we leave."

The stranger spluttered indignantly, "You don't come here and tell us how to run our penitentiary! You can do what…" His phone ran and he was obliged to respond. Taking the call, he turned his back to them, whispering furiously. His hands were shaking as he put the phone back in his inside pocket, and the steps were heard of another official coming round a corner, with two guards marching behind him.

The new, middle-aged arrival, who was more round of face and body than his deputy and looked even more officious, said to the one who'd been on the phone, "I'm relieving you of duty, after direct intervention by the Bureau." He ordered the two guards following, "Take him to my office and get the prisoners back in their cells."

Speaking to the mediums direct, the new man smiled congenially and said, "I am the governor and was not aware of what my deputy had arranged. My apologies. Please continue and I will set matters up as you request."

Taking the four mediums to one side, he explained, "You have to try and understand the raw feelings of the staff here. They see what you are doing as a threat to their job security. It causes unnecessary friction internally, but I can see long-term benefits if you succeed. I'll make sure this doesn't happen again."

He inclined his head to them and walked away, to supervise the queue as it was disbanding.

Each pair of mediums entered their designated room, to find the spectractor sitting on its stand, in one corner, and a rectangular, wooden table in the center with two chairs one side of it, facing the door, and one chair the other side, for the prisoner to sit on.

As Honey and Chuck were sitting down in the two adjoining chairs, Brains came in and said, "Hi! My assistant is going next door, to sit with Richard and Rose."

A guard entered and addressed Chuck, "If you are ready, I'm here to escort you and your male companion to our top security cells, for inmate selection. We don't think it's appropriate for the ladies to go anywhere else while they're with us; they'd cause a commotion."

Chuck got up, grabbing an A4 notepad and pencil, and called next door for Richard to join him, so they could select who they wanted to see.

The cells they approached were within easy walking distance, and they saw the familiar faces of those who had queued earlier pressed against the bars as they slowly passed. Chuck pointed out those who he wanted to process, while the guard wrote down the surname and inmate number of each them. Likewise, Richard made his selection, while the prisoners cheered and jeered loudly as the three of them walked by.

By the end, they had collected 33 names, and Chuck asked if they could move onto the cells containing the next lowest category of prisoners; that was to say, killers not on Death Row.

He was getting fed up with the chanting of dirty lyrics being directed at him. Someone had started the ball rolling by shouting,

> *I wanna be your lover baby,*
> *I wanna be your man,*

but it got worse when they started chanting their version of *The Teddy Bear's Picnic:*

> *If you come down to my cell tonight*
> *I'll give you a BIG surprise.*
> *If you come down to my cell tonight*
> *You'll hardly believe your eyes!*

It only petered out because the inmates didn't know how the rest of it went.

They returned with more than 60 identities on the list, with the guards instructed to escort them in pairs to the interview rooms.

Matt supervised the camera and sound recorder being set up in each room, checking progress by walking between the two. Finally, he requested another chair to be brought into the room occupied by Chuck and Honey and sat down on it. "We're ready!" he said, folding his arms on his chest.

Chuck had agreed with Honey that she should start each interview, at least for part of the day, while he took his turn verifying her decision. They beckoned to the guard standing by the open door, with Chuck ordering him to, "Bring the first prisoner in."

He dwarfed Chuck in height, having to duck to get through the doorframe, and was as broad as the two mediums combined. Chuck estimated that he must have been about 7ft tall, and his beam end was so big that he instinctively asked him, "Do you want two chairs to sit on, to feel more comfortable?"

The guard nervously gripped the handle of his truncheon as the prisoner glowered, debating whether to flatten the person opposite. Catching them unaware, he leant forward and banged the table with the flat of his hand, making everyone jump. This gave the impression to the people next door that the impact was causing the others to ricochet upwards.

When he saw the reaction this had caused, he let out a deafening roar of laughter and sat down gently.

The guard took advantage of the change in mood and told the man, "Sit down, answer all questions honestly, and only speak when you are spoken to."

He went to shackle the man to the floor, but Honey intervened, saying, "That won't be necessary."

The guard stood back from the table with an impassive expression on his face, and said, "I'll be here if you need me."

Chuck had already arched his back, to get out of reach of the prisoner. It was obvious to him that the man had lightning-fast reflexes and he might need to act quickly in self-defense.

Honey looked at the notes the guard placed in front of her and frowned. "This says your name is *Sonny Liston*." she said. "Surely not?"

He looked at her and grinned. "I got it changed by deed poll."

She studied his photo in the file and then stared into his liquid brown eyes; he didn't blink once or change his amused mask of an expression.

She commented, without removing her stare, "You don't look like the type of man who enjoys killing, or who is as capable of slaughtering as many innocent women and children as you have. Did you bother to tell your defense team that you did it out of revenge? That you did it because a cartel murdered your family first?

He looked back at her, with tears welling up in his eyes, and replied, "I haven't told anyone that, ever! What would have been the point of telling them? It wouldn't make any difference anyway. I'm glad I did it and that's a fact! Get this over with, please! I'm fed up with this useless way of life."

Honey looked at Chuck and whispered, "Over to you."

Chuck continued, "I've looked into the background facts" - meaning that he'd scrutinized Sonny's memories - "and agree that it was cruel to have your family wiped out by drug runners, but you shouldn't have taken revenge like you did. Now you must pay the penalty. You have two options but I won't tell you the second one unless you ask for it.

"My preference is for you to have your bad memories erased, and to be enrolled in the US army as a 'Universal Soldier', where you will be trained as a special operative to neutralize the cartels that still operate. The world will be a better place without them."

Sonny gave a bitter laugh, saying, "So that I have the chance to go on killing?"

He reflected before deciding, "At least, it will be the pigs who run these criminal gangs that I exterminate! Add a note to my file saying that I only want to get those who run the cartels and *not* the innocents, and I'm your man. Any money I get is to be paid to my parents."

Chuck added the note to the file and asked Sonny to sign and date the Acceptance Section of the Process Form, before saying to Brains, "Do it now!"

The spectractor was switched on, the lens was pointed at the big man, and Brains twirled a set of knobs to select the correct range of frequencies and bring them into sharp relief. "Come and look at this," he asked the two mediums, who gathered around him to peer at his screen.

Two main auras were visible; the central one around his head and shoulders being grey in color, and a larger, background one being almost black. He pressed a red button to begin oscillating the auras and when they separated into two distinct entities, he released it.

Focusing on the black aura, he looked at the two mediums for approval, and when they both said 'yes', he pressed a black button and the aura disappeared; they half-expected this action to be accompanied by a 'plop', but no sound was heard.

His final act was to seek the original grey aura; when he did, he cried out, "Would you believe this!" There in front of them was a clearly defined light green aura.

"I never expected that," he said, the image reflecting off his glasses. "This is not a 'husk' of a man we are witnessing, but the birth of a new spirit in an adult. Perhaps this person will not become the 'Zomboid' we were expecting to see, but a basic human untainted by any personality defects. This is far a better result than I hoped to achieve!"

"We'll see how the others we've yet to process turn out," said Honey, sitting back down, as the guard escorted 'Sonny' out of the room.

She asked Brains, "Could you add your recent comments to the Process Form and sign and date it?" He nodded, completed the details and handed it to Chuck, who added his signature and date.

"Where are you taking him?" Chuck asked the guard.

"To a holding area, where he can wait for the others you've got to deal with today."

With a newly found, sympathetic smile, the guard added, "He won't be going back to his cell, ever again!"

Chuck smiled back, and said, "Kindly ask for the next prisoner to be sent in." He placed the completed file in the Out tray.

The next prisoner to arrive was tall, slim, grey-headed, bespectacled and cold of countenance. His appearance exactly matched his profile, which made Honey shiver. She closed the file hurriedly and focused on reading his inner thoughts; what she saw were unpleasant in the extreme.

"You are one cold, unfeeling bastard, aren't you?" she said unemotionally. He didn't react at all.

She asked, "Why have you put the families of your victims through the agony of having to go repeatedly back into court? Why did you make them relive their ordeal as you challenged the validity of your sentence on technicalities? You know what you did, so did it add to your pleasure by making them suffer?"

He shrugged, looked away from her unflinching gaze, and said, "I want to live as long as I can, that's all."

Chuck added his voice, "That's because you're afraid of going to Hell. Look back at what you did: you raped, tortured and murdered five beautiful young women, without remorse. In their last moment on earth, you wrapped them up like mummies and bludgeoned them to death when they were conscious. No wonder you're afraid of your own death."

Honey concluded, "You've admitted to doing it, now you'll pay for your sins." With a resigned voice, she said, "Brains do it now!"

The prisoner closed his eyes and sat there motionless.

Brains started the spectractor, and the others gathered silently around him. This time, there was only one black aura visible, and Brains oscillated it; as his final act, he erased it. When he looked for any other aura that might be surrounding the man's upper half, there was only the faintest trace of a green aura to be found.

Brains sighed, and commented, "Whatever spirit is left in him is representative of what I expected to find. The body will function at the basic, zomboid level, controlling his basic bodily functions and movements, and will use his residual mental faculties to perform menial tasks.

"He will have no personality, thank goodness. His true spirit no longer exists."

Chuck ordered the guard, "Take him away to the medical unit, for castration, before transfer to the holding area. Please arrange for the next prisoner to be sent into us."

All three signed and added relevant comments to the Process Form and placed it in the case file. Brains dumped it disgustedly in the Out tray.

Meanwhile, Rose and Richard were tackling their caseload in a similar fashion.

After seeing the giant of a man confronting Honey and Chuck, they were glad when their first prisoner was led into their room.

Suddenly, they heard the giant net door bang the table with his hand, and that made them jump. It was probably their reaction that made him laugh loudly.

In contrast, this man was far less daunting in size, but even less prepossessing. His head was covered in crudely designed death's head tattoos, giving him a satanic appearance that the long expired Alice Cooper would possibly have envied. The rolled-up shirtsleeves revealed a medley of primitive curses on scrolls that he probably didn't understand.

In spite of the table width that separated the mediums from him, he exuded a strong body odor that made their noses wrinkle. He was repulsive and repellent, and Rose wished that she'd brought with her a perfumed hanky.

He had a habit of chewing, but there was no sign of anything to chew in his opening and closing mouth.

Rose had chosen to take the lead, and asked him, "What's that you've got in your mouth?"

"Nothing," he replied, "it's a habit I've got, chewing. I like it."

"Well kindly stop doing it!" she said crossly. "It makes you look like a camel!"

"Nope!" he said, baring an incomplete set of uneven, brown teeth, and breathing his stale breath in her direction. "Make me!"

Richard decided to take over and get some pace into the session. "Did you really enjoy killing those kids you fathered" Did you have no feelings of love from them when you burnt them alive?"

He made a gesture of no understandable significance with his hands and eyebrows, hoping to garner their sympathy, saying, "Didn't mean to. It was an accident."

Rose stared at his eyes, finding them empty of any sympathy or comprehension. "You have no love or feelings for anyone. You killed to get insurance money. There is no point in you serving any more time in prison, or be released afterwards. What do you think, Richard?"

"I think exactly the same. There is a better way than prison to make you useful to the community. Over to you, Igor!" Igor was the name they'd given to Brain's assistant on this mission, and he was eager to get on with his task.

As demonstrated by his boss, he started his spectractor, and focused the lens on the indifferent and still chewing prisoner while the two mediums completed the Process Form. He turned the dials to search for the frequencies of the auras surrounding the target prisoner, and invited them to join him.

Rose exclaimed, "Ooo, it's all black! Get rid of it!"

"I agree! Do it!" Richard affirmed, so Igor pressed the black button to comply.

The aura was erased immediately, and Igor searched the frequencies until a faint green version displayed.

"That I recognize!" he exclaimed, "It's associated with a typical Zomboid."

Richard ordered the guard, "Take him away, for castration, before transfer to the holding area. Please arrange for the next prisoner to be sent into us."

At least the prisoner had stopped chewing.

The second one to enter looked reasonably normal. He had no embellishments visible on his face or arms, and sported a 'short back and sides' haircut with a single parting to one side. He sat down, said, "How'd you do?" then relaxed with one knee crossed over the other, before adding, "I've been looking forward to this!" whilst beaming at them with pleasure.

Rose looked at his photo, read the case file briefly, and reached over the table to touch his hand. He gave a start as if he had felt an electric discharge, and she withdrew her hand hesitantly.

"You're innocent; why are you here?" she asked, as she and Richard studied him with increased intensity.

"Thank you!" he said, his lips quivering and eyes watering. "You've no idea how long I've been waiting for someone to say that to me!"

"What's your story?" Richard asked him.

The prisoner, who shall be identified as Spencer, stated that he had been alone with his wife, in a motel room on the second floor, when a volley of shots rang out and killed her instantly. The police identified they had been fired from a military-issue powerful rifle that used bullets capable of penetrating the walls of the motel.

The couple were on their way to a conference 500 miles away from their home on the west coast, and had stopped midway, to break the journey.

Only their room had been hit, and suspicion fell on the husband. This was reinforced when a witness came forward, testifying that the husband had paid him to kill the wife. As a result of the coast to coast publicity that the case attracted, a second person came forward and corroborated the testimony given by the first person.

All of this had been hotly denied by Spencer, claiming that he didn't know or ever had any contact with either person.

The husband was arrested on the charge of murder, solely on the basis of the evidence of the two testimonies, with nothing else to substantiate their claims. By a majority jury decision, he was sentenced to death, and had been on death row for 10 years as appeal after appeal was lodged, and the witnesses vanished.

He was still in prison, and continued being detained on suspicion that he had disposed of the witnesses, to get his sentence overturned.

Rose and Richard were stunned by the reality of the prisoner's circumstances. They conferred together as they researched the case, based on the details listed in the notes and the descriptions of the witnesses.

"It's lucky that we have photos and descriptions of the witnesses," Richard said, as they both examined them and the accompanying descriptions of the two men. These notes had been compiled during a nationwide search for them.

"I'm not accepting this situation!" Richard said angrily. "We've got to get him out of here!"

Rose suggested, "Put him in front of the spectractor, and see what he looks like, to confirm his story in accordance with our guidelines."

An inspection by Igor showed an aura that was entirely normal, and contained no trace of bad deeds having been performed.

Rose declared, "You're as clean as a whistle!" and told the guard, "Please take him out to the holding area, while we complete the Process Form and Discharge Permit."

Richard added, "Next case please!"

The next prisoner to enter was a twitchy individual of no real merit. He looked like a nobody, who no one would take any notice of if he passed them in the street.

His case file said otherwise; Rose looked at the first few lines and slammed the case file shut. It said that he was a cannibal who had killed his male victims like animals, dismembered them and boiled the body parts in a large saucepan.

She looked into his eyes, searched his memory banks, and found it to be a disgusting revelation. She and Richard checked the notes and found them to be a true and accurate account of what had been done.

"Hell, I feel like vomiting!" she said. "He ate them as well, claiming they taste like pork! What a monster!"

They completed their parts of the Process Form and instructed Igor, "Please go ahead!"

Igor complied, erasing the black aura without delay and handed the docile prisoner over to the guard, with the normal instructions for him to follow.

Richard leaned back in his chair to take a coffee break, and ruminated on their task. "I've been contemplating what we've got in front of us. At the rate of process we look like achieving, each team can go through one case every 15 minutes; multiply that by 2 and we have a total of 8 per hour. In an 8-hour work period, we can deal with 64 cases. That's at least 60 per day, allowing for slippage!

"Do you realize, Rose, that we will have cleared Death Row of inmates, and will be well on our way to clearing the prison of killers in less than two days?"

Rose did the sums herself, and said in reply, "We'd better start refining things to process those convicts who have committed lesser offences. We need to speak to Joe and get guidance."

As the workload continued to be tackled during the mentally arduous day, they had interesting feedback from the governor, who spoke to them personally.

"The bureau has investigated the background to the crime allegedly perpetrated by Spencer. An alternative explanation has emerged; immediately below the room occupied by Spencer and his wife, there was a drug gang in residence and they confessed that they might have been the intended target.

"They substantiated this by handing over the names of the two witnesses, who have been traced and are still alive. It was a set-up, by a rival gang, to distract the police from an attempted takeover of their district."

CONVICTED KILLERS PART TWO

THE ATONEMENT CENTER

"Where are we staying?" Honey asked, stretching her lithesome limbs to ease the aching inside her.

Chuck looked at her briefly, up and down, and commiserated, "I know how you feel. We've been using our brains most of the working day; it takes its toll on the body, sitting immobile for long periods." He raised his arms in a direct line above his head, straightened his back and stretched his muscles before giving an involuntary shiver. "That's better!" he said, sneaking another look at Honey.

Richard joined in. "Yeah, we'll have to ensure we take regular breaks between seeing people. My back is aching. I'll speak to Joe and tell him we need to pace ourselves, otherwise our health will suffer. 63 cases we processed today and we made great progress."

Rose was nodding off, so they quietened down, to let her rest.

Richard whispered to the others, "She's been fantastic. Her focus is superb."

He leant forward and asked the man at the wagon wheel, "Where are we heading?"

Until now, Richard hadn't bothered with anything or anyone surrounding his immediate circle, being all pooped out.

It was Jake, and Richard was surprised to see him lounging nonchalantly in his bucket seat, reading an ebook. He had his feet raised on the dashboard and was clearly making no effort to check on the controls.

"I don't know," he replied; "I'm too knackered to bother looking."

Richard looked at him and asked, "When did the studio have the wagon converted to self-drive?"

"Months ago," he replied, continuing to read. "Listen to the GPS if you're interested in our destination."

In other words, shut up.

The machine was droning out information, at a low level, and Richard couldn't fully hear what it was telling them, from the rear end of the vehicle. He looked at his watch and noticed that they'd been travelling for 25 minutes. "I'll wait and see," he decided. "Qué sera, sera!"

His body clock must have been telling him they were fast approaching where they'd be staying that night, like a dog recognizes his owner coming home from miles away. Within 5 minutes, they stopped at a booth with barriers blocking both lanes of the road they'd recently turned into.

Jake sat upright and opened his window, while the female security guard opened the door of her booth and walked up to him, after recording the car registration on the windscreen with her security mobile.

She peered in and looked at the occupants, scanning them with her face recognition app. They were holding up their ID cards and she scanned those too, scurrying back to the booth while her two male companions ensured her safe return. She gave a wave and they raised the bar with panels underneath, their side of the road, to let them through.

In semi darkness, as Honey peered out at the estate they were passing through, she remarked, "Everything is brand new here. I can see workmen putting the finishing touches to the interiors of the properties." The others joined in looking, and noticed that most of them had bare electric cables hanging from the porch ceilings, while the lights inside were illuminating painters and decorators hard at work.

Rose stirred, having heard the comments being made, and asked, "Where are we, are we near the hotel?"

Richard replied, "It's coming up shortly."

They passed a small brightly lit covered shopping mall, with a handful of people walking around doing 'window shopping'. "It's not fully open," Rose remarked. "What is this place?"

No one answered; they were unfamiliar with it as well. In minutes, conveniently close to the mall, they drew into an empty car park, and stopped close to the heavy looking, black polished double doors fronting their destination. It was a cream painted two-storey building with sash windows and constructed in the style of traditional 19th century buildings that fronted boulevards in cities like Boston.

"This looks nice," said Rose admiringly, "It's a boutique hotel if I'm not mistaken."

Out of character for this style of construction, the doors weren't hinged but slid wide apart, allowing them to enter four abreast. They walked into a substantial reception hall, to appreciate the ambience. The lower half of every wall was covered in in oak panels with a dado rail above. Each corresponding top half was covered in vertically striped wallpaper, in restful pastel shades of green and yellow.

There were deep upholstered Chesterfield two seater sofas sprinkled around, and classical music was being fed into the area from hidden speakers. The front of the half-moon reception desk was covered in matching oak panels, and the counter top was made of molded marble. Behind it was a young woman, who smiled and invited them to approach her. She was wearing a two-toned grey outfit and looked exceptionally smart and well groomed.

She trilled nasally, "Welcome to our home from home. My name is Marsha and you must be the guests we were expecting. If you could each place your ID card consecutively on this glass panel, that will complete our booking-in procedure."

"Ladies first," Jake said, and they took it in turns to comply, adding their thumbprint when requested by Marsha.

After they had finished, she delicately pressed an old-fashioned Dome bell and advised them, "A porter will be with you momentarily."

Chuck muttered to Honey, "I *hate* that word *momentarily*! It is so misused!" She showed her scorn by pouting at him and mouthing the words, "*Aw, diddums!*"

A smartly dressed porter, with a round, flat hat on his head, soon came out of a door labelled 'Staff Only' and walked towards them. Richard and Rose stood there gaping; it was the same convict that they'd processed at the start of the day! He was behaving respectfully for the first time, and standing there diffidently, waiting to take their baggage.

Rose whispered, "He looks ridiculous with that hat on his head."

It was true, when one took into account the hideous, death's head tattoos on his face.

Richard asked him suspiciously, "How did you get here?"

The ex-con replied with a polite smile, "By bus, sir."

Richard said, "Don't be funny. I'll rephrase that question: *what* are you doing here?"

Without a trace of sarcasm, the ex-con replied, "Waiting to take you to your rooms, sir."

Out of the 'Staff Only' door hurried another man, dressed in a two-tone grey suit, charcoal grey shirt with a Windsor-knotted crimson red tie, and shiny black shoes on his black socked feet. He interposed himself between Richard and the porter, saying politely, "Please don't interrogate our staff member, sir; he's only started today, and he's – how to put it? – somewhat restricted in his capabilities."

Chuck pulled Richard's sleeve and whispered to him, "You're talking to one of the guards who worked with us today. Don't you recognize him?"

Richard looked at him more closely and exclaimed, "Lord, yes!"

The ex-guard said in a hushed tone, "Okay, so you know who I am! That's good; we're being re-deployed to ensure that the ex-prisoners receive on-the-job training, for their new roles in life. It's part of the 'Atonement Program.'" He looked at him pleadingly and begged, "Please don't give me grief!"

"Okay," Richard agreed, and the newly appointed 'Trainee Training Supervisor' fetched another ex-con to act as porter 2. He instructed him to, "Get a four-wheeled trolley from the luggage room, load the pile of luggage on it, and push the loaded trolley after the group."

It took two trips to ascend in the elevator, and they all gathered on the floor above while the trainee porter, ex-con 1, studied the cards he was holding, trying to match them to the intended occupants.

Honey walked over to help him, and he watched bewildered as she snatched them from him. Thumbing through the cards impatiently, she selected her own, and handed it to him, saying, "Follow me."

She led the way to her room first, which happened to be the nearest as far as she was concerned. She watched as the porter studied the card from all angles, before instructing him impatiently, "Place it any way up, and either side. It should work any way round."

By this time, he had remembered what he had been taught to do with it, and he held it shakily against the matching outline, traced waist-high in the door.

The light above this outline went green. He looked at her with a grateful smile as the door swung open, and she entered. Then she remembered her travel bag, and went back out. She beckoned the other trainee porter – ex-con 2 – to push the luggage trolley to her.

The others stepped back hastily, to avoid being skittled-over as trainee porter 2 pushed the trolley ahead in a straight line, in her general direction. Rather than wait, when it came within reach, she grabbed her bag off it and hurried back into her room.

Before the door had a chance to close, she went out momentarily, slapped the remaining room cards in the immobile hand of the first trainee porter, and said to the others in the group, "You can sort yourselves out!" Then she pushed the closing door hard, to help it slam shut.

The other guests stood there nonplussed, looking as unsure as the two porters.

Honey threw herself on the comfortable four-poster bed, and cursed her luck, saying. "Welcome to the Adams Family residence!"

She allowed herself a brief period of relaxation, laying on her back in a trance, before leaping to her feet, stripping off her day clothes, and taking hot, cold and hot showers in sequence, to invigorate her circulation. Wrapping herself in the thick, cotton toweling robe hanging by the walk-in shower, she padded her body dry and unpacked her bag.

Within 15 minutes, she was dressed and ready to go downstairs and meet her fellow guests for the evening meal; it was precisely the time agreed. They were waiting for her as she walked cautiously down the main stairs in high-heeled shoes, drawing admiring stares from the film crew and two male mediums.

Oblivious to their attention, she breezed past them, saying, "I'm hungry, let's eat!" and headed towards the dining room.

They stood by the entrance, waiting to be seated, and checked the overall appearance of the room. It was more Spartan than Honey had hoped to find, with the furnishings, being … Honey didn't know how best to describe it all, and then the most apt description came to mind: homely! The walls, ceramic floor tiles, laid tables and wooden chairs looked the sort of things she would expect to find in a typical, family home for normal people with no great aspirations in their lives.

Richard was blunter in his assessment, and moaned, "Jeez, what a dump! This place is all fur coat and no knickers!"

Chuck was more moderate in his comments, but clearly felt the same, and said, "The outside is better than the inside, that's for sure! I wonder why?"

Rose said, "Look more closely; study the people already being fed; the answer is staring you in the face."

Sitting in groups at a few of the tables were old people in groups of two, three and four, attentively helped by smartly dressed waiters. These 'guests' were all pensioners, with limited mobility, and were being fed with spoons. Some had plastic baby bibs resting on their chests, into which food was dropping as it failed to lodge in their opening mouths.

The onlookers increasingly recognized the true identities of the waiters, as they got fed up waiting and walked further into the room.

Rose said, "See what I mean? Those are the prisoners we processed earlier."

At that moment, a few ex-prison guards dressed as Training Supervisors, walked into the room, to supervise activities.

"I get it!" Honey exclaimed. "We're slap in the middle of the biggest upheaval of the prison service in its history!

Chuck said, "Yes, and we are the instigators of all of this. However, is it reasonable for us to have to live with our work? Couldn't we have been taken to a decent hotel, instead of being put up in an old people's care home?"

A familiar voice was heard behind them. "Not good enough for you, is it? Too down-market for your taste, is it? You insisted on staying and threatened to leave if you couldn't do things your way. We have to live with our work, morning, noon and night; why shouldn't you as well?"

They turned round slowly, to face the Assistant Governor they had confronted that morning. He seemed to be somber, instead of sneering and patronizing in his attitude. Rose felt compassion for him, and said, "I feel sorry now, for us giving you the wrong impression. We *will* go and sit down with everyone else, to see what it's like to stay at this new facility. Everyone should do it, and learn a lesson in humility."

Chuck said, "Come on, let's go and pull some tables together. Would you like to join us?"

The Assistant Governor responded, "Thanks, but I've already eaten here, otherwise I would." He smiled for the first time, and wished them well before departing.

Honey looked at his back as he left, and stated, "Actually, he's a nice person, with no sharp edges to his personality. His mother is in here too, as it happens.

"Perhaps, Richard, you should be less abrasive and selfish when you develop relationships." He blushed red in embarrassment, as the group went silent at this public criticism of him. It had hit home.

The ex-con fledgling waiters struggled at first, until the ex-guards handed round menus, to take their orders. In clockwise sequence, they each wrote down on a single notepad, in capital letters, what they wanted for courses 1 and 2 and for final course 3, with soft drinks. To their surprise, they were also offered wine and beer, and used the same routine to order their alcohol.

Things went relatively smoothly after that, although they did spring up from the meal table quite a few times, to avoid trays being tilted and things dropped.

Honey was pleased with the simple but well prepared, abundant choices of courses and commented, "Do you know, this is absolutely delicious! I feel like congratulating the cooks who prepared all of this."

She mentioned her views to one of the ex-guards, who told her, "I'm not surprised, the man who put all of this together is a pupil of Jamie Oliver, who was famous for his expertise with cooking for the masses. Thank you for your praise."

After the meal, they went outside for a stroll. Rose, observant as always, said, "Look at all the cars passing; they're mostly small, and silent. Yes, look now!" She pointed at the road, where a short convoy of identical vehicles was swishing by, with the only noise coming from their tires.

"Isn't this exciting!" she remarked. "This is a new era, ushering in changes that we wouldn't have dreamt of a short time ago. It won't be much longer before wheels become obsolete and cars float along, perhaps even fly as well!"

A good night's sleep was enjoyed by all, in rooms that were of a four star standard, especially for a residential care home destined for pensioners. As Matt commented, "Add personal knickknacks, and the people who stay here, God bless them, will enjoy the rest of their lives to the full."

Whilst they were sitting eating at their breakfast table, they noticed the Assistant Governor sitting alone with an old lady, spoon-feeding her tenderly. Rose went over and sat with them for a few minutes chatting; he nodded as he replied, and she came back to inform the rest of the group, "He'll be over, after he's finished helping his mother."

They had all finished using the self-service breakfast facilities, when he joined them.

"I'm sorry we got off to a bad start. May I introduce myself properly? My name is Jeb Clarkson and I'm spearheading the changeover from the penitentiary to this complex, while the governor stays there for the interim period, until it is emptied.

"When this task is completed, he will retire, and the whole project will rollover to another location and be repeated."

Richard asked him, "Could you tell us the full picture? When we came here, our briefing was restricted to processing the prisoners. Perhaps our boss, Joe Fraser, chose to let us find out the rest for ourselves."

Jeb replied, "Oh yes, I've got to know Joe reasonably well, and that is the type of thing he'd expect from you, as mediums."

Rose commented shyly, "We don't always try and enter peoples' heads; it would be an invasion of their privacy."

Honey pitched in, "That's true! I tend to switch off when I'm not working. I'll tell him that, when we go back at the end of the first five days we spend here."

Chuck asked, "What is the end game? I'd love to know myself."

Jeb explained matters. "This care home is meant to impress, from the time that future residents and their families, or carers, set first set sight on it. Hospices will close and those who go to them, in their final days, will come here instead.

"The hospice staff will transfer to this place to supervise their terminally ill patients, and help oversee the trainee supervisors; these are the ex-guards who've joined us from the penitentiary. Their role is to monitor the ex-cons who you processed and are now of limited intelligence and devoid of personalities. You refer to them as 'zomboids'.

"The longer-term objective is to provide the so-called 'zomboids' with non-criminal personalities and higher IQs. In the meantime, security of the complex has to be very high, giving them less risk of being murdered by anyone who is seeking revenge for their past actions.

"Do you understand what I am telling you?"

They all nodded, and Honey stated, "Yes. They have no recollection of past events. Killing the murderers would be of no practical benefit to anyone."

Jake asked, "Who are the houses and flats intended for?"

Jeb answered, "Mainly, they are earmarked for all the managers, supervisors and other personnel, plus their families. They will also be reserved for ex-cons who will work in the shopping mall, and for those who will eventually be reintegrated into the broader community outside.

"I should add that all the buildings here are constructed with steel frames and bricks, and can withstand winds of over 200 miles per hour."

Walter asked, "How is it intended to process prisoners who have been convicted of lesser offences? As I see it, the spectractor is only capable of processing the dregs of society."

Chuck intervened. "I think I know the answer; we processed one prisoner whose 'aura' was found to be borderline; I'm referring to 'Sonny Liston'. Brains made some adjustments to his spectractor, and Sonny was left with an 'aura' that showed an enhanced level of basic intelligence. He was put onto the Universal Soldier Training Program. No doubt he will be monitored."

Jeb agreed and checked his watch, concluding, "I could go on, but I think you should ask Joe to give an update next time you speak to him."

Richard checked his watch too and asked for the session to end. "Yes Jeb, we've got to get back to work as well. Thanks for the briefing and we hope to see more of you before we leave in four days' time."

They bade each other farewell and went their separate ways. As the group of mediums and the film crew walked through the reception area, Honey's attention was drawn to a large framed plaque on the wall by the elevators. She decided, "*I'll have a look at that later.*"

There was a change in emphasis during this second day. They had completely processed all the long-term inmates who were guilty of murder, and called a halt while they pondered how best to deal with the next category of inmates, who were also serving long terms of incarceration.

Amongst themselves, they agreed that they would like to focus on prisoners who were serving 10 year+ minimum sentences, without parole, for committing acts of bodily violence and mental torture.

However, after consultation with the governor, they agreed to abide by the official categories. In future, they would be escorted past cells containing the next lower category of inmates. There they would apply telepathy to select individuals according to what was stored in their minds and evidenced by their deeds.

Brains gave them good news to help speed things along, "A straightforward adjustment has made the spectractor more flexible. I am now able to identify auras associated with individuals who suffer from lesser spiritual shortcomings."

Chuck asked, "How does that affect us?"

Brains explained, "It means you only have to supervise the streaming of inmates, for access to different types of correctional facilities. For example, you can enroll specialists to help identify if persistent, bad behavior has a root cause in the brain, or is based on the chemicals circulating in the body."

Chuck saw the light, "Ah, this opens up whole new disciplines for after-care! For example, an offender can be sent for a magnetic resonance brain scan, which these days can pinpoint *and* correct all manner of irregularities."

Rose added her views, "Comprehensive blood and urine tests can also be taken, to make sure that all the body organs are functioning correctly, the diet is correct, and there are no abnormalities occurring that would have an impact on behavior. It would also find any evidence of 'mind-bending' substance abuse."

Honey reached for her mobile, saying, "I'm going to ask Joe if he can arrange emergency funding for these extra facilities, while we're here."

"No need for that," Brains said, intercepting her. "I've asked already, it's been agreed, and teams of specialist staff are being assembled. Our benefactor has deep pockets, and has been recruiting hospital staff for years."

Honey mused, "He seems to anticipate our every move. I wonder who he is?"

A voice sounded in her head, "*You'll find out soon enough!*"

Rose looked startled, and said, "I heard that too!"

This new approach enabled them to process the inmates more

rapidly, almost at breakneck speed. Individually, as each medium stood in front of a prison cell, its door was opened by one of the accompanying guards, and key decisions made on the fate of the individuals inside.

Unusually, the occupants were silent; word had got round what was taking place, and they were anxious to know what would happen to them.

The less fortunate were considered to be those who were taken away for processing by the dreaded spectractor. Commiserations were mumbled to them as they parted company, and those who remained breathed sighs of relief, knowing that they were almost certain to receive beneficial check-ups and, possibly, remedial treatment.

It was a good sign for the mediums, who were normally ostracized by society, since they were now regarded as angels of mercy. Everyone in the penitentiary could see that harsh, mind-numbing punishment was being substituted with behavioral correction.

The only inmates taken to the holding area were the oddball cases processed by the spectractor, on full power. Those remaining were content to stay in their cells, with the doors left open so everyone could socialize freely.

It would also help the staff to monitor and weed-out any residual troublemakers. Fortunately, nothing to upset the tranquil atmosphere was reported, and the positive reputations that the mediums had acquired remained unsullied.

That second evening, when the group returned to the care home and walked through reception, Honey remembered the wall plaque and went over to study it.

It stated in gold letters,

'THIS EDIFICE IS DEDICATED TO OUR BENEFACTOR, THOMAS BECKON, WHOSE MUNIFICENCE KNOWS NO BOUNDARIES.'

She said to herself, "*That's narrowed it down. I wonder who Thomas*

Beckon is?"

By the end of the five-day mission, each medium had mainly dealt with an average of 12 inmates per hour, for 8 hours, leading to a rounded total for the four of them of 380 cases. They achieved an actual total over the ultimate four days of 1403 inmates, with allowance for the harder cases that had to be processed by the spectractor.

In theory, when the specialist medical teams and laboratories cleared the existing backlog of inmates, more than half the penitentiary would be empty. They and the staff would be taking up temporary residence in the secure, well-protected Atonement Center in the nearby countryside and learning new, legitimate ways of earning a living.

Richard yawned as he estimated, "We'll have helped to empty this forbidding dump in record time, possibly by the end of next week. Roll on the next assignment!"

On their way back, Jake informed his passengers, "Joe has asked that you attend an urgent meeting with him, at 7:30am on Monday, before we head back here."

LOOSE ENDS GET TIED

The wagon collected the four mediums from their homes and dropped them outside the headquarters of The Deaduction Agency. They were expecting to find it as they had left it, but the building was covered in scaffolding, and there were many workers milling around, starting work somewhere inside.

They wondered what was going on, but when they trooped inside and walked upstairs, they could see that the activity was confined to the floors above and did not affect them.

Joe was feeling chipper; that much was evident as they entered and went into his room. The mediums themselves were feeling buoyant as well, after a restful weekend.

Honey trailed behind as the others entered Joe's room, and mischievously went further along the corridor, to enter Richard's room. Knowing how punctilious he was about the placement of his furniture, she pulled one of the chairs away from his conference table and left it sticking out at an angle.

On her way back to catch up with the others, she did the same to a chair in Chuck's room, guessing it would make Richard react; she was sure he would notice.

"Ah, there you are!" Joe said as he saw her and smiled pleasantly. "Take a chair!"

She looked at him suspiciously, wondering if he had noticed her earlier, but a quick scan of his thoughts showed the comment was innocent.

He commenced the briefing by announcing, "You will have noticed that modifications are being made to the other floors in this building. That is because the Bureau has taken possession of them on our behalf. We are expanding!"

The others looked at each other in surprise, wondering what else was coming.

"Assuming you finish your current mission early, next week we would like you to begin selection of eight more mediums, to continue our program of spearheading the reforms of the prison service, nationwide."

Richard relayed his views silently to the others. "*This is getting interesting! When the mice were away, the cats did play!*"

"It is important that you select and train these recruits personally, since they will report to you as assistant partners. See, we are top heavy already! However, it will be a 'flat' organization structure, with only three levels internally."

Chuck joined in the fun and sent his own message. "*Hey hey, I sense a bonus coming up!*" The two women smiled and kept their counsel.

"Jeb told me that you have been asking questions, and I think there is only one thing left for resolution: how far do we go beyond the prison service? The answer is this: we have approval to go into young offenders' institutions, social care services, policing and schools. We want to nip anti-social behavior in the bud, by working with those professions that inter-relate with youngsters and fledgling adults.

"Implants to regularize emotions are beginning to improve behavior, by reducing the aggression and hatred that some types of personalities feel more than others. This type of approach has, so I am informed, been conducted for a long time and is altering the components of our DNA for the better, over the longer term."

Richard intervened and stated, "Joe, that admission that would cause outrage if it was publicly admitted."

He smiled and said, "Maybe, maybe not. It depends on how effective the implants are proving to be. Much of the population has accepted candid statements on things, like UFOs and aliens, and star wars weapons as reality, and presidential speeches made about them in the United Nations are generally ignored.

"No one fled their houses, like they did when Orson Wells made a spoof radio announcement that Martians had landed, and were sweeping across the country slaughtering the masses."

He checked his watch and concluded, "There is one last item on the agenda: we have all been invited to attend a Hollywood style glitzy gathering to be held by the film studio that employs Jake, Matt and Walter.

"It is re-christening itself, '*FLIEZ ON THE WALL*', and is promising it will be a must-attend red carpet affair. It will be staged on Saturday, in two weeks' time, and will introduce a new rock star to the world, who goes by the name of *Oliver Twist*. I'm looking forward to seeing this young man."

Honey thought, "*He sounds familiar!*"

Noticing that Richard had made a beeline for his office, she held back until the others had left the meeting, while Joe went to reception to speak to Alison. She pretended to be pre-occupied looking at paperwork until all of her companions had rushed out to board the wagon. Then she swiftly made her way to Richard's office at the far end of the corridor, noting with a smirk that all the chairs in there were in their original, symmetrically identical positions.

As she was exiting, it interested her to see that Richard had also straightened the chair she had re-positioned in Chuck's room. She wondered, "*Is he jealous of Chuck?*"

To her embarrassment, she saw that Chuck had decided to return; he ignored her as he strolled past, entered his room and pulled the chair back out, to conform with the angle at which she had set it! She stood there amazed at this puzzling behavior, as he sauntered back towards the stairs, showing no sign of recognition, and disappeared out of view.

"Well I never!" she exclaimed, and raced after him to board the wagon, for the journey to begin. She chose the empty bench seat next to him, staring into space with her heart pounding, and reflecting on her personal relationships. Richard was sitting behind them, with a space next to him that she had failed to see.

She felt conscious of him staring at her, which was probably the reason why she and Chuck failed to strike up a conversation during the journey.

She pondered the situation. "*Someone has been reading someone else's mind. How long has this been going on? Are they both at it?"*

Now that the worst offenders had been removed from the penitentiary, the remaining inmates were enjoying a more relaxed atmosphere. They could wander freely within their wings of the prison, mix amicably with one another and show their true natures.

This meant that the dwindling number of troublemakers could be snatched away unobtrusively, before they had a chance to howl in protest. Their former cellmates might notice they had gone, but guessed what was happening and were happy with the situation.

As one inmate succinctly put it, "Glad to see the back of 'em!"

The mediums felt truly safe, especially the women, as they were now working singly to keep up the momentum. The cell doors were opening in their wake, as they and their escorting guards made progress with selecting individuals for future treatment.

The opportunities this presented were immense, as they could now mix socially and read acquiescent minds without raising barriers.

During a coffee break late that morning, Brains asked Honey, "How does this new freedom help you?"

She replied, "Incredibly. For instance, in the last hour I've identified three men, with lighter sentences than they deserve, who have committed unrelated murders. I've also found two others who have the potential to be serial killers and are secretly making plans to start abducting youngsters."

Rose confirmed how the freedom benefited her as well. "I've been mixing with our own, home-grown religious fanatics. They too have provided me with information on plots they are involved in, descriptions of those who have committed atrocities abroad, *and* I've got a list of the networks they are aware of. All of this is being carried around in their heads. Can you imagine the impact when I follow the psychic trails?"

Chuck said, "I've found two men who have been framed for crimes they didn't commit, and another for the murder of his family, but not by him! He didn't do it and is unaware of the identity of the killer. They all need investigating."

Richard went off at a tangent, saying, "Yeah, I've found a few as well, with false rape charges.

"But do you remember the last time we were staying at the Atonement Center? Well, I began picking up other people's thoughts from some of the houses we were passing on the last day."

Chuck asked him, "What, as we were leaving the place, in the wagon? You mean from a distance?"

Richard nodded. "Yes, from a distance, and a lot of them were remote viewings."

Brains replied, "That's unusual. It suggests your skills are increasing, probably because of all those repetitive mind readings you've been doing. As the saying goes, 'Practice makes perfect'. I'll inform Joe."

As they were going their separate ways, Richard asked Brains, "Could you spare me some time? I've got an idea I'd like to run past you."

"Sure, fire away."

"It goes like this. Let's look at the human body as a biological entity."

"Okay."

"Let's look at the human spirit, or any other spirit, as a 'spirit entity', and assume it too is composed of a DNA and genetic structure, on a parallel plane to the biological entity."

"Yup, I'm following you so far."

"We both know that a computer is based on bits and bytes which are combined together to define words that describe specific things, very specifically."

"Yup."

"I have studied DNA strands and can see great similarities between how they work and how a computer works, at a fundamental level."

"I can see what you mean, but where's this heading?"

"Stay with me. The human brain works at different levels of consciousness. It pulls information from its own library of memories or 'memory bank'. True?"

"As far as we know, yes."

"What I would like you to experiment with is the possibility of not only accessing the human memory bank, but of adding more memories to it."

"That should be easy, considering the tampering that already goes on!"

"Right! What I want you to think of is the approach adopted by the authorities who unofficially read email traffic. What method do they use to pick out traffic that is undesirable?"

"Key words! I think I see where you're going with this."

"What I want is a set of key words that are associated with emotions of intense anger, sexual frustration and unnatural hatred."

"You mean those which are associated with humans?"

"Exactly! I would like you and your scientists to try to embed these key words in the memory bank, for use as triggers if a person suffers an attack of extreme emotions or unnatural desires. My idea is that they would function as a line of natural defense, and use DNA derived triggers, to intercept and calm these 'bad' emotions. This would be the reverse of the way that the brain malfunctions and blocks signals, when dementia develops as an illness."

Brains was getting excited. "Under your approach, it would be accomplished by looking for key words, associated with extreme emotions, in the memory library! But why bother to go that indirect route, when the emotions could be destroyed using 'DNA illness-focused' implants?"

Richard explained, his eyes feverish, "Because I don't want to lessen the range of human emotions, only to lessen the possibility of them occurring! They lead to extremes of behavior and could be controlled."

"Hmmm ... Melatonin could be a handy regulator, if generated automatically. I *lurve* the way you explain this concept! Let me record it as a scientific proposal and pass it to my boffins. We'll see what we can come up with."

As an afterthought, Richards said, "I wouldn't want to bypass the current techniques, which can associate behavior with an underlying physical problem. In my opinion, it should only be used after them, where nothing wrong has been uncovered.

"Understood! As a matter of interest, we have access to a

brand spanking new 'biological quantum computer'. Do the words 'biological', 'quantum' and 'computer' signify anything to you? I think we've found how to put this device to best use!

"Could you refresh my memory on the definition of 'quantum'?"

"It's a branch of physics. Quantum studies are conducted at a sub-atomic level, and these relate to the biological enhancements you propose making."

The four mediums continued setting a fast pace each day, with sustained mental effort. The last thing they wanted was unhappy staff demanding they come back, if things had been botched at the beginning.

One evening, after they returned to the care home at the end of yet another long day spent vetting prisoners, Honey entered reception and went over to gaze at the plaque dedicated to Thomas Beckon. Richard joined her; looking at her quizzically, he asked, "You're intrigued by this man, aren't you?"

"Hmm…yes. Why do I think I know him?" she responded."

He hesitated before admitting the truth. "I'm afraid you won't like the answer. Thomas Beckon is a man with a rare ability; he can inhabit a person's body, and does so when the desire takes his fancy. He does so irresistibly, and subordinates your will to his own."

He ended with a bitter comment. "He feels what you feel, to the full, and you are powerless to prevent him."

Honey looked at him aghast. "You're talking about yourself, aren't you? Did he do this when we were making love?"

He looked at her full in the face. "Yes, he did! He dominated me, totally. My spirit was pushed into the background; I was unable to intervene, while he took over."

She thought about the implications of this admission, using cold logic. "That makes him a rapist, but it's an unprovable crime! What's he like, as a person?"

Richard said, "Potentially, he's mankind's savior. He is revolutionizing transport, halving the population by sterilization and is ascending the political ladder ruthlessly. I don't know how he does it, but he seems to be a chameleon, and doesn't age.

"I think he can hop from one body to another as he sees fit, on a permanent basis, but this a supposition."

Honey said, "You make him sound like a monster! How will the sterilization be done?"

Richard said, "I don't know. It may be an airborne virus, or be spread by touch, or in the water we drink; who knows? I am reading in the press that reports are circulating of a widespread lack of fertility. The rate of baby births is dropping dramatically.

"The word is being spread that we shouldn't worry, that everything that is happening is done deliberately. Otherwise, if we don't take action, mankind will carry on over-populating everywhere it goes, and be wiped out as unwelcome pests."

She ignored his hyperbole, seeing it as unlikely scenario, and asked him, "Stick to the point and tell me one thing; was the decision yours alone to use hypnosis and make me act like a performing seal, or was it his?"

He looked down and admitted, "It was mine; I wanted you for my own, selfish pleasure. I have since realized how much I love you and feel deeply ashamed."

She looked at him sadly, and said, "I don't care. Your actions make you as much my violator as he was. Aren't you aware that a professional stage hypnotist went to prison for doing the same thing as you've done? I'm sorry but I feel dead inside and wish to move on."

She walked away, and he followed, gripping her arm. "You seem more forgiving of Beckon that you do of me. Is that fair?"

She replied cruelly, "Powerful men are ruthless by nature and get what they want by fair means or foul. It so happens that what he did to me may have been without my knowledge, but I don't think so.

"I wasn't unconscious, and I was sure at times I was with someone else when we did it. That person was attentive and gave me pleasure, whereas all you ever did was take! You surely haven't forgotten the talents that I possess? I know a charlatan when I see one, and that charlatan is you!"

She pulled her arm away and said over her shoulder, as she carried on walking, "Thanks for explaining the message on the plaque. It all fits into place, and I'm positive that the niggle at the back of mind has gone. You've confirmed I was with him, not you."

She rushed off in tears, her emotions in a jumble, while he stood there devastated.

At the end of the third long day, the four were sitting alone at the table after the evening meal comparing their progress, when Rose asked, "What about the guards?"

"What about them?" Richard queried, looking puzzled.

"We haven't studied them in any depth. What if they're not clean?" He was getting irritated with her use of slang.

Honey objected. "Are you implying that they may be up to the same tricks as the inmates? If you are, we'd look like a bunch of turncoats if we started singling them out for the same treatment ! Neither would it go down well with the prison authorities who vetted them."

Richard objected, "You should have brought this up at the start of the mission, not now. We're on the verge of leaving, so let it drop."

They all looked at Chuck, who raised his hands in the air and said, "Whoa, I'm not getting involved!"

Rose was still determined to continue. "Only today, I checked what the guards were thinking about. Guess what? One of them, called Slim Jim, is having secret trysts with a prisoner's wife; he's called Barney the Butcher because of his trade and criminal activities on the outside. Isn't it exciting?" she giggled, "All these nicknames they give each other!"

"To add to the excitement, he's also banging the two teenage daughters!" She frowned before asking, "Isn't that strictly against the rules?"

"*And* he's got a family at home, an attractive wife and three young children to support. *And* he's got a load of money stashed away in a safety deposit box; they're the proceeds of drugs he's been distributing inside, paid for by relatives and 'associates' on the outside."

She paused before asking, "Do you think he'd show up on the spectractor, or if a brain scan was done on him?"

Now fully exasperated, Richard leaned over and hissed at her,

"Let it drop! We've done good things here, so don't tarnish our reputations by getting involved. Try and appreciate what we've achieved!"

She shrunk back looking tearful, and whispered, "I was only trying to be helpful!"

"*Blast!*" thought Richard, "*She's making me look a heel!*"

Late afternoon the following day, the four were together again, for a coffee break. They had chosen to use the interview room previously reserved for Rose and Chuck. Three of them were already seated when Rose rushed in looking highly excited.

"Guess what? The guard I told you about, Slim Jim, has been thrown in the slammer!"

The others all leant keenly forward, as Honey asked, "How'd it happen?"

Rose explained, "He blabbed, he spilt the beans! His conscience compelled him to confess, and he couldn't stop talking as I recorded it all. What a snitch he is!"

She continued, unable to stop herself. "From what I can gather, when he told his wife, she cleaned out the contents of his safe deposit box and intends taking the kids to a new location where she's gonna buy a top of the range mansion and live like a queen."

She pondered on the other ramifications, before continuing. "He landed a load of other guards in the soup, and they are being nicked too. Although, he won't have any worries worth mentioning; he's being put on the witness protection program to protect him from all the people who are after him. Barney the Butcher intends leading the gang, after he found out about what Slim Jim was doing to his family."

Rushing over to Richard and giving him a kiss on the cheek and an embrace, she gushed, "Richard, sweetheart, I can't than you enough for everything you've done. You've helped us clear out a load of snakes in the grass from the service, so we can leave with our heads held high. Your use of hypnosis was a masterstroke, to wheedle out of Slim Jim the deposit box codes and get him talking. You're a real gem!"

He surprised her by brushing her arms away and rushing out

of the room. "I didn't do it!" he yelled back, dropping huffily onto a seat next door, with his back to them.

Honey murmured to Chuck, "He's a really creepy guy, even when he tries to act good."

Late, really late, that same evening, Chuck knocked lightly on Honey's door. When she opened it wide, after seeing who it was through the spyglass, he looked at her adoringly and dropped to one knee. He held out a little posey of flowers that he'd borrowed from the dining table, and popped the question, "Will you marry me?"

She hadn't seen that coming and was thunderstruck; he'd deliberately blind-sided her, knowing she'd say *no* if he asked her for a date. In fact, she had long suspected him of wanting to do exactly that and intended telling him to, "sod off!"

She approached him closely and stared at his eyes; she was looking for any sign that a certain evil spirit by the name of *Beckon* might be lurking in him. He looked at her bewildered and asked, "What are you doing?"

"Just checking!" she replied and slammed the door in his face. He leant against the other side with a huge smile; he knew enough about her to understand that she was going to say *yes*, in the near future and his heart started pounding.

Suddenly, she yanked the door open, causing him to fall into her arms. She said the magic word, and they kissed each other tenderly, as he pushed the door shut with his foot.

That was the trouble with mediums; they could read each other's minds.

It was the beginning of the final week for the team, and they had finished much earlier than the original due date.

The Monday morning start time for the meeting with Joe had been set for 8am sharp.

He began proceedings by making a special announcement. It began with the words, "You've done so well that you all deserve a break. You can collect your tickets at the airport, to stay at a 5 star hotel on the Mexican Riviera for the rest of the week. Don't forget, we have been invited to attend a premiere arranged by the film studio. It will be held on Saturday evening at 7pm. Be there!"

He was speaking to an empty room. They had all anticipated the offer, knew when to get to the airport, which airport it was, how they'd be chauffer-driven to and from each location, and everything else they needed to know by picking his brains.

That was the trouble with mediums; they could read minds.

A GLITTERING PREMIERE

The four constant companions were blessing their good fortune. They'd checked Joe's thoughts on their way back from the Atonement Center and found out that he intended giving them a week-long break at the agency's expense.

Had they waited until Monday of the next week, they would have missed the deadline he'd imposed; they were expected to get to the airport the Saturday before! Panic had set in, until they reached the conclusion that he'd done it deliberately. The suspicion was that he was trying to catch them out.

Hence, there were three scenarios: the first was the assumption by Joe that one or more of them had the capability to read his mind from a distance; the second was that one or more of them could anticipate what was going to happen in the future and foresaw his intentions in advance.

The third was that they would arrive to attend the meeting on Monday, as scheduled. If, on the other hand, they didn't arrive that morning, it would prove to Joe that at least one of them could either see the future, or read his mind from a distance.

Richard had probed Joe's memory deeper, and confirmed the existence of these devious ideas. He declared to the others, "Do I care? I do not!"

The prospect of a luxury break for six full nights on the Mexican Riviera had been irresistible.

He, Chuck and Honey set their hearts on windsailing for three days, and did so with gusto. Conversely, Rose had chosen to entertain the hotel guests with her skills as a psychic, and was playing to packed audiences for hours; she loved her work and was glad to console the living by hosting visits from their deceased kin.

On the fourth day, they all took a break from their pastimes, and went to a special event. Chuck married Honey, with Richard putting on a brave face and acting as best man, and Rose attending as the main witness.

From that moment on, the loving couple stayed out of sight, leaving Richard and Rose to go their own independent ways.

On their symbolic but otherwise meaningless wedding night, Honey snuggled up to Chuck and softly said, "I owe you a big thank you."

"For what?" he asked, gazing adoringly into her eyes.

"For throttling that monster who was attacking me in the park."

"How'd you know it was me?" he asked playfully.

"Bless you for keeping watch over me," she continued, ignoring his retort and instead asking. "What did you do with the body?"

He kissed her on the cheek, and said, "Sent him for a frogman's swim, to say sorry to his victims."

On the seventh day, Friday at 1pm, the four refreshed companions reunited; three of them were bronzed, but the sun had not touched Rose. They were ready to be taken to the airport for their flight home.

After an uneventful journey, the first action that each took after stepping over the threshold was to make a series of urgent appointments, according to their gender.

The men arranged to get haircuts and hire tuxedos; the women booked appointments with hairstylists, and then with upmarket shops specializing in the prompt supply and fitting of full-length evening gowns.

Honey had not yet made the move to Chuck's pad, wanting to clean her own place and put it on the market by the Monday. Her attitude to attending the upcoming premiere that evening was typical; she was not going to splash out a dollop of money on the event. They were only there as spectators, to make up the numbers in the audience. It was not worth the effort; when all was said and done, the studio was only a bit player in the film industry, showing crime series on a scarcely watched TV channel.

After satisfactorily completing all the tasks she had set for herself, she had time to relax before applying her makeup and getting dressed.

At 6:15pm, she answered a knock on the door and was impressed to see a uniformed chauffeur waiting for her. He gave her an admiring glance from head to foot, and a subdued whistle.

"Honey, or peach, isn't it? If so follow me."

He led her outside, and opened a passenger door half way along a highly polished white stretch-limousine. She lifted her shimmering blue gown to step in, showing more thigh than was decent, to see Chuck, Rose and Richard already sitting there.

She sat next to her new husband, in the place he had reserved for her opposite the other two, who were sitting on an identical backward-facing, sumptuous red leather bench seat. They seemed to be fixated by the shiny 24-carat gold rings of the newly weds, and the single-stone huge diamond engagement ring on the same, fourth finger of her left hand.

An awkward silence lasted for barely a minute, broken only when Honey asked Rose, "He's been at you, hasn't he?"

She had the grace to suppress a nervous giggle, replying, "I don't know what you're talking about!"

"Yes you do," Honey continued. "You've had sex with him." She inclined her head in Richard's direction; he shifted uneasily and stared out of the one-way side window.

Chuck sent her a private message; that is to say, he was sending it for access by her mind only, screened from the two sitting opposite.

"*Let it drop, love; he did it as an act of compassion towards her. She'd never in a million years have expected him to want her as much as she wanted him. Remember the film actor Clark Gable? He did the same once to an ageing actress, for something to remember him by. Don't be too judgmental!*"

She replied, "*I wonder if he or she was the most active? Did he use hypnosis on her?*"

Rose butted in to clarify the situation, making Honey realize she'd been overheard.

"*I'm not capable anymore of gymnastics! He was the one on top, and he kept his eyes on me to see if I was enjoying myself.*" Honey judged from Richard's lack of awareness, he hadn't overheard anything being conveyed, and Honey felt a sense of relief.

For Chuck's ears specifically, she commented, "All's well that ends well!"

Richard faced them and returned their smiles with a sickly one of his own.

Honey communicated to Chuck, "*He's developed a sense of decency, at long last!*"

Silence descended as the journey continued.

At last, the chauffeur announced over the internal comms system, "We're approaching now!"

They all looked ahead, to see flashes of light going off from cameras being used by the assembled press, and a red carpet with white ropes suspended both sides to keep a massing crowd from trampling over it.

"Woo, it's a bigger ceremony than I expected!" Rose exclaimed, her body twisting to see what they were approaching. "Stop, stop!" she insisted as they drove slowly past the crowd and parked in front of the carpet.

A security guard opened the nearside door and invited them to leave the limo; and walk along the carpet. Celebrities could be seen signing autographs for member of the crowd standing the other side of the ropes. Some were also engaging others in conversation, causing Rose to shrink back.

"This is awful!" she moaned, "How embarrassing, to get off in the wrong place, where everyone's looking at us!"

The other three concentrated for a moment. Before Richard gave her a reassuring hug and said, "I don't think this was a mistake Rose. Somehow or other, we were meant to get off here. Come on, let's face the music!"

He was referring to repetitive background music coming from a row of musicians in the open-fronted vestibule. Saxophones and big double bass violins played, their volume amplified by loudspeakers. It was making his back tingle, and went something like:

Dee dum dum dum,

being strummed by the Bass violinists, followed by

Dah dee dah dee dah,

blown by the saxophonists.

This went on repeatedly, penetrating his sub-conscious. He noticed that his companions had begun to hum along with it too, so it was having a contagious effect on them all.

Someone in the crowd shouted, "Hey that must be Chuck! Hi Chuck, will you give me your autograph?" A dozen hands were held out, as Chuck approached; he meant to ask how they knew who he was, but was being intercepted.

A young female shouted, "There's Richard! Do you see him? Come over here Richard and sign your name for me!"

Mixed male and female voices shouted for Honey and Rose to come nearer, and people held out bouquets of flowers for them to take, in exchange for their autographs, a chat and photo opportunities.

This sudden leap to fame bewildered them all, but they decided to wait until later for an honest explanation from Joe.

By the time they reached the end of the red carpet, the tune

Dee dum dum dum
Dah dee dah dee dah

was stuck in their minds, but all of a sudden there was a pause, which caused the crowd outside to go silent in expectation.

For the first time, they turned around and could see a sizeable number of youngsters standing at the outer fringes; they had been waiting patiently until then, but suddenly they began to jump and down in eagerness.

A huge scream went up, deafening everyone else within earshot, as an open-topped vintage yellow Cadillac drew up and the guards rushed forward to give its occupants protection.

Some of the girls shouted, "There he is!" and others tearfully put their hands to their mouths, saying, "Oh my gawd, it's him!"

The recipient of this overwhelming desire was a slim, outstandingly handsome young man dressed in a gold lamé suit and sitting raised on the rear boot lid of the car, with his feet on the rear seat. Two cheerful men dressed in blue cowboy outfits sat either side waving to the crowd, with another dressed the same in the front passenger seat.

Someone could be heard to comment loudly, "He's got the *Ollyards* with him!" and this caused another bout of jumping and screaming.

Soon there were chanting, "Ollie, Ollie, Ollie!"

A deep male voice announced of the loudspeakers, "Ladies and gentlemen, we have for your entertainment tonight a new, incredibly talented singer who has had a spectacular hit with his debut song *The Hunky Dunky Man!* Yes folks, it is none other than our latest signing, *OLIVER TWIST!* Give a big hand to welcome the reincarnation of the late, great King, *Elvis Presley!*"

The object of their adulation gave a wave to the crowds, aiming specifically at those near the back and causing a crescendo of scream. In the blink of an eye, he leapt athletically onto the carpet and landed in a crouch, revealing his ornate cowboy boots as he gave a mock snarl aimed at his fans.

The reaction was a mad rush of the younger members of the audience from the back to the front, so they could get nearer to their idol. They didn't care how they got there, by fair means or foul, as they shouldered their ways past the protesting adults, many of whom were their parents, who decided prudently to make way.

Some of the younger generation even tried to crawl between the adults' legs, as they tried to steady themselves and lock arms, to no avail. The human tide was unstoppable, and it was lucky that no one got seriously hurt.

It was controlled pandemonium, and the security men linked arms to protect their young charge as he sauntered up the red carpet, into the relative safety of the vestibule, as the repetitive tune commenced once again. The three Ollyards bounded up the carpet behind him, waving and smiling to everyone as they passed in Olly's wake

The musicians had resumed playing

> *Dee dum dum dum*
> *Dah dee dah dee dah*
>
> *Dee dum dum dum*

Dah dee dah dee dah

With bass violins and saxes. This time, however a new interlocking melody joined in from a row of trumpet players who had stood at the front.

They blasted out a rhythm that matched the first two lines of Oliver's hit single, *The Hunky Dunky Man*, which go:

> *I went to her apartment on a Monday at one*
> *A-singing do lolly, lolly Shaky bum, Shaky bum*

"I recognize this rhythm; it's the same as a very old tune called *The Telephone Man!*" Honey said, shouting to be heard.

"Yes! It's the debut song of this *Oliver Twist*; it's been rechristened *The Hunky Dunky Man!*" Rose shouted back. She'd obviously heard it.

Seamlessly, two of the Ollyards picked up their guitars, and the third sat behind his drums, placed centrally in front of the backing orchestra, which now played at a decreasing volume.

Oliver picked up his own guitar, placed the strap over a shoulder, and thanked a teenage girl for placing a microphone on a stand in front of him. The band briefly tuned their instruments and began playing *The Hunky Dunky Man*. while the new, emerging star started singing the lyrics in an astounding rendering of the King's voice:

> *I went to her apartment on a Monday at one*
> *A-singing do lolly, lolly Shaky bum, Shaky bum*
> *Started twisting in it, on a Tuesday at two*
> *A-singing do lolly, lolly Shaky do, Shaky do.*
>
> *Wednesday at three I woke up with a craving, singing:*
> *"Hey baby, come and start a'twisting with me!"*
> *Thursday at four she came up to me a-singing:*
> *"Hey, baby, I'm your number one fan*
> *You just show me how to twist and I'll do it if I can.*
>
> *We did it in the bedroom,*
> *We did it in the hall,*
> *We did it in the bathroom,*

Leaning up against the wall.
A-singing do lolly, lolly Shaky bum, Shaky bum.

One of the sax players had joined the group, and played solos as the tune progressed, with the crowd joining in the singing. They went hysterical as Oliver twisted his hips, and the fainting started amongst the female fans.

Rose noticed that a row of men in blue overalls had gone to the far end of the red carpet, and were rolling it up, away from the curb and towards them. Rose pointed at them and said, "Look, they're clearing the carpet away. That means there are no more celebrities arriving!"

The crowd, now entirely consisting of younger fans, swept forward as the fully rolled-up red carpet was heaved away by the heavily sweating team of men in overalls. This allowed a double line of security men to form and protect Ollie and The Ollyards from those who literally wanted to take him home in huggable chunks.

Oliver bowed in gratitude as he finished performing, and the announcer broadcast a message: " Hi y'all! For those who'd love to hear more, Oliver's soon gonna be singing his next big hit. Do you want more?"

The crowd responded by screeching, "YES!" and chanting, "Ollie Ollie Ollie!"

"Good good good!" The announcer yelled back, temporarily quietening them.

"I've got more good news to share with you. We have booked a stadium for Oliver to keep you entertained, at OUR cost for the next hour, while we continue here with our premiere. Its five minutes walking distance and members of our security team will guide you there.

"BUT FIRST LET YOUR PARENTS OR GUARDIANS KNOW WHERE YOU'RE GOING AND HOW LONG YOU'LL BE THERE. Details will be handed out to you when you start queueing, at the roadside in front of us."

The crowd retreated from the front of the vestibule and rushed towards the roadside, where they were starting to line up as advised.

Although forms were being handed out or taken from boxes,

many were dialing persons unknown and chatting away excitedly; clearly, they were already phoning friends to get them to hot foot it down and join them for the concert!

Within minutes, vehicles were drawing up in the vicinity and disgorging hordes of youngsters who anxiously joined the end of the queue, after they were refused permission to be with their friends.

Watching what was going on, Rose commented, "I wonder what they'd have done if it was raining?"

An unexpected male voice responded, "They've got a hangar-sized empty building to house them!"

Honey spun round and smiled with delight; it was Roland, the father of the singing star!

She had only just recognized Oliver as the 'prodigal son' in a case she had dealt with originally, on her own. She noticed that his mother Mary was engaged in conversation with Oliver and his band, while they were helping a support team to pack their kit, ready to make the transfer to the stadium.

Roland proudly told Honey, "I'm handling all of Oliver's business affairs and advertising, and things are great! Thanks for all the help you gave us."

Mary came over to join them, and they all introduced themselves. She looked at Honey's wedding ring and enthused, "Well I never, You're married already! Who's the lucky man?"

Chuck replied with a grin, "Me, as it happens! I'm so pleased to meet you."

Mary replied, "If you two ever want a romantic break, come and stay at our ranch, for nothing. Oliver has ploughed some money into our home and we've updated everything."

Honey said, "We might just do that! I promised myself a vacation when I stayed with you, and I'd love to come and see you. Where are Nathan and Rebecca; are they here?"

Mary replied, "Nathan is running the ranch as my acting manager, and Rebecca is at a special boarding school in Switzerland getting a good education."

Richard looked at his watch and said, "We'd better get moving;

people are heading into the main building."

"See you in there!" the couple enthused, as they all brought out their invitations to get them checked on entry.

"*I wonder why they've been invited?*" Honey wondered. "*We really ought to take notice of general things and not be so focused.*"

They were given a seating plan and escorted by a waitress to their reserved table, near the front. Joe and his wife were already sitting there, at the round table when the four of them arrived, with an unknown couple of similar ages alongside. Place cards were in front of each guest, and theirs said that Joe's wife was named Jenna Fraser, and their companions were Bill DiCaprio and Tara DiCaprio.

Jenna was a slim, blond middle-aged woman with shoulder length wavy hair, a smooth complexion and quiet smile. She was wearing a subdued dark blue dress that sparkled as she moved under the overhead lights. Joe, on the other hand, was wearing a tuxedo that he must have bought years ago; it had clearly seen better days, being shiny and worn at the elbows; this became evident when he leant on the table.

The DiCaprio's were a different proposition and he looked a stern and foreboding figure. His physique was wiry, and he had a receding hairline with thinning straight hair combed backwards away from a high forehead. He also wore thin-framed varifocal glasses perched on thin nostrils with thin lips underneath. His skin looked waxy and the veins on the back of his hands stood out, as if he'd done hard, physical work in his earlier life.

His wife was an angular blond-haired woman with a jutting jaw, whose attitude looked resigned, as if she no longer cared what fate had in store for her. Honey did notice that Tara was wearing a cream and gold colored robe, with an embossed pattern in it. It had a high collar, and she had attached a string of pearls to hang down the hidden cleavage between her small breasts.

From the outset, Honey refrained from studying the DiCaprios, fearing for some indescribable reason what she might find as she succumbed to curiosity.

"*Oh to hell with it!*" she thought as she settled down, wanting to enjoy the evening.

The table itself was set for eight people, so there were no spaces available for Jake, Matt and Walter, the film crew, which was a disappointment. It promised to be a good meal, with the elaborate layout of silver cutlery and cut-glass wine goblets, placed on a white linen tablecloth, raising their hopes.

Snapping out of her self-absorption, Honey looked into the soul of the silent Bill DiCaprio and asked, "Sir, what brings the illustrious Director of Communications to grace our humble presence?"

Chuck, Richard and Rose also stared at the DiCaprios and nodded in agreement, as if possessed by one mind.

Tara looked taken aback, as did Jenna, while Bill DiCaprio took on a fixed glare, like an angry eagle. Joe was trying hard not to laugh at their reactions, and the atmosphere melted away as Bill unexpectedly burst out laughing. He got up from his chair, went around the table, and gave Honey a friendly hug, before shaking hands with Chuck and Richard, and finally embracing Rose as well.

"Damned brilliant, all of you are!" he said as he sat back down, to share his merriment with Tara, his wife. She, on the other hand was looking distinctly uncomfortable.

Chuck addresses her directly, saying, "Don't worry, it was only a party trick, and we respect your privacy." He gazed across fleetingly, privately indicating that her secrets were safe with him and the others in their circle.

She mouthed to him a brief, "*Thank you*" and turned to talk to her husband, while fingering her pearls as if they were rosary beads.

The mediums silently agreed between themselves that the food was as good as that they'd enjoyed at the Atonement Centre. Indirectly, it was a compliment, since they considered that the chef concerned was as good as Jamie Oliver, whilst more refined in his approach to adding spices to the ingredients.

They sat there having enjoyed the meal and feeling contented with life, and were settling down when the curtains at the end of the room nearest them opened. There was a rostrum to one side, which lit up, and an older man in a dinner suit walked to it and addressed them through a microphone. A full-sized cinema screen occupied the main space.

"Welcome to the re-launch of our studios and we hope you enjoyed the meal. Was it alright?"

There was a sprinkling of handclaps and shouts raised in appreciation.

"Good!" said the man. "I'm Geoff Davis, the head of the studio, and this occasion is in honor of two major events. The first was our launch of the career of a new star, Oliver Twist, whose parents are here tonight. If Mary and Roland could stand up so we can see and thank them?"

They were near the table occupied by the mediums, and gave a wave as the spotlight was directed at them while they stood, blinking and waving blindly to all and sundry.

He looked ahead at his 3D speech reader and continued speaking.

"Henceforth, we will be known as the studio that produces real-life documentary-style shows under the name *FLIEZ ON THE WALL*."

"I now wish to show you some trailers of our shows about to be released." He lowered the rostrum light and left the stage, to rejoin his table and enjoy the show.

The audience gasped as the screen sprang into life. The colors were spectacularly lifelike and vibrant, and the legend *A FLIEZ ON THE WALL PRODUCTION* almost leapt from the picture in full 3D. The wrap-around music, although loud was not deafening, and filled the seating area without becoming overbearing.

The main title appeared next, and the four mediums blinked when they saw it appear:

THE DEADUCTION AGENCY

"*Oh dear!*" Richard communicated to the others.

"*It's hardly surprising our film crew have not yet appeared!*" responded Chuck.

"*What are we in for?*" asked Rose.

Honey gaped, as the trailers started showing them in operation, in authentic 3D and astoundingly natural colors.

"It's like real life!" she commented.

Tantalizing highlights of cases like *THE DERANGED HUSBAND, THE DECEASED COURSE GIRL, THE HONEY TRAP, THE PRODIGAL SON,* to *THE ATONEMENT CENTER* and now, *A GLITTERING PREMIUM* they were filmed in action.

Two of the snippets were, of course, opportunities to highlight Oliver Twist!

"*How did they do it?*" Richard queried silently with his partners. "*They've captured our activities even when they weren't recording!*"

Honey marveled, "*It's all so steady too! There's none of this camera jerkiness you normally get with 'Fly on the Walls' alleged documentaries!*"

After a half-hour of this skillfully edited patchwork-quilt exhibition of the mediums at work, the main characters felt like hiding under the table. This included not only the four main characters on whom the trailers concentrated, but also Joe himself; he had been featured holding it all together

As the head of the studio, Geoff Davis, returned to the rostrum and waved a hand to switch the light back on, he spotlighted their table and invited them to join him on the stage.

Collectively, they all groaned and were most unwilling to budge, until their ultimate boss, Bill DiCaprio hissed at them, "Get up of your butts and march onto that stage!"

"Yes! Do it!" Joe insisted.

Bill gave a wicked grin and said, "You as well, Joe!"

The five ascended to meet their living hell, and walked towards their nemesis.

"*The last thing we need is publicity!*" Honey moaned to her other, similarly gifted partners.

"*Console yourself with this thought: it didn't do Uri Geller any harm!*" Richard responded.

They each took their turn to shake hands with the boss man, who handed out small, golden statues that imitated those presented at The Oscars. Joe was the last to receive his, and held it aloft triumphantly to a big cheer from the audience.

After they had left the stage, Geoff Davis invited the camera crew to join him. Jake, Matt and Walter were standing in the wings, and walked across to be presented with similar awards. Each statue was a representation of a single camera operator, standing behind his equipment.

"*Their statues are bigger than ours!*" Rose hissed.

"*All the better to ram up their arses!*" Honey responded angrily.

Their male partners chuckled.

At the end of the presentation, Geoff sidled up to Jake with a microphone, and asked him, "Tell me Jake, how did you manage to film all that footage without the mediums knowing?"

Jake turned to the audience, put a finger to the side of his nose, and said in a conspiratorial way, "*That* remains our secret!"

Towards the end of the evening, the three reprobate characters strode up to the mediums' table and put their hands out, saying, "Forgive us our sins, we were under orders!"

They all laughed and shook hands in a public gesture of reconciliation. However, while maintain a smiling exterior, Bill DiCaprio made a point of ushering the three camera operators to one side.

He spoke in a low menacing voice. "I'm having you picked up by my agents now, outside. You won't be away for long, if you cooperate with us."

TESTS ARE SET

Joe called Richard into his office and drawled amiably to him, "Well, that was an interesting experience, wasn't it?" He was referring to the premiere they had attended last weekend.

He invited him to sit down and outlined the reason for inviting him there, on his own.

"I've had a phone call from Bill DiCaprio, you know, my director at the Bureau? It seems he made a point of interviewing the three stooges from the film studio, *Fliezzz on the Wall*." He extended the word *Fliez* to make it sound like a buzzing noise.

"He reminded them of how, when they were in the military, they had willingly signed their allegiance to their country. He held them to it, and swore he'd send them to another war zone, unless they coughed up the lowdown on their secret filming."

He paused before announcing, "They confessed to how they'd filmed our activities. They had nano implants planted in their skulls, permitting them to record everything they wanted to see and hear around them.

"We have thus acquired the technology we want to use." He pointed a finger at Richard and said, "We want to use it on you, as a matter of pressing urgency. An appointment has been made with our surgical team for the implants to be made in your head this morning."

Richard felt butterflies in his stomach; he didn't like the prospect of undergoing surgery and opened his mouth to say so. Joe intercepted him, saying, "Don't be a baby! There's a criminal out there who must be caught." He looked at him and said, "Jake is waiting for you at the wagon wheel. He'll reassure you, if you need to ask any questions. It's painless."

Joe's eyes were half closed, like a snake, as Richard left, feeling vulnerable but important.

Joe's promise was true, as Jake confirmed; the operation was fairly pain free, under the influence of local scalp anesthetic above the right rear cortex of the brain. Half an hour later, after leaving a darkened room, Richard began to apply mental instructions that operated his embedded recorders.

When he played back the recordings, the imagery and sound systems were spectacular, and his elation was tinged with a sense of relief; he had survived a medical experiment conducted by the military!

Joe greeted him on his return with a 'told you so' attitude and began his briefing.

"We have a mass murderer on the loose. Normally I wouldn't distract you from the important tasks you are performing nationwide, but this case is alarming the general public in our neighborhood. If we can't catch the shooter, who can?

"To bring you up to speed; three people were gunned down in a bar, which was scorched to the ground after. Either before or after - we don't know which – three more people were slaughtered in a convenience store right next door.

"This nutter has to be stopped. I have no doubt he or she will kill again, unless caught. We have recovered spent shells at both sites, indicating that a gun was fired until all the bullets were expended.

"We have established the identities of all the victims, and there is no logical connection between them. That is, apart from that fact that they seem to have been innocent bystanders who got in the maniac's line of fire. Please help us and visit the crime scenes."

As he departed in a hurry, Joe urged him, "Go catch the person concerned, Richard, before we lose our credibility."

Richard arrived at the shell of the razed bar, in Joe's driverless saloon, and stood outside watching senior firefighters inspecting the charred remains. One of the police officers recognized Richard as a colleague; he reported to Joe himself and was aware of Richard's importance to the investigation.

"I've got some photos of the victims for you," he said, handing them over for Richard to look at. "Relatives came forward after seeing the blaze reported on the news. They realized that members of their families frequented or worked at the bar being shown, and had not come home."

Richard murmured his thanks and began rubbing his fingers over the smiling faces they showed. Then he asked the officer to take him to the convenience store, where other bodies still lay. He looked down at them, and touched their lifeless heads, before moving over to the counter where the till and its computer screen were situated, untouched by the drama that had unfolded around them.

He called the officer to stand next to him, as he accessed the main system screen on the computer, before reciting the facts he had gleaned at both scenes, using his psychic powers.

"The killer is a man in his early thirties. He used a caliber 22 pistol and he lives locally. This is his picture:" He activated his nano implant, which beamed an invisible data stream into the MS Office Image folder. From there, using the keyboard he displayed a sharply detailed picture of the murderer onto the screen, aiming a gun and shooting at people.

The officer stood there, stunned by what he had witnessed, until Richard brought him to his senses by saying, "I'll go to my car, and beam the information to your station, for it to be transmitted to all the investigating officers. I suggest you start the search by visiting all the delivery stores in the neighborhood, and the mail delivery people, and show them the photo on your smartphones."

As Richard was departing, he shouted back to the officer, "Make sure you miss no one! This man does not appear on any of our data bases of known offenders."

Within three days, the man was identified by a pizza delivery man, his address was found, and he was cornered by a SWAT team in his apartment, where he committed suicide. In a drawer in his bedroom was an ancient Ruger Mark 2 caliber 22 pistol that proved to be the murder weapon.

What truly upset Joe was the man's social background and

upbringing; he was a lifelong member of the Scout movement and had attained the rank of Eagle Scout, whose elitist members were supposed to uphold the highest moral values in society. The acts this man had performed were heinous and evil. He wondered how he could have sunk so low, and was then informed by those who knew him that he had begun sniffing cocaine regularly.

That was the only thing that could explain it, to Joe as a police officer. It brought to mind the warped behavior of Nicky Lestrange's ex-husband, in 'The Case of the Deranged Husband'.

After a break, during which Richard temporarily joined his partners in their ongoing, public work Joe asked him to return to the agency post-haste and undertake another special mission. He also suggested that Richard say his fond farewells to Chuck, Honey, and Rose, in the eventuality that the split became permanent.

That caused a stir, when Rose in particular began invading Joe's mental privacy. Consequently, he asked Richard to tell him, Joe, how to keep his mental guard up and avoid others reading his mind. That did the trick, allowing him to concentrate on what was most important for the agency, like recruitment.

The next test that Richard had to undertake required him to read the Official Secrets Acts and sign endless forms committing him to secrecy. He had no bother doing this, being a free agent, in terms of personal relationships and having a selfish disregard for everyone else.

After he had signed all the paperwork, Joe said to him, "I am now passing you to another agency, at the recommendation of Bill DiCaprio. This one is primarily concerned with matters external to the homeland, if you get my drift, and does not contain the word 'Bureau' in its title.

"You have my best wishes and congratulation in your new role." Joe shook his hand vigorously, and they embraced for the last time, before Richard walked out of the building.

Somewhat later in the future, after several weeks of intense training at a secret establishment in Virginia, Richard passed his initiation course and had to report to a specialist center, where he would be allocated his first mission.

An unmarked car took him to the base he would presumably call home for the foreseeable future; he had no idea exactly where it was located. Upon entry, he signed the register and descended by elevator with a female agent, three levels down.

He walked along a corridor until he reached a door guarded by two military men holding rifles. They electronically unlocked and opened it, allowing him to enter, and he cast eyes on the person to whom he was expected to report.

"*Aw crap!*" he thought, as a person he had met before rose from the one desk in the room, and approached him to shake his hand warmly.

It was the hard-faced, angular Tara DiCaprio, whose words on this occasion said one thing and her attitude another. With a false smile, she said, "I am really pleased to welcome you to our intelligence agency! Long ago, we employed agents like Uri Geller; now we have you! To start the ball rolling, I want you to influence a crucial decision that a certain foreign Head of State is about to make . . . "

THE END

Don't forget, if you want to contact the author, you can do so via

www.terrytumbler.com

Have a good life!

PLEASE LEAVE A REVIEW ON AMAZON

Lightning Source UK Ltd.
Milton Keynes UK
UKOW04f1101100615

253250UK00001B/20/P